DEATH ON THE RIM OF SPACE

Calver motioned with his pistol. "Go on. Lead the way."

She sobbed as she turned from him and reluctantly walked toward the door at the far end of the passage, opened it, and passed through it. Calver followed. The room beyond the door was large and, like the approach to it, was lit with oil lamps—and by the ruddy glow of a brazier from which the handles of . . . of implements protruded. There was the smell of blood, and of sweat, of fear and of agony. Against one wall there was a thing like a narrow bed, but spiked. Against another wall there hung a pallid . . . something that writhed feebly in its chains, that was mewing weakly.

A dreadful fear almost stopped Calver's heart. He started to run toward what had once been a woman—then realized that the skin, where it was not burned, was not blood-covered, was green. But he did not stop. He approached the thing and, when he was close enough to be sure that he would not miss, pulled the trigger of his automatic.

When the echoes of the shot had died away, the mewing had stopped.

SF

THE RIM OF SPACE

THE SHIP FROM OUTSIDE
A. BERTRAM CHANDLER

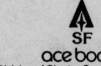

SF
ace books
A Division of Charter Communications Inc.
A GROSSET & DUNLAP COMPANY
51 Madison Avenue
New York, New York 10010

THE RIM OF SPACE

An ACE Book

Cover art by Attilla Heja

2 4 6 8 0 9 7 5 3
Manufactured in the United States of America

THE RIM OF SPACE

1

SLOWLY AND CAREFULLY—as befitted her years, which were many—the star tramp *Caliban* dropped down to Port Forlorn. Calver, her Second Mate, looked out and down from the control room viewports to the uninviting scene below, to the vista of barren hills and mountains scarred by mine workings, to the great slag heaps that were almost mountains themselves, to the ugly little towns, each one of which was dominated by the tall, smoke-belching chimneys of factories and refineries, to the rivers that, even from this altitude, looked like sluggish streams of sewage.

So this, he thought, *is Lorn, industrial hub of the Rim Worlds. This is the end of the penny section. This is where I get off. There's no further to go . . .*

Captain Bowers, satisfied that the ship was riding down easily and safely under automatic control, turned to his Second Officer. "Are you sure that you want to pay off here, Mr. Calver?" he asked. "Are you quite sure? You're a good officer and we'd like to keep you. The Shakespearian Line mightn't be up to Commission standards, but it's not a bad outfit . . ."

"Thank you, sir," replied Calver, raising his voice slightly to make himself heard over the subdued thunder of the rockets, "but I'm sure. I signed on in Elsinore with the understanding that I was to be paid off on the Rim. The Third's quite capable of taking over."

"You want your head read," grunted Harris, the Mate.

"Perhaps," said Calver.

And perhaps I do, he thought. *How much of this is sheer masochism, this flight from the warm worlds of the Center to these desolate Rim planets? Could it have been the names that appealed to me? Thule, Ultimo, Faraway and Lorn . . .*

"The usual cross wind, blast it!" swore Bowers, hastily turning his attention to the controls. The old ship shuddered and complained as the corrective blasts were fired and, momentarily, the noise in the control room rose to an intolerable level.

When things had quieted down again Harris said, "It's always windy on Lorn, and the wind is always cold and dusty and stinking with the fumes of burning sulphur . . ."

"I'll not be staying on Lorn," said Calver. "I've been too long in Space to go hunting for a shore job, especially when there's no inducement."

"Going to try Rim Runners?" asked Captain Bowers.

"Yes. I hear they're short of officers."

"They always are," said Harris.

"Why not stay with us?" queried the Captain.

"Thanks again, sir, but . . ."

"Rim Runners!" snorted the Mate. "You'll find

an odd bunch there, Calver. Refugees from the Interstellar Transport Commission, from the Survey Service, the Waverley Royal Mail, Trans-Galactic Clippers . . ."

"I'm a refugee from the Commission myself," said Calver wryly.

Port Forlorn was close now, too close for further conversation, the dirty, scarred, concrete apron rushing up to meet them. The *Caliban* dropped through a cloud of scintillating particles, the dust raised by her back-blast and fired to brief incandescence. She touched, sagged tiredly, her structure creaking like old bones. The sudden silence, as the rockets died, seemed unnatural.

Harris broke it. "And their ships," he said. "Their ships . . . All ancient crocks, mostly worn-out *Epsilon* Class tubs thrown out by the Commission just before they were due to collapse from senile decay . . . I'm told that they even have one or two of the old Ehrenhaft Drive jobs . . ."

"Wasn't *Caliban* once *Epsilon Sextants?*" asked Calver mildly.

"Yes. But she's different," said Harris affectionately.

Yes, thought Calver, remembering the conversation, standing at the foot of the ramp to the airlock, *Caliban* was different. A worn-out *Epsilon* Class wagon she may have been—but she still had pride, just as her Master and officers still had pride in her. This *Lorn Lady* was a ship of the same class, probably no older than *Caliban*, but she looked a wreck.

Calver looked down at his shoes, which had been highly polished when he left his hotel, and saw that they were already covered with a thick film of dust. A sidewise glance at his epaulettes—the new ones, with their Rim Runners Second Officer's braid, on the old jacket—told him that they, also, were dusty. He disliked to board a ship, any ship, untidily dressed. He brushed his shoulders with his hand, used a handkerchief, which he then threw away, to restore the shine to his shoes. He climbed the shaky ramp.

There was no airlock watch—but Calver had learned that the outward standards of efficiency diminished, almost according to the Law of Inverse Squares, with increasing distance from the Galactic Center. He shrugged, found the telephone.

After studying the selector board he pressed the button labelled *Chief Officer.* There was no reply. He tried *Control Room, Purser* and then *Captain,* then replaced the useless instrument in its clip, and opened the inner airlock door. He was agreeably surprised to find that the manual controls worked easily and smoothly. He picked up his bags and went into the ship. He was familiar enough with the layout of this type of vessel and went straight to the axial shaft. The newer *Epsilon* Class vessels boasted a light elevator for use in port. Calver was not amazed to discover that *Lorn Lady* did not run to such a luxury.

There was somebody clattering down the spiral stairway in the axial shaft, the stairway that led up to the officers' accommodation. Calver stood there and waited. The owner of the noisy feet dropped into view. He was a man of Calver's age, no longer young. His uniform was tight on his stocky frame; he wore Rim Runners epaulettes—the three gold bars of a Chief Officer with, above them, the winged wheel—but his cap badge was an elaborate affair of stars and rockets surmounted by an ornate crown.

He looked up at Calver when he reached the deck, making the tall man suddenly conscious of his gangling height. He said, "You'll be the new Second. I'm the Mate. Maclean's the name. Welcome aboard the *Forlorn Bitch*." He grinned. "Well, she looks it, doesn't she?"

They shook hands.

"I'll take my bags up to my cabin," said Calver. "I've seen enough of Port Forlorn to last me a long time so, if you like, I'll do the night aboard."

"Night aboard? There's no shipkeeping here," laughed Maclean. "And there's no cargo working tonight, either. The night watchman will be on duty in an hour or so, and he's fairly reliable."

Calver looked as shocked as he felt.

"I know how you feel," said the Mate, "but you'll get over it. I used to feel the same myself when I first came out to the Rim—after the Royal Mail it seemed very slovenly."

"I'm afraid it does."

"You're out of the Commission's ships, aren't you?"

"Yes."

"I thought as much. You're a typical Commission officer—middle-aged before your time, stiff and starchy and a stickler for regulations. It'll wear off. Anyhow, up you go and park your bags. I'll wait for you here. Then we'll go and have a couple or three drinks to wash this damned dust out of our throats."

Calver climbed the spiral staircase and found his cabin without any trouble. It was, to his relief, reasonably clean. He left his bags under the bunk, went down to the airlock to rejoin Maclean. The two men walked down the ramp together.

"You'll not find Commission standards here," said the Mate, taking up the conversation where he had dropped it. "Or, come to that, Royal Mail standards. We keep the ships safe and reasonably clean —and reasonably efficient—but there's neither money nor labor to spare for spit and polish."

"So I've noticed."

"So I noticed, too, when I first came out to the Rim. And if I hadn't told Commodore Sir Archibald Sinclair to his face that he was a blithering old idiot I'd still be in the Royal Mail, still keeping my night aboard in port and making sure that a proper airlock watch was being maintained, and all the rest of it . . ." He paused. "There's a not bad little pub just outside the spaceport gates. Feel like trying it?"

"As you please," said Calver.

The two men walked slowly across the dusty apron, past cranes and under gantries, through the gates and into a street that seemed lined with factories and warehouses. The swinging sign, the big bottle with vanes and ports added to make it look like a rocketship, was, even though sadly tarnished and faded, a note of incongruous gaiety.

The pub was better inside than out, almost achieving coziness. It was, at this early hour of the evening, practically deserted. Calver and Maclean sat down at one of the tables, waiting only a few seconds for attention. The slatternly girl who served them did not ask for their order but brought them a bottle of whisky with graduations up its side, two glasses and a jug of water.

"They know me here," said Maclean unnecessarily. He filled and raised his glass. "Here's to crime."   •

Calver sipped his drink. The whisky was not bad. He read the label on the bottle, saw that the liquor had been distilled on Nova Caledon. It wasn't Scotch —but here, out on the Rim, the price of the genuine article would have been prohibitive.

He said, "Would you mind putting me into the picture, Maclean? They were very vague in the office when I joined the Company."

"They always are," the Mate told him. "They're never quite sure which way is up. Besides—you hadn't yet signed the Articles; you had yet to bind yourself, body and soul, to Rim Runners. I suppose you noticed the Secrecy Clause, by the way?"

"I did."

"I suppose you thought it a rather odd clause to find in a merchant ship's Articles of Agreement. But it's there for a reason. Your predecessor signed it— and ignored it. That's why he's doing his spell in the mines, under guard . . ."

"What! Surely they wouldn't . . ."

"They would, Calver—and in his case they did. Bear in mind that Rim Runners is just about a government shipping line and that all of us are, automatically, officers of the Rim Naval Reserve . . .

"Anyhow . . ." He glanced around him, made sure that there was nobody within earshot. "Anyhow, this is the way of it. Until very recently Rim Runners owned only a handful of ships and served only four planetary systems—those of Thule, Ultimo, Faraway and Lorn. Just puddle-jumping by *our* standards, Calver—our old standards, that is. Even so, they had to keep on recruiting officers from the rest of the Galaxy. They don't like Deep Space, these Rim Worlders; they're scared of it. I suppose that it's because for all their lives they've been hanging over the edge of the Ultimate Pit by their eyebrows.

"But the Rim Government wants to expand, wants to become sufficiently powerful to be able to thumb its nose at Earth and the Federation. As you know, the Survey Service has always neglected the Rim. So Rim Runners put their own survey ships into operation. They made a sweep to the Galactic West—and found the anti-matter suns and planets. There was no room for expansion there. They ran to the East and found normal matter and quite a few stars with inhabited worlds. There's Mellise, which is practically all water and inhabited by a race of intelligent amphibians. There's Tharn, which has yet to build an industrial civilization but whose people are as near human as makes no difference. There's Grollor, where the natives can just be classed as humanoid and have the first beginnings of space travel. There's Stree, with its philosophical lizards . . ."

"I can see," said Calver, "that I'll have to do some heavy boning up on the Pilot Books . . ."

Maclean laughed. "There aren't any Pilot Books, Calver. Not yet. When there are, it'll be the likes of us who've written them." He splashed more whisky into the glasses. "Anyhow, we're loading zinc and tin and cadmium tomorrow for Port Faraway on Faraway. We load at Faraway for the Eastern Circuit. How does that suit you?"

"The Eastern Circuit? The new worlds?"

"Aye."

"Sounds interesting. But you still haven't made this secrecy business clear."

"The Rim Government," said Maclean patiently, "wants to form its own Federation, out here on the

Rim, wants to have the whole thing sewn up tight with pacts and treaties and trade agreements before any Survey Service ship comes nosing out this way. All known Federation agents have been rounded up and are being kept in protective custody. Pickering, your predecessor, was an ex-Lieutenant Commander out of the Survey Service and had the odd idea that he still owed them loyalty—in spite of the Court Martial that was the cause of his leaving them . . ."

"And are you loyal to the Rim?" asked Calver. "I know that there's no likelihood that the Kingdom of Waverley will ever cast covetous eyes on this sector of the Galaxy—but suppose they did?"

"I'm a Rim Worlder," said Maclean at last. "I wasn't born out here, but the Rim has always had its appeal for me. It's a last frontier, I suppose, and will be until some genius comes up with an intergalactic drive . . . And out here one can be a spaceman, a real spaceman, without all the time being tangled up in red tape . . . And now there are the new worlds, and there'll be more of them . . ." He looked around. "The dump's filling up. No more shop talk."

As he said, the place was filling up. There were roughly-dressed men from dockside, mines and factories, a few overly-neat men from offices. There were women—some of them drably and dowdily respectable, others whose skimpy dress, too red lips and overly made-up faces were like a uniform. There was a slim girl who began to wring a plaintive melody from a piano accordion. She flashed a smile at the two spacemen as she played.

Maclean sang softly in time to the music:

"Exiled from home

> *By woman's whim,*
> *We'll ever roam*
> *And run the Rim . . ."*

"This," said a female voice, huskily attractive, "is where he usually starts to cry into his whisky . . ."

"That's a lie, Arlen," said Maclean, "and you know it."

Calver turned in his chair. He saw the Purser, whom he had already met, and, beside him, a tall woman with the silver bars of a Catering Officer on her epaulettes. She was a little too slim for conventional prettiness and her features were too strong and bore the ineradicable marks of past strain. There was a startling silver streak in her burnished, dark hair.

She said, "You'll be Calver. The new Second."

"I am," said Calver.

"I'm Arlen. Chief cook and bottle washer."

She extended a slim, strong hand. Calver took it. Her eyes, he noticed, were a blue so deep as to be almost black. Her smile was a little crooked, which made it no less attractive.

Pender, the little Purser, bustled up with two extra chairs, set them in place noisily. The sullen waitress brought more glasses.

Arlen sat down gracefully. She said, "Try to imagine that you're back in the Royal Mail, Maclean. Be a gentleman and pour me a drink."

The Mate poured drinks.

"We're all lushes on the Rim, Calver," said Arlen. (She had, he decided, already taken more than a few on board.) "We're all lushes, even though we've learned the hard way that drinking solves nothing. But we don't like happy drunks. The last Second

Mate but one, Wallis, he was a happy drunk. He was so happy that he could never be trusted with the loading. It was all one to him if the center of gravity was up in the control room or somewhere under the main venturi. But Maclean's not like that. Maclean will cry into his whisky, and pour a little of it over that absurd Royal Mail cap badge that he insists on wearing, and will stagger back on board tonight full of the woes of all the Universe as well as his own—and God help the stevedore if he stows one slab of zinc a millimeter out of place tomorrow!"

"Stow it, Arlen," said Maclean.

"Are you a happy drunk, Calver?" she demanded.

"No," he said.

"Then you're one of us. You'll make a real Rim Runner, skimming the edge of Eternity in a superannuated rustbucket held together with old string and chewing gum, and taking a masochistic pleasure in it. You've run away from yourself until you can't run any further, and there's a sort of desperate joy in that, too. You don't drink to forget. You don't drink to get into a state of maudlin, mindless happiness; you drink to intensify your feelings, you . . ."

"Stow it, Arlen!" snapped Maclean.

She got to her feet. "If that's the way you feel," she said coldly, "I'd better leave."

"Can't a man have a drink in peace without all this amateur psychiatry?" complained the Mate. "I drink because I like drinking. Period."

"Goodnight," she said.

"I'll see you back aboard," said Calver.

"No thanks," she told him. "I'm a big girl now. I'm not afraid of the dark. Would I be with Rim Runners if I were?"

Calver saw that the woman with the accordion was drifting towards the table, was smiling at Maclean, that Pender was already exchanging glances with one of the bold-eyed girls. He knew how the evening would develop and he wanted no part of it. He stood up, put his hand under Arlen's elbow and began to steer her towards the door.

"Goodnight, Maclean," he said. "Goodnight, Pender."

"What's the hurry, Calver?" asked the Mate. "The night's a pup."

"I'm rather tired," said Calver.

"All right. See you in the ayem."

The musician and the other woman slid into the vacated seats as Calver and Arlen reached the door. The waitress was bringing another bottle of whisky.

Calver glanced back to the table. "It looks like being a dog of a night . . ."

"What night isn't?" countered Arlen bitterly.

2

It was cold outside, and the gusty wind filled their eyes with dust. It was not the sort of night on which one finds pleasure in stargazing—yet Calver looked to the sky. The great, gleaming lens of the Galaxy was almost set, only one last glimmering parabola of cold fire visible low in the west. Overhead the sky was dark, the blackness intensified by the sparse and dim nebulosities that were the unreachable island universes.

Calver shivered.

"It's . . . It's frightening," whispered Arlen. "It's worse, somehow, seen from a planetary surface. Yet it has something . . ."

"Something?" he asked. "Or . . . nothing?"

"There are easier and faster ways of finding nothing," she said.

Calver felt a flare of anger and began to appreciate how, at times, her shipmates found this woman hard to live with. He asked brutally, "Then why didn't you take one?"

"Why didn't *you?*" she countered. "I'll tell you. Because you're like the rest of us. I don't know your story, any more than you know mine, but something happened to smash the career that you were carving out for yourself in the Commission's service—something that was your fault, and nobody else's. You hit rock bottom—but you refused to admit it. You decided, quite probably on a subconscious level, that the only salvation lay in a voyage—real and symbolical—to the very edge of the night . . ."

Calver laughed harshly. "And does this fancy theory of yours apply to all the Rim Runners?"

"To most of us. Not to the Old Man—he was born out here, on Thule. The only thing that he's running away from is the Grim Reaper; he's two hundred years old if he's a day. Pender's a Rim Worlder, too. So's Levine, our Psionic Radio Officer.

"But there's Bendix, the Interstellar Drive Engineer—he's out of Trans-Galactic Clippers. There's Renault, the Rocket King—he was Reaction Chief of a *Beta* Class liner . . ."

"I've heard of him," said Calver. "I've never sailed with him."

"Brentano, Electronic Radio, used to be in a respectable little outfit called Cluster Lines. Old Doc Malone had a flourishing practice in Port Austral, in the Centaurian System. Maclean, as you know, was with the Waverley Royal Mail . . ."

"And you?" he asked.

"Another refugee from the Commission," she said. "But I was ashore, on Earth, for a few years before I came out here . . ."

Calver realized with a start that they had walked the distance from the tavern to the spaceport gate.

The guard on duty—alert in spite of his slovenly appearance—looked at them, at their uniforms.

He said, "Good evening, Mrs. Arlen. Back early tonight."

"Somebody has to be up in the morning to cook breakfast for these space-hounds," she said.

"And this gentleman?"

"Our new Second Officer."

The guard looked from the photograph that he had produced from his pocket to Calver's face, nodded curtly. He pressed the button that opened the gate. Arlen and Calver passed through. Ahead of them was the ship, black against the dark sky, only a dim glimmer of yellow light shining from the airlock.

"The *Forlorn Lady*," said Arlen. "The poor old *Forlorn Bitch*. When I hear people talking about her I always wonder if they're referring to the ship, or to me . . . But I have every right to be forlorn. Do you know what they used to call me? Calamity Jane Lawler. But that was before I was married. It's Calamity Jane Arlen now . . ."

They walked slowly up the rickety ramp to the airlock, Calver steadying the girl with his arm. They got past the watchman—an ex-spaceman by the looks of him, and a heavy drinker—without waking him. They climbed the spiral staircase to the officers' flat.

Arlen led the way into the little pantry adjoining the messroom, switched on the percolator. In a matter of seconds it began to chuckle softly to itself. She drew two mugs of the bitter, black brew.

"Sugar, Calver? Cream?"

"Just sugar, thanks."

"I don't know why I drink this muck," she said. "It'll sober me up, and I don't want to be sober.

When I've had a few drinks I can accept the coldness, the loneliness, and make them part of me. When I'm sober, they . . . They frighten me . . ."

"Lawler," said Calver slowly, ignoring what she had just said. "Lawler . . . Calamity Jane Lawler . . . The name rings a bell. Weren't you in *Alpha Scorpii* at one time?"

"Yes," she said flatly. "I was. It was when there was the outbreak of food poisoning, and some fool pointed out that something horrid always happened aboard any ship that I was in. Hence the name. It stuck. The worst of it is that I do seem to be an accident prone sort of person, even ashore. When I left the Commission's service, when I married, the calamities still kept on coming. So . . ."

"So? What did happen?"

"What happened to *you?*" she demanded in reply. "We don't know each other well enough yet to start swapping life stories. I doubt if we ever shall."

Calver finished his coffee. He said, "Goodnight, Arlen."

"Goodnight," she replied dully.

Feeling suddenly both helpless and useless, Calver left her there in the little pantry, went to his cabin and turned in.

He was surprised at the speed with which he was able to adjust himself to the rather slovenly routine of *Lorn Lady*. She was pitifully shorthanded by the standards to which he was accustomed; there was no Third Officer, there were no junior engineers for either the Interstellar Drive or the Reaction Drive, and the Surgeon was also the Biochemist and, as such, was in charge of hydroponics, tissue culture and the yeast and algae vats. There were no cadets to do all the odd jobs that were beneath the dignity of the officers. Such jobs were done, if they were essential; otherwise they remained undone.

Safety first, Maclean had said. Safety first. Efficiency second. Spit and polish this year, next year, some time, never. Yet the gleaming, ever-precessing gyroscopes of the Mannschenn Drive Unit sang softly and smoothly, with never a stammer; and the pumps that drove the fluid propellant into the furnace of the Pile functioned with a reliability that could have been the envy of many a better found vessel. Old Doc Malone was an efficient farmer, and there was never a shortage of green salads or fresh meat in the mess; the algae served only as air and water purifiers, never as article of diet.

Yet she was old, was *Lorn Lady*. Machinery can be renewed part by part, but there comes a time when the shell plating of the hull holding that same machinery is almost porous, when every structural member is weakened by the fatigue that comes to all metal with the passage of the years.

She was old, and she was tired, and the age of her and the fatigue of her were mirrored in the frail body of Captain Engels, her Master. He was the oldest man whom Calver had ever met, even in Space where, barring accidents, extreme longevity is the rule rather than the exception. A few sparse strands of yellowish hair straggled over the thin, transparent parchment covering his skull. His uniform was too big for the fragile, withered body it covered. Only his eyes, pale blue and bleak, were alive.

He worried the officers very little, keeping to his own accommodation most of the time. Yet any minor malfunctioning, any deviation from normal routine, no matter how trivial, would bring him at once to the control room. He would say nothing, yet his mere presence would induce in the mind of the officer of the watch a sense of gross inadequacy and, with it, the resolve not to let the thing, whatever it might have been, occur again.

There was very little camaraderie aboard the ship whilst she was in Space; watch and watch routine gives small opportunity for social intercourse. But, Calver decided, there would not have been much social life even if the ship had been adequately manned. She carried too heavy a cargo of regrets. With Maclean he might have struck up a friendship, but the only times they met were at the changes of watches. He would have liked to have gotten to know Jane Arlen better—but she kept him, as she kept all the others aboard the ship, at arm's length.

The voyage to Faraway passed, as all voyages pass. There were no emergencies of any kind. The landing at Port Faraway was slow and painful, old Captain Engels refusing to trust the auto pilot and treating the ship as though she were an extension of his own aged and brittle body. Once she was berthed, discharge and loading progressed according to plan.

Calver had free time when *Lorn Lady* was in port. He did not particularly want it, but realized the folly of staying aboard the ship. On the evening of the day of arrival he changed into his least shabby uniform and then went to Arlen's cabin to see if she would come with him; she told him curtly that she was busy and that one Rim World city was as bad as the next anyhow. He left her checking stores, walked down the ramp from the airlock and on to the apron. He was obliged to admit that Arlen was right. From the spaceport Faraway looked like Lorn. The air was a little purer, perhaps, but was just as chilly and as dusty. There was no warmth in the westering sun, no light and color in the world.

He took the monorail from the spaceport to Faraway City. It was hard for a stranger, like himself, to tell where the industrial suburbs ended and the city proper began. All the buildings were low, all drab and in various stages of dilapidation. Even though the sun was down when his journey was ended, there was a marked shortage of bright lights.

Across the street from the monorail station was a hotel—*Rimrock House,* proclaimed the flickering neon sign. Calver walked across to it, went first into the bar. The whisky, he soon discovered, was inferior to the rotgut distilled by old Doc Malone. After his second drink he went into the hotel restaurant, ordered a meal. He did not enjoy it. Whoever had cooked it could have taken a few lessons from Arlen, with advantage.

He was grimly amused to see that the couple at the next table shared his low opinion of the Rimrock House cuisine. He could not help overhearing some of their comments. Their accent was familiar, and brought a wave of nostalgia with it. *Earth,* he thought. *But what are they doing here? They must be tourists. But who'd come out to the Rim for pleasure?*

The man got abruptly to his feet, stalked out of the restaurant. The girl remained seated, caught Calver's eye and grinned ruefully. She said, "Grim, isn't it? It was too much for my brother. He's gone up to his room to nurse his indigestion . . ."

Now that the girl had spoken to him, Calver was able to look at her without rudeness. There were pretty women, and even beautiful women, on the Rim Worlds—but all of them were lacking in finish, all of them ruined what had been given them by Nature with unsuitable clothing and accessories. This girl, obviously, had been brought up to regard the adornment of her face and body as an art, as a fine art. *No beauty doth she miss,* thought Calver, remembering the words of an old poet, *when all her robes are on. But beauty's self she is when all her robes are gone . . .*

"We thought that we should be playing safe by having something simple," she went on. *"Steak Diane* . . . That wasn't asking too much, was it?"

"One would think not," admitted Calver.

"I saw you making faces over your dinner," she said.

"Lobster Thermidor," he told her. "But I'd hate to meet the arthropod that was masquerading as a lobster. My guess is that it was just an oversized cockroach . . ."

Her face, even with the grimace of disgust, was attractive—and her laugh was even more so, its silvery, tinkling quality somehow matching the gleaming platinum of her hair. She said, "Will you join me for brandy and coffee in the Lounge? I'll get them to bring down a bottle of the real stuff from my room. Even though Napoleon never dipped his beak into it, it's still the produce of France . . ."

"Thank you," said Calver.

He got to his feet when he saw that the girl was about to rise, escorted her from the restaurant to the Lounge, to a table in a dimly-lit corner. He heard her ask the waitress to send somebody to her room, heard the other woman say, "Certainly, Miss Verrill . . ."

He said, "From Earth, Miss Verrill?"

"How did you know?"

"I heard the waitress address you by name."

"I meant, how did you know that I was from Earth?"

"The accent is obvious. You're from Earth, from one of the English speaking nations. North America . . . In fact, Virginia . . ."

"You're right, Mr. . . . ?"

"Calver."

"Mr. Calver. Also from Earth. With the indefinable accent, the amalgam of accents, of the true spaceman. But I didn't know that there were any big ships in port."

"There aren't."

"I must be slipping. When I saw you sitting there I thought that you were a typical I.T.C. officer out for an evening's slumming, seeing how the poor live . . ."

"I *was* in the I.T.C.," said Calver shortly.

"And now?"

"Rim Runners."

"Oh, yes. Rim Runners. They're the local shipping line, aren't they?"

"They are."

The waitress brought the coffee. With it, on the tray, there was the bottle of brandy, the two balloon glasses. The coffee was vile. The brandy was not.

Calver felt its warmth creeping through him. It was pleasant here, away from the ship, pleasant to be seeing a new face, listening to a fresh voice. Even though the meal had been almost inedible, there were compensations. This was the sort of life that he had run away from (or been driven away from?)— the pleasant chatter over a glass of good liquor, the companion at whom other men looked with envy. And perhaps . . .

Perhaps . . .

And why not? he asked himself. A beautiful woman, unattached, lonely . . . So she's got her brother with her. So what? No matter what the *mores* of the rest of the Galaxy might be, Earth had left the Victorian era centuries behind.

"I envy spacemen," the girl was saying.

"Why? The life's not bad at times—but at times it's not good."

"What I envy," she said, "is the here today and gone tomorrow philosophy."

Promising, he thought, studying her face in the dim, flattering light. He decided that she was not as young as he had first thought, but that did not matter. She was an attractive woman, and an available woman, and he, despising the spaceport trollops, had been too long without a woman.

"Love 'em and leave 'em . . ." she went on.

"Too right," he agreed. Then, "This is rather absurd. I don't even know your given name."

"Does it matter? 'Darling' is safe. Stick to that and you can be as absent-minded as you please." She smiled again—and there was definite promise in the smile. "But if you must know—it's Sonya . . ."

"It rather suits you," he said. "If it wasn't for that Virginian accent—but I like it—you'd look fine with one of those Russian hounds, a Borzoi, on a leash . . ."

"So I'm the Grand-Duchess-in-exile type?"

"You could be, at that. But a human Grand Duchess, not a female with a mixture of ice water and indigo in her veins. As for the 'in-exile' part— any civilized person is in exile out here." He added, "You especially."

"And you. You belong to big ships, not the scruffy little tramps that run the Rim." She sipped her drink, looking at him over the rim of her glass with violet eyes in which there was more than a hint of promise. "Fair exchange is no robbery. What do they call you when you're up and dressed?"

"Calver. But take away the uniform and it could be Derek."

"It rather suits you. Derek . . . Derrick . . . Puts me in the mind of something tall and angular . . ."

"The original Derrick, after whom derricks were named, was a public hangman," Calver told her.

"Need we be so morbid, Derek?"

"We needn't, Sonya."

"Then let's don't. Or don't let's. You know what I mean, anyhow." She raised a slim wrist, looked at the tiny, jeweled watch that seemed more ornament than precision instrument. "If I know my darling brother he's away by now, drowning that vile dinner in one of the low groggeries he's so partial to. If you don't mind, I'll slip upstairs and make sure. His room's next to mine, and he's inclined to be just a little old-fashioned and stuffy . . . Don't bother to get up. I shan't be long."

Calver watched her walk towards the door. She walked as a woman should walk—not flaunting the slendernesses and the curves below her beautifully-cut clothing, but not making any secret of them, seeming to move to inaudible music. He thought,

She's what I've been needing. It's a pity that the old Forlorn
Lady *will be such a short time in port, but Sonya might still
be here when we get back. Or she might come to Lorn . . .*

He thought, *Careful, Calver, careful. You know what
these rich bitches are like—or you should know. Once bitten,
twice shy. Don't get too deeply involved again. You heard
what she said—'Love 'em and leave 'em . . .'*

He saw the other woman standing by the door
through which Sonya had passed—the tall brunette,
handsome rather than beautiful (but who, given the
correct stimuli, would be beautiful), slimly elegant,
too elegant (as Sonya had been) for her surroundings, somehow familiar.

She was looking at him intently, and her gaze was
accusatory.

He wondered what specter this was from his past
come to haunt him—then realized that it was Jane
Arlen, strange in her civilian clothes.

3

In uniform she was a handsome woman. In her tailored gray costume, with the little, bright accessories detracting from its severity, she was a little more than handsome. *Beautiful?* Calver decided—although not rapidly—not. She would never be beautiful until she lost that hardness.

She walked slowly to the corner where Calver was sitting. He got to his feet, sketched the suggestion of a bow.

She said, "Doing yourself proud, aren't you?"

He said, "I'd offer you a drink—but it's not mine to offer." He added, "But I don't suppose Sonya would mind."

She said, "*Sonya!* Why not Olga Popovsky?"

"What the hell are you getting at, Arlen?" demanded Calver.

"The original innocent abroad," she sneered. "I suppose you think that she's after you for your good looks. Or your bankroll. It's a well-known fact that all Rim Runner Second Mates are millionaires."

He retained a precarious grip on his temper. He said reasonably, "Listen, Arlen, there's no need to be a dog. I asked you to come ashore with me, and you refused. Now, just because I'm having a few drinks with an attractive woman, you go off at the deep end . . ."

She sat down abruptly.

She asked, her manner serious, "Calver, just what have you been telling that tow-haired canine?"

"It's no concern of yours," he replied. "But, if you must know, we've just been exchanging light, civilized conversation—one of the commodities that's in very short supply out on the Rim."

"And that's all?"

"That's all."

She relaxed a little then, allowed herself to sink back in the chair. She said, "I think I will have some of this excellent brandy. Ask the waitress for another glass, will you? We may as well finish the bottle; your precious Miss Verrill won't be taking it where she's going."

"Arlen, what is this?"

She ignored the question, continued, "And if anybody wants to know in whose company you've passed the evening, it's mine."

"I still don't get what you're driving at."

"You will," she told him. "You will." Her eyes, that had been fixed on his, shifted their regard, looked towards the door. A faint smile played over her firm mouth.

Calver followed her glance. He saw the two men who had just come in, the two men who, in spite of their civilian clothes and casual manner, could only be police officers. They looked at him and at Arlen, their faces expressionless, walked purposefully towards the table.

One of them said, "Good evening, Mrs. Arlen. At first I didn't recognize you in your finery."

"Hardly finery, Colonel Trent. I've had this costume for all of five years."

"The age makes no difference to the cut," said Trent. Then, "I don't think that I've met this gentleman."

"Colonel Trent, Mr. Calver," said Arlen. "Mr. Wayne, Mr. Calver."

"New to Rim Runners, Mr. Calver?" asked Trent.

"Yes."

The police officer's keen eyes were making an inspection of what was on the table—the bottle of French brandy, the three glasses.

He said, "Been having a slight party, I see."

"Yes," said Calver, feeling the need for caution but still not knowing why. "Care to join us in a drink?"

"Some other time, perhaps, when we aren't on duty. As a matter of fact we are looking for Miss Verrill."

"She went upstairs to powder her nose," said Arlen.

"Thank you, Mrs. Arlen. We'll find her there."

When they were gone, Arlen said, "Yes, they'll find her there. And they'll also find the concealed tape recorder that was supposed to record everything you said . . ."

"Are you crazy, Arlen?"

"Far from it," she remarked, sipping her brandy. "Far from it. I got the buzz that the Verrill wench and her partner were in town, sniffing around and on

the look-out for somebody, anybody, from the ship.
The pair of 'em will sleep in jail tonight—and as
many nights hereafter as the trumped-up charge will
hold 'em. My dear, innocent Mr. Calver—that woman is one of the slickest operators in the Federation
Secret Service. We, of course, are still in the Federation—but the big boys have heard rumors of our
impending secession and it's got 'em worried.
They've heard rumors of the new worlds to the
Galactic East, too, and suspect some kind of a tie-up.
So . . ."

"You mean," said Calver, "that she is a spy?"

"You could call her that—although, at the moment, with the Rim Planets among the Federated
Worlds still, she hasn't quite got that status . . ."

"But Trent and the other fellow were very . . .
gullible."

"They know me."

"But what about the hotel staff?"

"They know me, too. I asked them to do me a favor, to say that I had dined here with you. They
knew that if they didn't do that small favor I'd be
doing no more small favors for them." She smiled her
attractive, crooked smile. "After all, I've never regarded smuggling as a sin."

"I see," said Calver tiredly. "Anyhow, thanks for
saving me from the mines."

"I didn't want the ship to be held up," she told
him. Then, "I'm afraid this has rather ruined your
night on the tiles."

"It has, rather. But it could have been much
worse. Thanks to you, it wasn't. Well, I suppose that
we'd better get back to the ship."

"The night," she said, "is young, and neither of us
is senile."

They finished the brandy between them and, as he was sipping the last glass, Calver thought regretfully of the woman whose gift it had been—regretfully, but not too regretfully. After all, whatever had happened to her was merely one of the normal hazards of her profession. She would suffer a little indignity, a little discomfort, and that was all—and then, her usefulness at an end insofar as this sector of the Galaxy was concerned, would be returning to Earth or some other civilized planet.

Even so—it could have been good.

And how much, wondered, Calver, would he have told her? A man in love—or a man infatuated—will babble foolishly. But how much would there have been to tell? He had browsed through the log books covering past voyages of *Lorn Lady*, had been told by Maclean and the other officers much about the commercial side of the Eastern Circuit trade. He knew that large shipments of machinery were being made to Tharn—and that was a contravention of Federation law. He knew that the people of Grollor—who already had interplanetary rockets plying between the worlds of their own system—were importing manuals concerning the manufacture and operation of the Interstellar Drive. That was another crime by Federation standards.

"There is only one word for this conversation," said Arlen, breaking into his thoughts. "Scintillating."

"Sorry," he said. "I was thinking."

"Poor boy," she murmured. "Did Mummy take away his little platinum-haired doll?"

"Mummy did just that," he grinned.

"That's better. As long as you can see the funny side of things there's hope for you yet." She signalled to the waitress. "Oh, Sue, we seem to have finished Miss Verrill's excellent brandy. I know that you can't supply another bottle of the same—but have you any of that tiger's milk of yours?"

"We have, Mrs. Arlen. I'll bring it right away."

"That's a good girl, Sue." She turned to Calver. "It's a local liqueur. It's got a fancy name—*felis tigris*. Don't ask me how they get that striped effect, because I don't know. Just drink it and enjoy it."

They drank it and enjoyed it—but it did nothing to loosen Calver's tongue.

At last Arlen asked abruptly, "How do you like the *Forlorn Bitch?*"

"Which one do you mean?" he countered, grinning.

"The ship, of course."

"She's . . . a ship."

"I know that. But how do you like her?"

"She feeds well."

"I know that, too. Perhaps I should ask, how do you like the Rim?"

"I don't," he said frankly. "Even though I'm no telepath I can feel the weight of the mass fear, the dread of the cold and the dark."

"Then why don't you go back where you came from?"

"You should know the answer to that question, Arlen. You were with the Commission yourself. I was Chief Officer of one of their big ships, and by leaving them I insulted them. That's the way that they always look at it. I can never get back."

"There are plenty of smaller lines, far superior to Rim Runners."

"I know. And they run to ports also served by the

Commission. I should always have the reminder of what could have been (what should have been?) if . . . I'd always be seeing some big *Alpha* or *Beta* Class liner and thinking, *I could have been Master of her, if . . .*"

"If what?"

He said, "I like you, Arlen, but I'm damned if I'm going to do a psychological strip-tease just for your amusement."

She said, "I hate to have to admit it—but I like you." She paused, sipped her drink thoughtfully. She went on, "As you know very well, it's customary for the average spacewoman to have her steady from among the officers of whatever ships she's serving in. I'm no prude—but I've never been like that. Maclean tried hard when I first joined *Lorn Lady*, but never got any place. Now, as you've seen, he's well content with the cheap little trollops he finds in every port. Pender tried, too. The engineers and the radio men have made passes."

"So?"

"I'll be frank. Do you want me, Calver? If you do, I think that we should know a little more about each other's backgrounds before we start anything."

Calver looked at her. He thought, *Such an arrangement could take the keen edge off the loneliness for both of us. It can never replace what's been lost, but it could be . . . comforting. For her as well as for me.*

He said, "There's not much to tell. I was, as you know, in the Commission's service. I was Mate of one of the big *Beta* Class wagons. I was married, fairly happily, with two children . . ."

"Go on," she told him gently.

"Oh, it's an old story. It's always happening to

somebody. It's the sort of thing that always happens
to somebody else—until it happens to *you*. Anyhow, I
met *the* woman, the only possible woman, you know
—she was a passenger from Caribbea to Port Austral. (Funnily enough, her name was Jane, the same
as yours.) There was the usual mess—resignation
from the Commission's service, divorce and all the
rest of it. Dorothy—my wife—remarried, happily I
hope. Jane and I married. Her father found me a
shore job—a well-paid sinecure, actually—in the
firm of which he was president. What the hell does a
spaceman know about the design and manufacture of
personalized wrist radios?"

"Sweet Fanny Adams, I should imagine," said
Arlen.

"How right you are. Anyhow, it all worked out not
too badly for a while until Jane began to realize that
a spaceman aboard his ship and the same spaceman
holding down an office chair are two different
animals. Then the glamor began to fade . . ."

"Glamor has nothing to do with pretty uniforms,"
she told him.

"Perhaps not. But there's the other, more real
glamor—the glamor of authority over men and machines. In a job in which I could have pulled my
weight it might have been different. In a job where I
was no more than the boss's pampered son-in-
law . . ."

"You should have struck out for yourself."

"I should have. I realize that now. But there was
so much that I wanted to be able to buy for Jane—
and so much that I could never have afforded if I'd
started again at the bottom in some worthwhile employment. Anyhow, as I said, the glamor began to

fade. And it went out like a snuffed candle the night that she went alone to a party to which I had not been invited, returning unexpectedly to find me with a girl I'd picked up in a bar. Cutting a long story short, I didn't bother to pack. I just got out. Since then I've been drifting out towards the Rim. And now I'm here."

She said, "I'm rather sorry for her. I'm rather sorry for both of them."

"Thank you," he said. "And what about me?"

"You're sorry enough for yourself," she told him. "Any sympathy from me would be superfluous."

"If that's the way you look at it . . ."

"That's the way I look at it."

"All right. Well, what's your story?"

She shrugged. "Nothing much. Just that I've always been Calamity Jane, and always shall be . . ."

"Fair exchange," he insisted, "fair exchange."

"All right, then. You know about the reputation I had when I was with the Commission; it always amazed me that they kept me in their employ. There are accident prone people to whom accidents happen —and there are accident prone people around whom accidents happen. I come in the latter category. But I thought that the jinx was licked at last. Like you, I met the only possible person during a voyage. I left the Commission's service to get married. We were very happy. And . . ."

"And?"

"As I said, my marriage was very happy. A drunken surface car driver smashed it. He got off without a scratch. So did I."

He said, acutely conscious of the inadequacy of the words, "I'm sorry."

"So was I. So am I." She stared into her empty glass. "Pour me another drink, Calver, will you?" He obeyed. She went on, "You know, Calver, I like you. I think that I like you rather too much to see anything happen to you. I'm afraid that if we do start anything between us, the old Calamity Jane business will begin again . . ."

"What have I got to lose?" he asked bitterly. Then—"That was rather selfish, wasn't it?"

"It was," she said. "It was." Again she was silent. She almost whispered, "But you've been warned. If you still want to go through with it . . ."

"If you do," he said.

4

THE PEOPLE of Tharn, where *Lady Lorn* made its first call, are human, except for very minor differences. There is a greenish tinge to their complexions and the coloration of their hair is usually either blue or dark green. (There are, of course, other differences, but these are obvious only to the biologist.) Their women, however, are indubitably mammalian.

It was on Tharn that *Lorn Lady* discharged the parcel of such tools and instruments as would be of value to a people with only the beginnings of an industrial technology. There was, for example, a large consignment of magnetic compasses; these would be in great demand among the fishermen and seamen. There were such items as needles and scissors; and there were hammers, planes, chisels and saws. There were scientific text books for the Temple University.

It was on Tharn that *Lorn Lady* discharged these goods—and others—and on Tharn that she lay idle until the commencement of loading the morning following completion of discharge. So, after the evening meal, Calver and Jane Arlen went ashore together. The Mate and the Purser were already ashore—they did not ever, as Renault, Reaction Drive Engineer caustically remarked, waste one second of boozing or wenching time. Renault, aided by Bendix and Brentano, was having to stay on board to overhaul his propellant pumps. Old Doc Malone was playing chess with Captain Engels. Levine was in his cabin with his dog's brain amplifier, trying (but in vain) to find out if there were any practicing telepaths on the planet.

Calver and Arlen walked slowly from the primitive spaceport—no more than a field with a few warehouses around its periphery—to the town. The shortest way lay over rough heathland, but it was pleasant to walk after the weeks of Free Fall. The westering sun, bloated and ruddy, was behind them, and in the planless huddle of buildings ahead of them the soft yellow lights, primitive affairs of burning natural gas, were already springing into being. Blue smoke from the chimneys of the town hung in layers in the still air. There was the smell of frost.

"Things," said Arlen softly, "are a lot better now. I used to dread going ashore just as much as I dreaded staying aboard. Now, I'm beginning to enjoy it . . ."

"I'm glad," said Calver. Then— "But I'm a stranger here, Jane. Where do we spend our money? And on what?"

"We'll have a quiet evening in one of the taverns," she said. "The liquor here isn't at all bad; as you know, we're loading a fair consignment of it tomorrow . . . There's usually a musician or juggler or conjuror to amuse the customers. And there'll be a blazing fire, as like as not."

They were in the town now. They walked slowly along the rutted street, between the stone houses with their high, thatched roofs. Shops were still doing business, their open windows illumined by flaring gas jets. It could almost, thought Calver, have passed for a street scene in the Middle Ages back on Earth. Almost . . . But gas lighting was unknown in those days, and the women did not wear dresses that exposed their breasts and most of their legs, and any small animals abroad would have been dogs and cats, not things like elongated, segmented tortoises. Even so, there must have been very similar displays of ambiguous-looking meat, of glowing fruit, of gleaming fish (gleaming *and* reeking), of rich cloth and of cloth far from rich, of jewelry both clumsy and exquisite.

They stopped at a shop and Calver, with Arlen translating, bought for her a bracelet of beaten silver, paying for it what seemed to be an absurdly small number of the square copper coins. The robed shopkeeper bowed low as they left his premises.

"He," said Arlen, "is one of those who like us." She lifted her slim arm so that the bracelet caught the flickering light. "He gave you quite a good discount on this . . ."

"One of the ones who likes us?" asked Calver. "I'd have thought that everybody would have liked us."

"Always the innocent abroad," she jeered. "When are you ever going to grow up, Derek? Anyhow, the shopkeepers are pleased to see us here. Naturally. So are the fishermen and sailors, to whom our compasses are a godsend. The artisans, who buy our fine new tools, welcome us. The priests at the University look upon us as a source of new knowledge that will not run dry for centuries."

"Well, then—who else is there?"

"The peasants, who have the typical peasant mentality, the distrust of any and all novelties. The landowning noblemen who sense, and not altogether without justification, that we are ushering in the forces of evolution and revolution that will destroy them . . ."

"Aren't we taking a bit of a risk coming ashore here?"

She laughed. "This is a University town. The priesthood maintains a very efficient police force. If anybody were fool enough to harm any of us, the High Priest, personally, would see to it that he died very slowly. *Pour encourager les autres* . . ."

"Voltaire didn't say it, or mean it, in quite that way."

"Is Voltaire buying the drinks tonight? If he's not, he can shut up."

They paused outside the door of one of the taverns, looked up at the swinging sign, the sign that shone bravely silver in the light of the flaring gas jet. Arlen chuckled. "This is new. It wasn't here the last time that we were on Tharn. It used to be some sort of dragon, done in red. Now it's a spaceship."

"The innkeeper," said Calver, "is obviously one of those who like us. He might even stand us a drink or two. Shall we go in?"

They went in.

The place was warm and the air was blue with smoke. Calver thought at first, foolishly, that it came from pipes and cigars and cigarettes, then saw that it was eddying from the big open fireplace. Even so, there was a distinct aroma of burning tobacco in the air. Puzzled (for smoking is a minor vice practiced

only by Earthmen and their descendants) he looked
around, saw Maclean and Pender sitting at a table in
the corner of the big room. A giggling girl, who was
trying to smoke a cigarette and who was making a
sorry job of it, was perched on the Purser's lap. The
Mate, as usual after a sufficient intake of alcohol, was
singing softly.

> *Goodbye, I'll run to seek another sun*
> *Where I may find*
> *There are worlds more kind than the ones*
> *left behind . . ."*

Another girl stood beside him, trying to pick out
the notes on a stringed instrument like a small harp.

Arlen frowned. She said, "I suppose it's all right—
but those two are liable to get themselves into serious
trouble one of these days . . ."

"Nobody here seems to be worrying," said Calver.

Nobody was. Everybody present seemed to be
worrying about one thing—the maximum intake of
liquor in the minimum time. They were a rough
crowd—most of them, obviously, seamen and fishermen; knee- or thigh-boots combined with clothing
of dark blue seemed to be almost standard wear
throughout the Galaxy for those who followed the
sea. Most of them had girls of their own with them—
and those who did not were not the type to allow
women to interfere with serious drinking. Almost all
of them raised their mugs to the spaceman and
spacewoman in salutation. Room was made for them
at one of the larger tables and tankards of the dark,
sweet brew were pressed upon them.

Calver felt a little out of things as Arlen entered

into a spirited conversation with the tough, grizzled seaman on her left. She did condescend, now and again, to translate some of his sallies.

"He's Master of a schooner," she said. "You may have noticed her as we came in, the quite large ship at the quay just below the bridge. He says that he'll sign me on as his cook any time that I want a change . . ."

"I'd starve without you, Jane," said Calver. "In more ways than one."

He let his attention wander from the incomprehensible conversation, looked to the corner where Maclean and Pender were sitting, saw that they were getting along very well indeed with the two native girls. He felt smugly superior to them, then thought, *But I wonder what it would be like? There must be some difference . . . And that green skin, and the blue hair . . .*

He started as the door opened with a crash.

A young man strode arrogantly into the hall, followed by half a dozen others, obviously servants or retainers. He wore emerald trunks, scarlet boots and a scarlet jacket. A great silver plume bobbed and nodded above his wide-brimmed, black hat which, like the rest of his clothing, was lavishly ornamented with gold embroidery. A long, slender sword swung at his left side. He was neither seaman, fisherman nor artisan. He could not, thought Calver, possibly be one of the priestly scholars from the University. He could be only one of the landowning nobility of whom Arlen had spoken.

He glared around him, looking for somebody. He saw the two spacemen with their girls in the far corner. His mouth tightened and his yellow eyes gleamed dangerously. "Sayonee!" he called in a voice of command. "Sayonee!"

The woman on Maclean's lap looked up and around. Her lip curled. She spat like an angry cat.

"Oh, oh," whispered Arlen. "I don't like this. She told him to run away and get lost . . ."

The young man, his followers at his heels, pushed to the corner of the room, careless of the overset bottles and tankards in his wake. He stood there, glaring down at Maclean and Pender. The Mate matched him, glare for glare, his face flushed and angry under the carroty thatch. The girl, Sayonee, looked frightened, whispered something to Maclean, tried to slide off his lap. Maclean said, in English, "You're my woman for tonight. I've paid for you. I'm not giving you up to any damned planetlubber!"

Pender said, "Mac, hadn't you better . . . ?"

"Shut up!" snapped Maclean.

"Maclean!" called Calver. "Don't be a fool!"

"Stay out of this, Calver!" shouted the Mate in reply. "And if you're scared, get the hell out!"

The aristocrat said something. It must have been insulting. Maclean, obviously, knew what had been said—the spacefarer usually learns the curses of any strange language long before he is capable of carrying out a polite conversation in it. The blood drained from his face, leaving it a deathly white. He got to his feet, unceremoniously dumping Sayonee. Her little harp jangled discordantly as she fell. He picked up his mug from the table, let the Tharnian have the contents full in the face. He took a step forward, his fists clenched and ready. Drunk as he was, he would have used them, and used them well—if he had been allowed to do so.

The nobleman's sword whipped out from his scab-

bard, ran him through before he could make another
gesture either of offense or defense.

There were shouts and screams; there was the
crash of overturned furniture and shattered glass-
ware. From somewhere above there was the furi-
ous, incessant clanger of a bell. Calver was on his
feet, about to go to Maclean's help—although he
knew that the Mate was beyond help—when he remembered Jane Arlen.

"Get out of this!" he snapped.

"No."

"Then keep behind me!"

The aristocrat was pushing towards the door, his
men on either side of him and behind him. He held
his sword, still unsheathed, and the blood on it
gleamed scarlet in the flaring gaslight. His bullies
had drawn long knives. One of them staggered as a
flung bottle struck him on the temple. Another bottle
shattered in mid-air as the long sword leapt up to
deflect it.

He saw Calver and Arlen. A thin, vicious grin split
his face. At Arlen's side, the old sea captain growled
something that sounded like a curse. Calver saw that
he, too, had drawn a knife. For a moment he feared
attack from this quarter, then realized that this was
an ally, that most of the fishermen and seamen in the
inn were allies.

But they were not trained fighters—not trained
fighters of men, that is. With wind and weather, with
straining, refractory gear and with the monsters of
the deep they could cope, but all their fights with
their own kind had been limited to the occasional
tavern brawl. This was more than a mere tavern

brawl. This was a one-sided battle against soldiers, experienced and ruthless killers, intelligently led.

The swordsman was close now. The old captain shouted and jumped forward to meet him. He fell into a crouch, holding his knife for the deadly, upward thrust. The blade of the sword flickered harmlessly over his left shoulder. Had he been fighting one man only he might well have won—but one of the retainers jumped him from behind, driving his blade deep into the old man's back.

Calver picked up a chair, held it before him as a shield. He jabbed the three legs of it at the aristocrat's face, felt a savage satisfaction as flesh and cartilage gave beneath the blow. He swung his makeshift weapon down and around, felled the man who had stabbed the old seaman in the back. He brought it up again just in time to intercept and to deflect the vicious sword.

He heard Arlen scream.

He dared not look around, but from the corner of his eye he saw that two of the bullies had seized her, were dragging her towards the door. Hostage or victim? He had no time to reason it out. He was fighting for his life, and he was very conscious of the fact. He was fighting with a clumsy weapon, held in unskilled hands, against a finely balanced instrument of murder in the hands of a master. His body and head he could protect, but his legs were already bleeding from a score of wounds, some of them deep.

He fell back, saw the smile that appeared on the bloodied face of his enemy, the twisted smile under the broken nose. He fell back farther, as though in terror. He hoped that the Tharnian would be in no hurry to follow, that he would elect to play a cat and mouse game, to finish his victim almost at leisure.

Calver thought, *I'm no swordsman, but I do know something about ballistics* . . .

With all his strength he hurled the chair, followed it before it had reached its target. He saw the Tharnian, foolishly, bring up his sword to parry the heavy missile, saw the point of it drive through the thick wooden seat. Then the other man was down, and Calver was on top of him, his hands seeking the other's throat. But somebody was pulling at his shoulders, trying to drag him off his enemy. He tensed himself for the sharp agony of the blade in the back—but it never came. Muscular hands closed over his own, pulling them away from the Tharnian's bruised neck. He was jerked to his feet. He glared at the men who surrounded him—the hard, competent-looking men who wore uniforms of short black tunics over yellow trunks, who carried (and used) polished wooden clubs. He saw new-looking, shiny handcuffs being snapped on the wrists of those of the nobleman's bullies who were still standing.

He saw—and he found it hard to forgive himself for having forgotten her—Arlen. She was pale, and her uniform was torn from her shoulders, but she seemed unharmed.

"The party's over," she said with a sorry attempt at flippancy. "These are the University police. They'll see us back to the ship . . ."

"And Maclean?" he asked.

"Dead," she replied flatly. "But Pender's all right. He kept under the table."

"And what will happen to . . . him?" asked Calver, nodding towards the swordsman who, like his followers, was now handcuffed.

"I don't know. I don't want to know. His father, who's the local baron, might be able to buy him back from the High Priest before justice has run its full course . . . But I doubt it."

"I feel rather sorry for him," said Calver slowly. "After all, poor Maclean did steal his girl . . ."

"And he," she flared, "did his best to steal yours!"

"I forgot that," he muttered.

"You'd better not make a habit of it," she told him coldly.

5

THE FOLLOWING DAY was a busy one. In spite of the events of the previous evening, in spite of the tragedy, the ship's work had to go on. There was cargo to load —casks of the local liquor, ingots of gold, the baled pelts of the great, richly-furred mountain bears. There was the inquiry held by Captain Engels into the death of his Chief Officer, the inquiry at which, in addition to Calver, Arlen and Pender, the High Priest was present.

The old Tharnian—he seemed more aged than Captain Engels himself, his green skin deeply wrinkled, his sparse hair faded to a pale yellow—was sorrowful.

He said, speaking in English, "There are those on Tharn who hate and fear you, Captain, who hate and fear the knowledge that will set all men free."

"I am afraid, Your Wisdom," said Engels, "that my own officer was in part to blame for what happened."

"The girl was not Lanoga's property," said the

priest. "She was free to go with whom she would. Lanoga's actions were aimed as much against the University as against your people."

"And Lanoga?" asked Calver.

"If you delay your departure," said the High Priest, "you will be able to witness the execution tomorrow."

"We have to maintain our schedule," said Engels.

"And so do I," said Jane Arlen. "If I am not required any farther, I will see to the business of the next meal, Captain."

"You may go, Mrs. Arlen."

"And if I may be spared, sir," said Calver, "I have the stowage to see to."

"But of course. I forgot that you're the Mate now."

Calver and Jane left the Captain's day room, left the two old men who, although of different races, had so much in common, the two sad old men voicing their fears and regrets over a glass of wine.

Calver said, "I feel sorry for the old priest. If he's not careful, he'll bring his world tumbling about his ears. The way I see it, the Barons are just itching for an excuse to crush the University and all that it stands for . . ."

"He's no fool," Arlen told him, "and he's tougher than he looks. I think that he rather hopes that the Barons will march on the town. There are quite a few things you don't know, Derek. Now that you're Chief Officer, you'll be finding them out . . ."

"Such as?"

"It's not for me to tell you. I'm only the chief cook and bottle washer. But you'll find out."

They parted company then—Arlen proceeding to

her own domain, Calver to see to details of the loading. His first task was a melancholy one—to make space for Maclean's body in one of the ship's deep-freeze chambers. It had been decided that he would not be buried on Tharn, in the soil of an alien planet, but in Space, as a spaceman should be.

Then there was a session of work at the Ralston, the ingenious instrument which was, in effect, a two-dimensional model of the ship mounted on gymbals, upon which shiftable weights represented stores, propellant, personnel and cargo. After a few trials and errors he had the center of gravity where he wanted it for the next leg of the voyage—in theory, that is—and then busied himself, aided by little Brentano, Electronic Radio Officer and now Acting Second Mate, in ensuring that his calculations were carried out in practice.

What remained of the morning passed rapidly. When the stevedor's help ceased work for the midday meal, Calver was ready for his own lunch, as were the other officers, all of whom, in their separate departments, had been making all ready and secure for Space.

But in the messroom the table was not laid. In the galley the stove was cold, the pots and pans all hanging in their proper places with none in use. Calver thought that Arlen must be ill, perhaps suffering from some sort of delayed reaction to the previous night's events, hurried to her cabin. The bunk was neatly made and empty, however. Of Arlen there was no sign.

Calver reported to the Captain the absence of the Catering Officer.

Engels was worried. He said, "Do you think she

could have jumped ship? Such cases are not uncommon . . ." He looked sharply at Calver's face, remarked drily, "But I was forgetting, Mr. Calver. I'm sorry. She has no reason to desert, has she?"

"She has not," said Calver. "There must be something seriously wrong, sir. I'll go into town straight away, start making inquiries . . ."

"Not so fast, Mr. Calver. We start making inquiries here. Call all officers into the messroom. We will find out who saw Mrs. Arlen last, and in what circumstances."

Calver did as he was told. They sat around the table—the burly, swarthy Renault, the Rocket King; the gangling, balding Bendix, Chief (and only) Interstellar Drive Engineer; the dark, compact and competent Brentano; little, weedy Levine, looking (as he always did) as though he had just been dragged away from his crystal ball; the monkish Doc Malone; pudgy Pender with his fat, sulky face. At the head of the table sat Captain Engels.

"Mr. Calver," he asked, "when did *you* see Mrs. Arlen last?"

"I exchanged a few words with her after we left your cabin this morning. I haven't seen her since."

"Mr. Renault?"

"Captain," said old Doc Malone, interrupting. "I think that I can throw some light on the matter. The last time that we were here Mrs. Arlen asked me to analyze some of the local fungi. I found that they were not only non-toxic, but quite delicious. She told me this morning that she was going out to gather some for our lunch . . ."

"And where was she going to gather them?" demanded Calver.

"I'm not sure. But I think that she found the last lot in that little wood about a mile to the west of the landing field . . ."

Calver jumped to his feet. "Sir," he said, "there's no point in wasting further time. With your permission . . ." (and he made it plain that the asking of permission was a mere formality) ". . . I shall go to the woods at once. Somebody had better come with me. She may have twisted her ankle, or may have been attacked by some wild animal . . ."

"All right, then, Mr. Calver. But report to my cabin first."

"Sir, there's no time to waste . . ."

"Report to my cabin, *now*." He paused, seemed to be making mental calculations. "And bring Mr. Bendix and Mr. Pender with you."

Impatient, gnawed by anxiety, Calver followed the Captain to his quarters. He, with Bendix and Pender, stood there while the old man unlocked the big, steel cabinet, opened the door to reveal the neatly-racked weapons. As he did so he was speaking softly, saying, "I understand your feelings, Mr. Calver; that's why I'm letting you go. But I can't strip the ship of all effective personnel. In a pinch, Brentano can be Acting Mate. And, if things blow up in our faces—as the High Priest said they might— Renault can get the ship up and in orbit, while Levine yells for assistance . . . But take an automatic each, with spare magazines . . ."

Calver buckled belt and holster around his waist, took one of the heavy weapons from its rack and hefted it appreciatively, then tested the action. He rammed a clip of 10-mm cartridges into the butt, snapped back the slide to load the pistol, thumbed on the safety catch, holstered the gun. He filled his pockets with spare magazines. While he did so, he was thinking of what the Old Man had been saying —and his thoughts were not pleasant ones. The sprained ankle was still a possibility, but it was remote. And evil men were more to be feared than wild animals.

He hurried down the spiral stairway in the axial shaft, followed by the others. He walked hastily towards the little copse, as hastily as the roughness of the terrain would permit. And as he walked he stared at the hill on the horizon—the hill upon which stood the rugged, domineering pile of the castle.

"And that was all you found?" asked Captain Engels tiredly.

"That was all we found," said Calver. "Her basket, one shoe, the signs of a struggle . . ." He said, almost as an afterthought, "There was no blood . . ."

"Why should there have been?" asked Engels sharply. He added, more softly. "I appreciate your feelings, Mr. Calver. I know that you're all in favor of leading an armed assault upon the castle. But it would be futile. Oh, I know that it would be a case of modern automatic firearms against bows and arrows —but the people with the bows and arrows outnumber the crew of this ship a hundredfold, and they will be firing from behind stone battlements . . ." With thin fingers he filled a pipe of polished porcelain, a pipe as old and fragile as himself, lit it with the glowing coil of the lighter that he pulled from its socket on his desk. He said, "I sent Levine into town with a message to the High Priest. He should be back at any time now."

"The High Priest," said Calver bitterly. "What can he do?"

"Plenty," snapped the Captain. "This is his world. Furthermore, he is in a position to bargain . . ."

"To bargain?" echoed Calver. Then— "Oh, I begin to see . . . This is all just a matter of filthy local politics, isn't it? That arrogant murderer Lanoga will be returned to his father intact—and in exchange we get Jane in like condition . . ." A dreadful doubt assailed him. "I suppose that the High Priest will play?"

"That, Mr. Calver, can be decided only by himself."

"Damn it all, sir, can't we force him? Can't we threaten to lift ship and juggle lateral drift so that we pass over the town? A tongue of incandescent exhaust gases licking around his precious University would soon make him see reason!"

"Mr. Calver! Get it into your head that there's more at stake than the safety of one woman!"

"More politics!" sneered Calver. "More politics! Don't let's be nasty to the poor, dear aliens . . . Who knows? In ten thousand years' time they might be our allies against the wicked Federation . . ."

"Mr. Calver!"

"I warn you, sir, that if you won't do it, I shall. The other officers will be with me. This won't be the first time that a Master has been relieved by his subordinates."

"Perhaps not," replied Engels—and Calver was suddenly shocked by the strength that was an almost visible aura about the feeble old man. "Perhaps not, Mr. Calver. But it would be the last thing that you ever did. The old penalties for piracy and mutiny still exist . . ."

They were interrupted by a knock at the door. It was Pender—still armed, still wearing the belt with its holstered automatic with the air of a small boy forced, against his will, to participate in a game of Cowboys and Indians. It was Pender, who said, "His Wisdom is aboard to see you, sir." It was Pender who stood aside to let the High Priest pass.

The old Tharnian walked slowly into the room, faced Engels. He said, "Captain, this is a serious business."

"A masterly understatement!" flared Calver.

"Mr. Calver!" snapped the shipmaster. Then, "Please be seated, Your Wisdom."

"Thank you, Captain."

"Can I offer you refreshment?"

"Thank you, no. This matter is better discussed in absolute sobriety."

"You may stay, Mr. Calver," said Engels. "Sit down. And now, Your Wisdom, what can you tell us?"

"Little more than you already know. I have received a message from Baron Tarshedi to the effect that your woman officer will be returned unharmed if his son is returned in like condition. On the other hand—if the execution is carried out as planned your officer will be killed. Slowly."

"So you will return Lanoga," said Calver.

"I am afraid," said the priest, "that that is impossible." There is so much at stake, sir. Cannot you see that such a capitulation will weaken the power of the Temple and the University?"

"Damn your Temple and University!"

"Mr. Calver! Any further outbursts and I shall be obliged to order you to leave!"

"The woman," said the priest gently, "is your woman?"

"Yes."

"Then the anxiety is understandable. But, sir, you must try to understand too. You must try to understand that the future happiness and prosperity of this world are of far greater importance than the life of one individual . . ."

"To you, perhaps!"

The High Priest ignored this, went on, "Even so, there are so many factors that must be weighed. Firstly, there is the inevitable loss of face if I accede to Tarshedi's demand. Secondly, there is the inevitable loss of face if I do not accede to his demand, if I allow it to become obvious that I can do nothing to save those under my protection. The time is ripe for what your people call a showdown. The time is ripe to smash the power of the first of the baronies . . ."

"So you intend," said Engels quietly, "to assault the castle?"

"I so intend, Captain."

"This last cargo of ours should have built up your strength sufficiently . . ."

"I think that it has, Captain."

"This last cargo . . .?" echoed Calver without comprehension.

"Yes, Mr. Calver. This last cargo. All is not ploughs that comes in cases stencilled *Agricultural Implements* . . ."

"But, sir, Federation Law . . ."

"We make our own laws on the Rim." Engels

turned to the priest again. "My officers will be willing to help, Your Wisdom."

"Your offer is appreciated, Captain—but I am safe in saying that my own men are better trained in the use of arms than your people. However . . ." and he smiled slightly . . . "this gentleman has a personal interest . . ."

Calver was already on his feet.

"When do we start?" he demanded.

"There is no hurry," said the priest quietly. "The execution is not taking place today. Furthermore, in this matter you are displaying an understandable impetuosity. What, do you think, will be the fate of your woman when my forces breach the walls, break through the outer defenses? Will Tarshedi let himself be robbed of his revenge?"

"Then . . ." In desperation Calver turned again to the Captain. "Damn it all, sir. We have to make this man agree to an exchange! It's the only way!"

"There are," said the priest softly, "other ways . . ."

6

CALVER WAS a spaceman and the solution of problems of spacemanship and astronautics was, to him, second nature. When it came to the problems of warfare—and warfare on a planetary surface at that—he was obliged to admit his deep ignorance. Even so, he was amazed, and a little shocked, at the High Priest's mastery of the subject. A man of any god should be a man of peace. (But it is at times necessary, and for the highest possible motives, to fight.)

He walked with the priest into the town, and through the town to the University. They talked on the way—but not of the impending assault on the castle. Gently but persistently the High Priest drew him out, questioned him about the worlds that he had visited, the civilizations of Earth and her colonies, of the non-human cultures. The Tharnian was curious, too—although not offensively so—about the relationship existing between Calver and Jane Arlen. It was somehow a relief for Calver to be able to talk about it.

The University—it was, Calver realized, more like a fortress—stood on a rise to the east of the town, overlooking the broad river and, a few miles to the northward, the wide expanse of the sea. As they approached it, Calver looked up at the turrets standing to either side of the great gate, noticed the searchlights and the ugly, eager snouts of heavy machine guns. The guards who came to smart attention were armed—but not armed as had been those guards who had broken up the tavern brawl. It was not polished wooden truncheons that they wore at their belts but vicious automatic pistols.

After he had acknowledged the salutes of his men, as he and Calver were walking across a cobbled courtyard, the High Priest said, "As you see, Mr. Calver, we are in a state of preparedness. If Baron Tarshedi should march upon the University . . ."

"I believe," said Calver slowly, "that you'd welcome it."

"I should. The barons have to go—and if they are the aggressors in any trouble *we* shall be all the more highly regarded by the people. And it is essential—you understand that, don't you?—that we retain our leadership by respect, not by force of arms . . ."

They passed through another gate, into another courtyard, a larger one.

Calver gaped. He stared at the light tanks, the mechanized field artillery, the rocket launchers on their half tracks. He ejaculated, "An arsenal!"

"Yes, Mr. Calver. An arsenal. Unluckily we have no flying machines yet. They are on order, of course, and the first of them should be delivered here by *Rimhound,* together with an instructor, in three weeks' time. But, you will appreciate, one of your helicopters would be of great value to us tonight. Even so, some of my priests have been studying books on the history of aeronautics and one of them—although he could not possibly have had an emergency of this nature in mind—has done more than merely read the books . . . But come with me. We still have much to discuss, to plan."

Calver followed the old priest through a doorway, up a flight of stone stairs, into a large room. From the glazed window of it—even though the local glass was translucent rather than transparent—he was able to see the courtyard, the ranked vehicles of war. He found the sight of the massed weapons comforting and, after he was seated, kept glancing out at them.

There were others in the room—Tharnians, some of them in the uniform of black tunic and yellow trunks, some of them in priestly robes. There was a girl, too—a girl with impudent breasts and long, arrogant naked legs—a girl whose frightened face belied the careless bravery of her body. Calver recognized her. It was Sayonee, the woman who had been with Maclean when he had been murdered.

The High Priest said, "I shall not bother to introduce you. Very few of those here understand spoken English—although most of them have a grasp of the written language. And Sayonee, I think, you already know."

"He was there," said the girl sullenly. "He was there when Mac was killed."

"And you will help our friend to rescue his woman," said the priest.

"If you say so, Your Wisdom. But it will not bring my man back."

The High Priest ignored her, went on talking to Calver. "These," he said, "are my officers, who will lead tonight's assault on the castle. In spite of all our reading and all our drills we can think of nothing better than a simple, frontal assault. We have the firepower, and we shall use it. We shall batter down the defenses, force an entry and smash opposition as we meet it."

He paused. "Meanwhile, while all this is going on we have to consider what thoughts will be passing through Tarshedi's mind. If it is obvious to him from the beginning that there is no hope, then it is fairly certain that he will take his revenge on the girl as soon as possible. (Of course, there is another possibility—he may barter her safety for his own. But Tarshedi, to give him his due, has never cared much for the safety of his own person, or the safety of any other person. With the exception, of course, of his pampered pup.) So this is what I have decided. Our first attack will be a diversion only. We shall refrain from showing the full strength of our hand. Tarshedi will think himself secure behind his stone walls. Meanwhile you, Calver, will drop into the fortress, taking Sayonee with you as a guide. You will rescue your woman. Then, when you are out and clear, the real assault will begin."

These, thought Calver, *are an incredibly simple people.* He demanded, "And how do I get into the fortress? Do I fly?"

"Yes," said the priest.

"But you said that you had imported no aircraft yet."

"I said that we had imported books on the subject. Totesu!"

"Yes, Your Wisdom?" said one of the scholarly men.

"Totesu, tell Mr. Calver what you have achieved."

"Your people," said the scholar, "obsessed by idea of heavier than air flight. Why? Inefficient. Power of engine used to keep machine airborne. Yet, on your world, beginnings of lighter than air flight. First of all Montgolfier, then balloonists who used gas and not hot air, then, at last, your Count Zeppelin. We, here, have gas. Can make balloons. So far, no proper engine, but . . ."

"A balloon?" asked Calver.

"Yes. Balloon. Hold four people and plenty ballast. Take you, me, this woman to castle. Lift you, me, two women away from castle . . ."

"It could be done . . ." whispered Calver.

"It can be done," said the High Priest. "There is much to be worked out—some sort of a timetable, signals. Meanwhile, I suggest that you familiarize yourself with Totesu's contraption." He looked distastefully at Sayonee. "And take the girl with you."

The sun was down when the long column clanked and rumbled through the gates of the University, down the slope and into the streets of the town. The beams of headlights were reflected from armor and armament, from grinding track and swiveling turret —and from the pale faces of the townspeople who, alarmed by the noise, had come out, were standing in the doorways of their houses to watch. There was a cheer from a group of men outside the *Spaceship* tavern—a cheer that was drowned by the snarling machines. But, on the whole, the crowd, although not hostile, was not enthusiastic. Calver remembered something he had read about one of the old wars on Earth, one of those futile conflicts that had been fought, in somebody else's country, between two great powers each of whom was convinced of its own essential rightness. A peasant had been asked what he thought about it. He had replied, bitterly, "What difference does it make to a blade of grass if it is eaten by a horse or a cow?"

But who ruled Tharn was no concern of Calver's. All that concerned him was Jane Arlen's safety—and her safety depended upon such a fantastic, flimsy device. He felt between his fingers the bundled fabric upon which he was sitting, looked at the clumsy gas cylinders from which that same fabric would be inflated, at the pile of bags of sand ballast. He looked at his companions—at the young priest, Totesu, whose face wore the expression of a small boy with his first working model rocketship, at Sayonee, who was obviously terrified by the growling, jolting monster in which she rode. A little fear was justified, Calver thought. What if the motion of the half track should chafe holes in the balloon fabric?

They were clear of the town now, striking out across the heathland. Away to his right Calver could see the spaceport, could see the floodlit, silvery tower of *Lorn Lady*. He knew that his shipmates would all be in the control room, would be watching through the big mounted binoculars. He knew, too, that most of them would be wishing that they were with him—but Captain Engels had refused to allow his ship's complement to be depleted any further. *Lorn Lady* was secured for space and, at a pinch, could blast off without her Chief Officer or Catering Officer. And Engels, fanatically loyal to his own world, would blast off without hesitation—although not without regret.

They were striking out across the heathland, pitching and rolling over the rough, uneven surface, their headlamps probing the night like the questing antennae of great insects. Ahead of them was the castle, the grim bulk of it in silhouette against the glowing arc of the westering Galactic lens. Ahead of them was the castle—and from turrets and battlements glowed the ruddy watchfires. *The watchfires,* thought Calver. *The watchfires, and the cauldrons of molten lead and boiling oil . . . Every time that anybody uses atomic weapons against some primitive and unpleasant race there's a squeal goes up to High Heaven from the humanitarians—but what's the difference between being fried in oil and fried by hard radiation?*

He realized that Totesu was speaking, his voice barely audible over the growl of the motor. He said, "What?"

"Wind just right," said the priest. "Good." He grinned broadly, his teeth startlingly white in the chance beam of another vehicle's headlight. "First use of flying machine in Tharn warfare."

"At least," said Calver, "you know what you're doing. Which is more than the Wright brothers did . . ."

"No understand."

"Skip it."

"Still no understand."

"It's cold," complained the girl.

"If you put some clothes over that shapely carcass of yours you wouldn't feel the cold," said Calver roughly.

Sayonee glared at him, hugging herself. Her long legs, under the short skirt, glowed greenly luminous. She repeated, "It's cold."

"Oh, all right."

Calver took off his jacket—first of all transferring

the spare clips for his automatic to his trousers pockets. He draped it over Sayonee's slim shoulders —and felt the chill wind striking through the thin fabric of his shirt. He looked at the girl with distaste. He thought, *This is all your fault. Because of you, how many men died last night? And how many men will die tonight?* He stared at the pale green oval of her face, said, "Is this the face that launched a thousand ships and burned the topless towers of Ilium?"

"What do you mean?" she asked.

"Skip it," he said, thinking that the use of those two words was becoming a habit.

But Jane's is the face that's launched the thousand ships, he thought. (And it seemed, briefly, that there were phantom masts and square sails in silhouette against the sky over the lurching war vehicles, that the rolling heathland was Homer's wine dark sea.) He thought, playing with ideas to try to dispel his fears, *But I'm no Menelaus. And Tarshedi's no Paris, and that ugly castle of his is no Troy . . .*

He thought, *Even so, there's truth in all the old stories. Whenever there's bloodshed and upheaval there're always women involved somewhere, somehow. Helen . . . Cleopatra . . . What historian was it who deplored the disproportionate influence that a few square inches of mucous membrane have always had upon the course of human history?*

"Balloons used in warfare on your world," said Totesu, making light conversation. "Siege of Venice. Montgolfier balloons. Dropped bombs."

"Really?"

"Airships used, too. In First World War. Zeppelins. Dropped bombs."

"Fantastic."

"Pity tonight no bombs." The priest waved his

hand at the column of tanks and artillery ahead of them and behind them. "All this—useless. Cost too much. Few bombs—much better. Cost less."

"You're wasted in the priesthood," Calver told him.

"No. Not waste. As say in your religious books—Church Militant."

"Who," demanded Calver, "will rid me of this turbulent priest?"

"No understand."

"Just a quotation."

The castle was closer now and the vehicles were climbing the hill upon which it stood. The castle was closer and, drifting down against the wind, came the thin high notes of a trumpet, the rattle of kettle drums. The castle was closer, towering black and seemingly impregnable against the dark sky, sullenly contemptuous of the mobile armor that was advancing against it. And Calver, suddenly, thought again of the flimsy affair of fabric and wickerwork in which he and his two companions would ride, the frail contraption that, according to its pilot, was more deadly a weapon than the land ironclads.

7

THEIR HALF TRACK, the specialized vehicle with the winch and the gas cylinders, halted, as did its next astern. The rest of the squadron rumbled by, ignoring them. Totesu clambered out, dropped to the ground, followed by Calver and the girl. The priest began giving rapid orders to the men from the troop carrier.

Working with smooth efficiency, they pulled the balloon fabric from the half track and, with it, the sections of basketwork that fitted together to make the car. Flexible pipes were run from the gas cylinders to the balloon. Calver heard a faint hissing noise, saw a gray mound growing upon the dark ground, a gray mound that heaved and stirred as though alive. He watched the clumsy, formless bulk struggling to lift, watched its wrinkled skin smoothing out, watched it swell to a dull-gleaming rotundity. It was clear of the ground now, held only by the mooring lines. It was well clear of the ground, straining against its moorings, seemingly resentful of the burden of the basket that men were securing beneath it.

Calver stood with Sayonee, watching. He was rather grateful for her company. She knew as little about what was being done as he did—and could hardly distrust the contraption more than he did. In a way, she was lucky. She took such things on trust. Whereas he, Calver, whilst not knowing enough at the same time knew too much.

"Ready," said Totesu.

"If you say so," said Calver.

"I can't!" cried Sayonee suddenly. "I can't go in that thing. It's . . . It's not safe!"

"Be quiet," said Calver roughly.

He picked the girl up, threw her into the basket, followed her. Totesu was close behind him, saying, "All right. Everything good. All right." The priest shouted an order to those on the ground—and suddenly the dark heathland, the black shapes of the two vehicles and the bright beams of the headlights were far below them, were diminishing with every passing second.

Calver gulped, trying to conquer his queasiness. He heard Sayonee being noisily sick over the side of the basket. He could sympathize with her. This was so different from a powered ascent in aircraft or spacecraft; the unsteady swaying of the basket was worse than Free Fall to a first tripper.

To occupy his mind, he pulled his torch from his belt, began to make an inventory of the car's contents. There were the bags of ballast. There was the line depending from the gasbag that controlled the valve and the other, heavier line that was the ripcord. There was yet another line that ran from the car down to its own reel in the truck, a line that, at intervals, passed through rings spliced into the cable. It was a signalling device and Calver did not trust it. One pull meant, "Pay out"; two pulls—"Stop paying out"; three pulls—"Heave in." But if the line should foul it did not much matter. He had arranged for flashes from his electric torch to hold the same meaning.

"Good," said the priest happily.

"Mphm," grunted Calver noncommittally.

"I . . . I feel sick . . ." complained the girl.

"Like seasick," explained Totesu. "Soon better."

"But I'm *always* seasick . . ."

Calver looked down from the basket—and as he watched, the battle was opened. He could see the flashes from the guns, could hear the thud and rattle of heavy and light weapons. He hoped that the gunners were following the High Priest's orders—the direction of the fire of the light automatics against the castle walls, where it could do no possible damage; the use of reduced charges and practice ammunition in field pieces; the holding of rocket fire until the order was given for the real assault. Meanwhile, it was spectacular enough—the column of vehicles, headlights blazing, roaring around the castle just out of bowshot, pouring in streams of prettily-colored tracer. It reminded him of films he had seen of the old days of the American West—the mounted Redskins riding in a circle around the encampment of the pioneers—and seemed no more deadly than the cinematic make-believe.

And Tarshedi's boys, he thought, *will no more think of looking up than those old pioneers would have done . . .*

The castle was almost below them now. Calver,

turning his attention back to the interior of the car, saw Totesu jerk the signal line twice, saw him standing there, the line in his hand, waiting. Abruptly the worried frown was erased from his face. "Good," he said. "Good."

With his other hand he reached for the valve cord, pulled it gently. There was the faintest sigh of escaping gas and the balloon began to drop, began to sag down to the center of the dark rectangle that was the flat roof of the main building of the castle. There would be nobody there, thought Calver hopefully. There would be nobody there. They would all be on the battlements, shooting off their arrows and dying for the opportunity to use their boiling oil and molten lead. They would be thinking, optimistically, that the new-fangled weapons that the High Priest had imported were fine for making a noise, but for little else . . .

And what happens, he wondered, *when our cable falls across the battlements? It's bound to be noticed . . . Or is the tower high enough to carry it clear? Even so, there's a considerable catenary . . .*

"Jump," Totesu was saying urgently. "Jump!"

Calver checked his equipment—the pistol, the spare clips of ammunition, the torch. Not without misgivings he made the end of the line that he would carry down with him fast to his belt. He clambered on to the rim of the basket, gripping the rigging firmly as his foothold shifted and tilted. He looked down, saw that the flickering light of the fires on the battlements was being reflected from the underbelly of the balloon, was falling upon a reasonably level surface, only a few feet below him. He was grateful for the light—and frightened by it. There was, perhaps, lit-

tle likelihood that any of the defenders would look
behind him, would see the ruddily-illumined shape
hanging over the central keep. But if one did, his action would be followed almost immediately by a
shower of arrows, and the means of escape for Arlen
and himself would be destroyed.

But, he thought, *the main thing is that I've got here. I've
got here, and I've a pistol and ample ammunition, and Arlen
and I should be able to hold out until the priests take the
castle . . .*

"Jump!" Totesu was urging. "Jump!"

Calver jumped.

He fell more lightly than he had anticipated; the
balloon, freed from his weight, surged upwards, taking up the slack of the line that he carried. He was
dragged to the parapet, almost carried over it, throwing both arms around a chimney to halt his uncon-
trolled rush. He recovered his breath at last, was able
with one hand to cast off the hitch about his belt, to
throw another hitch of the mooring line around the
stone flue. He looked up, saw that the red-gleaming
shape (he thought, *There's far too much light from those
fires . . .*) was descending steadily. Then he heard the
noise of a scuffle in the basket, heard Sayonee cry out
in pain and anger. He saw her figure appear over the
edge of the car, saw her descending jerkily to the roof
—an undignified flurry of arms and legs—as Totesu
lowered her at a rope's end.

Quickly he released her.

"Which way?" he demanded. "Which way?"

"I'll scream," she snarled. "I'll scream, and
then . . ."

"You'll not scream," he said coldly. He pushed
the muzzle of his pistol against her, feeling the soft

flesh give beneath it. "You'll not scream. You know what this is for. If you give any trouble, I'll use it."

"You . . . would . . ." she whispered, with a certain wonderment. Then, "That turret . . . There's a stairway. Follow it down, all the way down, and you come to the dungeon . . ."

He said, "You are leading the way."

"But I don't want to. Not any longer. At first I thought that I was avenging Mac—but now I see that it's wrong to do so. It's you spacepeople who're ruining this world, who're turning priest against noble and both of them against the people. Until you came . . ."

He put his free hand on her shoulder, turned her so that her back was towards him. He felt the foresight of his pistol graze her skin as he did so. He pushed the muzzle into her back, said, "Lead the way."

"But . . . It's dark . . ."

With his left hand he pulled his torch from his belt, adjusted the control so that it threw the feeblest of beams. He switched on, let the pool of faint light fall before her feet.

"Lead the way," he said again.

She led the way.
She led the way into the little turret, to the stone spiral stairway that wound down, and down, and down. Calver was reminded of the spiral stairway in *Lorn Lady*'s axial shaft and, with his gift for remembering odd things at odd times, recalled how filthy he had thought it when he first joined the ship. But, in spite of the odd cigarette ends and scraps of waste paper, it was a model of cleanliness compared with

this noisome corkscrew. The people of the town had seemed to be reasonably civilized in their sanitation; it was obvious that the people of the castle were not.

Down they went, and down, the feeble glow of the torch their only light, the noise of the battle (still the mock battle? Calver wondered) muffled by the thickness of the stone walls. Down they went, and down—until at last they could go no farther. Sayonee fumbled with the latch of the heavy door ahead of her, muttering to herself, spitting a curse as Calver prodded her with his pistol. At last the door swung open. There was light beyond it, yellow light, the flickering illumination of crude, smoking oil lamps set on shelves on the rough stone walls of the passageway. At the end of the passage there was another door.

Ignoring the gun, Sayonee turned. There was fear on her face, fear and horror. She asked, pleadingly, "Must I come any farther? I'll wait for you here. I promise that I will. I promise . . ."

"Go on," said Calver, motioning with the pistol.

"But I promise. I promise. Lanoga made me come down here once. He made me watch what they did to a woman—one of the castle wenches—who'd been unfaithful to his father . . . Please let me wait here . . . Please . . ."

Calver said coldly, "A bullet in the guts is more painful than the most painful memory. Lead the way."

"But . . ."

With his free hand he slapped her viciously, *"Lead the way!"*

She sobbed as she turned from him, her slim shoulders drooping. She dragged herself towards the door at the far end of the passage, opened it. Her head hanging low, she passed through it. Calver followed. The room beyond the door was large and, like the approach to it, was lit with oil lamps—and by the ruddy glow of a brazier from which the handles of . . . of implements protruded. There was the smell of blood, and of sweat, of fear and of agony. Against one wall there was a thing like a narrow, spiked bed. Against another wall there was hanging a pallid . . . something—a something that still writhed feebly in its chains, that was mewing weakly.

Nausea filled Calver's throat and a dreadful fear almost stopped his heart. He started to run towards what had once been a woman—then realized that the skin, where it was not burned, was not blood-covered, was green. But he did not stop. He approached the thing and, when he was close enough to be sure that he would not miss, pulled the trigger of his automatic.

When the echoes of the shot had died away the mewing had stopped.

Calver turned back, caught Sayonee by the shoulders, shaking her. The girl was dumb with fear, with horror, at first could only stare past him with wide, blank eyes at the dreadfully dead woman. She began to moan a little as he continued his rough treatment —then turned away sharply.

"Sayonee," he almost shouted. "Sayonee! Where is she? Where's Arlen?"

"The cells," she muttered. "The cells. Through that other door . . ."

He left her standing there, ran for the door to which she had pointed. It opened easily enough. Beyond it was a long corridor, once again oil-lit, with rows of stout doors on either side, each one of which had a heavily barred opening in its upper part.

"Arlen!" he shouted. "Arlen!"

He was answered by a chorus the like of which he never wished to hear again—a cacophony of screams and animal howlings.

"Arlen!" he shouted again. "Arlen!"

He didn't hear her answer—but he saw her hand —slim, white—extended through the bars, beckoning him. He ran towards her, saw her face behind the grill. Still looking at her, still trying to make himself heard above the uproar being made by the other prisoners, still trying to hear her, he fumbled with the door. He realized that it was (as it had to be in this place) locked. He shouted, "Stand back and away! I'll have to blow this open!"

This time the noise of the pistol shot was almost inaudible, was drowned by the tumult from the other cells. Calver pushed the door, almost fell through it, found himself in Arlen's arms. He wanted to stand back, wanted to look at her, wanted to assure himself that she was unhurt—but it was some time before he was able to do so. It was as well that he was able to break away from her at last, able to pull her out of the noisome cell. He saw, in time, the brutish fellow who was hurrying along the passageway with a cudgel in his hand, a bunch of keys dangling at his belt. He saw him in time to bring his pistol up and to snap off two hasty shots—one of them at the man as he was advancing, the other as he was running in full retreat.

Both of them missed.

And it was very shortly after that the great bell, somewhere above, broke into clangorous life.

* * *

They found Sayonee standing where Calver had left her, still seemingly dazed. Calver let go of Arlen, grabbed the Tharnian girl, pushed her roughly toward the door to the corridor to the turret stairway, sent Arlen stumbling after her before she was able to look at the dead woman, at what had been done to her. Something whirred past his ear, something vicious and deadly, something that fetched up with a crack and a clatter against the farther stone wall.

Calver turned, saw the bowmen standing in the entrance to the cell corridor, shooting from the doorway. He raised his pistol fast—and yet, it seemed to him, with slow deliberation. He had time to think, to count, before he pulled the rigger. *Two from eight leaves six* . . . He fired again. And again.

He realized that Arlen was beside him.

He said, trying to jest, "Get up them stairs!"

She said, "But that stupid girl. She says it's dark."

"Then take my torch. And hurry. I'll be close behind you."

Again he fired, at an incautiously exposed head, then ejected the spent clip. His hand went down to his pocket for a fresh one, found only emptiness. He remembered his descent from the balloon to the roof, his involuntary gymnastics. So he was out of ammunition. But it didn't matter; the enemy could not know that and the pursuit would be made with caution.

He walked backward, carefully, the menacing but useless pistol held before him. He hit the wall a couple of feet to his left of the doorway, stepped sidewise until he was in the opening, backed through it. He shut the door, sorry that there was no means of bolting or otherwise securing it.

He ran to the doorway to the turret stairs, ran through it. He slammed the door behind him—then thought that he should, perhaps, have left it open. He could hear the footsteps of the women above his head, but the curvature of the stairway cut off the light of the torch that Arlen was using. But it was of no real importance. A spaceman, he was trained at working by feel, in pitch darkness.

He started confidently up the stairs.

He slipped on something, on some nameless filth, and fell heavily. For what seemed a long time, too long a time, he could only crouch there where he had fallen, waiting for the pain in his side to ease. He heard noisy feet in the corridor, heard voices. He saw the dim, growing light as the door started to open— slowly, cautiously. Groaning, he staggered erect, drove himself to the ascent of the stone stairs.

Light suddenly flooded the stairway, reflected from the walls. The others must have taken a lamp from one of the shelves, were bringing it with them. As yet, the direct source of the illumination was hidden from him—but unless he hurried this state of affairs would not last for long.

He tried to hurry—and each step was like a knife driven in deep just below his heart. He tried to hurry, and he did hurry—but haltingly, lamely—and the light around him grew brighter and the voices of his pursuers louder.

He tried to console himself with the thought that bows and arrows would not be effective weapons in this locality—and knew that the Tharnians would have swords or knives, whilst he had nothing.

Not even a chair . . . he thought bitterly.

He drove himself up the stairs, forcing his legs into a steady rhythm, ignoring the pain in his injured side. He climbed, gasping for breath, staggering, falling against the stone walls, bruising himself more with every impact. Above the roaring in his ears he could hear the shouts of the soldiery, imagined that there was a note of triumph in their voices. But of course, there would be; they would have found the pistol that he had dropped, would have realized that he was weaponless.

He wondered if he should take one of the side doors, leave the stairway for one of the floors or galleries of the tower. But he still retained the ability to think logically, decided against it. The Tharnians could not possibly know of the waiting balloon, would think that once he was on the roof they would have him—and the women—at their mercy, would be able to drive them to the parapet, to the sheer drop to the cobblestones below.

He hoped that Jane would have the sense to tell Totesu to cast off the balloon before it was too late. It was too risky for the others to wait for him now, whether or not he succeeded in reaching the roof before the soldiery. A flight of arrows, however hastily directed, and the balloon would be useless.

Again he fell—and this time he didn't get up.

He was too tired and his side was hurting too badly. He half-closed his eyes against the glare as the glaring oil lamp was carried around the last bend below him, saw, through slitted lids the advancing soldiers, the triumph on their faces, the short swords that they held in their hands.

So I've run to the edge of night, he thought, *and soon I shall be over the edge . . .*

He saw the men hesitate, start to fall back.

In the confined space the deadly chatter of the machine pistol was deafening. He looked around, and by the flickering light of the dropped lamp he saw Jane, her face set and hard, the vicious, smoking weapon in her hands. She fired one last short burst and the light died—and with it the man who had carried it.

There was a steady light then, the light of his torch, and Jane, holding it, was kneeling beside him, "Derek," she was saying, "Derek. What's wrong? Are you wounded?"

"Just a fall," he said tiredly. "One or two ribs cracked, perhaps . . ." He began to recover. "Where did you get the gun?"

"From your pilot, that aeronautical priest. *He* wouldn't come. He thinks that the only civilized way of making war is to drop bombs on people . . ."

"But you came . . ."

"But of course. Now, if you can manage the rest of these stairs, the carriage waits, my lord."

With Jane supporting him, Calver managed the last of the stairs up to the roof of the tower. The balloon was still there, hanging with its basket just clear of the flags. Totesu was having a heated argument with Sayonee about something—about what, Calver neither knew nor cared.

He ignored the balloon at first, walked unsteadily to the parapet, looked out and down. The High Priest's motorized column was still circling the castle, still pouring in an ineffectual fire. But the rate of fire had slackened. Ammunition was not too plentiful—and it would all be needed for the real assault. Meanwhile, the apparent loss of enthusiasm on the part of the

attackers was all to the good. It would lull the defenders into a state of false security.

Arlen said, "There's somebody else coming up
those stairs. It's time that we weren't here."

"All right," said Calver. He raised his voice.
"Totesu! We're coming aboard!"

"Ready. Always ready."

He and the girl walked back to where the basket
was suspended. His foot struck against something
small, something that rang metallically. *One of the
magazines,* he thought. *It's not much good finding it now.*

Jane clambered into the basket. The balloon
dropped, with her added weight, until the car was
touching the flags of the roof. Calver tried to follow,
found that stiffness was setting in around his bruises.
Jane cursed him softly and, aided by Totesu, pulled
him in over the wickerwork rim.

There was a growing light in the turret doorway.
The priest saw it, began to make impatient noises,
began to throw out the bags of ballast. Jane helped
him. Calver asked, "Where's your pistol? A couple of
bursts will keep them down."

The girl answered, "I . . . I thought that you had
picked it up and brought it . . . It must still be
there . . ."

"Ballast," grunted the priest. "Finish. No lift."

Calver found his torch, flashed it around the interior of the car. Inadvertently he held the beam for
a second on Sayonee. She cringed away from it, whispering, "No. Please. No. Not me."

"I'm tempted," said Calver.

There was a spare magazine for Totesu's lost
weapon. He threw it out. There was his uniform
jacket, that Sayonee had again draped around her

shoulders. He pulled it from her, dropped it overside. There was the flare pistol—but that would be needed. It would be needed—but only one cartridge. There were six in the carton—but why waste them?

The light in the turret door was bright now, the voices loud. There was a certain reluctance on the part of the owners of the voices to show themselves, but that was understandable. However, sooner or later they would pluck up courage and charge upon the helpless balloon.

Hydrogen, thought Calver, *is a light gas. It rises. So, if there're any leaks in the fabric of the gasbag, as there must be (unless the sky pilot's calculations were all to buggery, which is a possibility) the gas will be well clear of the basket . . . But what about a mixture of hydrogen and the atmospheric oxygen?*

He broke the fat pistol, inserted a thick cartridge into the breech. He closed the gun with a snap, drew back the hammer. As he did so, the light in the turret was extinguished. He thought, *So they're going to come creeping out under cover of darkness* . . . He aimed, fired. There was a scream as the incandescent flare found its target and Calver saw a man rolling inside the doorway, his chest a mass of red flame. Calver hesitated before reloading—then remembered the woman whom he, mercifully, had shot. He fired again—and a screaming wretch, his clothing ablaze, flung himself over the parapet.

Totesu cried out in pain, clutching his shoulder. By the light of the flares Calver saw that the priest had been hit by an arrow, realized that the archers on the outer battlements now had the tower—and the balloon—under fire. He sighed. There was only one thing for him to do. Perhaps, with luck, he would still be here, would still be alive and kicking, when the defenses crumbled before the real assault and the priestly armor swept into the fortress. He said to Jane, "Take this pistol. As soon as you're up and clear, fire one flare . . ."

"What are you doing?"

He said, "What else is there to do?"

He got one leg over the rim of the basket, heard Totesu cry out again. He heard Jane call, "Derek, stop! Look!"

Calver looked. The priest was dead; of that there could be no doubt. No man can take an arrow through the eye and live. Calver scrambled back into the basket. He knew that there was no time for sentiment, but he felt strangely guilty as he helped the two women to tumble the body of the young man— the man who was going to revolutionize Tharnian warfare and who had been killed by one of the primitive weapons he despised—out of the car. The balloon lifted suddenly, springing aloft on the end of its cable, rising above and clear of the driving storm of arrows.

Calver pointed the flare pistol downwards, fired. Almost at once, it seemed, there was a new note in the thunder of the mobile artillery below them—a deeper, more deadly note. The streams of tracer were sweeping the battlements, no longer expending themselves harmlessly on the castle walls. And the rocket launchers were bursting into action—and even at their altitude those in the balloon could hear the roar of the explosions, the crash of falling masonry.

The beams of the headlights white in the smoke and dust showed the High Priest's armor advancing, crawling over the rubble, probing every possible shelter with the fire from the light automatic weapons. The balloonists could see the milling men and machines in the courtyard around the central tower —until, after only a short time, there were no more men.

Sickened, Calver wondered about the ethics of selling modern arms to these people—then remembered what he had seen and what he had been obliged to do in the castle dungeon.

He went to the signal cord, gave it three sharp jerks. It was slack and and unresponsive in his hand. He tried to find his torch to give the light signal, realized that it must have been dumped during the attempts to lighten the balloon. He thought of valving gas, came to the conclusion that, should he do so, the aircraft would fall again on or in the neighborhood of the tower—and the tower (there must have been wood, somewhere, in its construction) was now burning.

But it didn't matter. The men at the winch would have a rush of brains to the head sooner or later and reel the balloon in. He sat with Arlen on the floor of the basket, made no objection when Sayonee, seeking warmth, huddled against his other side.

And he went to sleep.

8

THE FOLLOWING morning, before daybreak, *Lorn Lady* lifted from Tharn.

When Calver and Jane Arlen returned on board, delivered to the ramp of one of the triumphant tanks, they found the ship secured for Space, ready to blast off at a second's notice. Old Captain Engels had greeted them at the airlock, had allowed a momentary warmth to dispel his usual coldness. He had said, briefly, "I'm glad," and then, with a swift return to his old manner, "Go to your quarters, Mr. Calver, and remain there until sent for."

Calver felt a sudden chill. Was his mutinous outburst of the previous day being remembered, being held against him? He realized that he knew little of the shipmaster's psychology, knew only that it was a complex one.

"But, sir . . ."

"Go to your cabin, Mr. Calver. I think that the old girl is capable of clambering upstairs this once without her Chief Officer to hold her hand."

"But sir, I'm perfectly fit."

"You don't look it. You look all in. I'll have Doc Malone look you over before we raise ship."

"But sir . . ."

"Go to your cabin!"

Calver went.

He tried to climb, unassisted, up the spiral staircase in the axial shaft from the airlock to the officers' flat. Then he was remembering that other spiral staircase, the one in the tunnel—and with the memories the numbness left him and all the pain of his bruised side came back. Jane supported him, tried to assist him, then stood to one side as Brentano and the Purser, sent down by the Captain, took over. He was practically carried to his cabin, let himself collapse thankfully onto the bunk. He was dimly conscious of old Doc Malone's probing fingers, of his voice saying, "Nothing broken. He'll be as good as new once we're in Free Fall. But you'd better stay with him during blast-off, Arlen."

He heard her reply, "I already had every intention of so doing."

It was strange for him to ride the rockets to the sky as a passenger, with Jane beside him—strange, but not unpleasant. Even so, it felt . . . *wrong*. His place was in Control, sitting in the co-pilot's chair, ready to take over in a split second should anything happen to the Master himself. (And Engels was so very old, so very fragile.) Brentano was keen, and efficient—but Brentano was an Electronic Radio Officer, had no training in ship handling . . .

"What are you grinning at?" Jane had demanded, speaking with difficulty as the acceleration tended to squeeze the air from her lungs.

"Already," he had told her, "I'm beginning to think like a Chief Officer again. Already I have an acute attack of Mately indispensability . . ."

"As far as I'm concerned," she had whispered, "You *are* indispensable . . ."

They heard the rockets give a last cough, heard the whining of the big gyroscope as *Lorn Lady* swung about her short axis, as she was lined up for the sun about which revolved Grollor. They felt the weightlessness of Free Fall, tensed themselves for the short burst of acceleration that would put them on course, that would send them falling down the long trajectory. It came—but the expected dizziness, the loss of temporal orientation following upon the activation of the Mannschenn Drive, did not come.

Calver started to fumble with the straps holding him to the bunk.

He said, "There's something wrong. I'd better get up to Control."

The door opened. Captain Engels stood there. He said, "Mr. Calver, I fear that your first duty as Chief Officer will be a melancholy one. Take Mr. Brentano and Mr. Pender with you and bring poor Maclean's body to the airlock."

Calver understood, then. The burial could not take place once the interstellar drive was in operation. Changing the mass of a ship during temporal precession can—and will—have catastrophic consequences.

He saw that the Acting Second Mate and the Purser were standing behind the Captain. He led them to the deep-freeze chambers, watched as they slid Maclean's shrouded body from its temporary icy tomb. The frost crystals on the sheet that covered him sparkled in the glare of the lamps, reminded him of the stars on the ornate cap badge that the dead man had always worn.

He led them to the axial shaft, to the spiral stairway. It would have been faster to have made the passage of the shaft the way that it always was made in Free Fall—a swift, swimming motion from one end to the other. It would have been faster—but lacking in dignity and respect. So he and the others used the stairs, the magnetic soles of their shoes clinging to the metal treads, walking slowly, walking almost as though the corpse had weight.

They carried the body to the airlock, outside which the Captain and the other officers were waiting. They placed it in the little compartment. Smoothly, silently, the inner door shut. There was the sobbing of pumps as the airlock pressure built up to four ship atmospheres. It ceased. Engels, in his dry cracked voice, began to read from the Book in his hand.

Calver listened to the solemn words, to the ancient ritual. He wanted hard to believe that this was not for Maclean the end, the ultimate nothingness, but he found himself incapable of doing so. This was not the first Deep Space funeral in his experience—but the others had been in towards the Center, with the bright stars above and below and to all sides, where it was easy to regard those same stars as the veritable Hosts of Heaven. Here, on the Rim, the final negation was too close to the living. It must be closer still to the dead.

"We therefore commit the body to the deep . . ." read the Captain.

Calver pulled the lever. The light over the airlock

door changed from green to red. The structure of the
old ship shook ever so slightly. Maclean—or what
was left of Maclean—was now Outside. Would he,
wondered Calver, plunge into some blazing sun years
or centuries or millennia from now? Or would his
frozen body circle the Rim forever? The maudlin
words of the song of which the dead Mate had been
so fond echoed in his mind:

> *We'll ever roam*
> *And run the Rim* . . .

Calver pulled the second lever. Again the pumps
sobbed. The light changed from red to green. The
needle of the gauge trembled, crept to One Atmosphere, steadied. Calver opened the inner airlock
door, looked inside, making sure. He shut the door.

"Mr. Calver," said Captain Engels stiffly, "secure
for Interstellar Drive." He made his slow way to the
axial shaft. The others began to follow.

Jane Arlen caught his sleeve. Her face was white.

"Derek," she said, "I'm frightened. I thought
when I came out to the Rim that I'd shaken off my
jinx . . . But now . . . Maclean, and all those
others . . ."

Calver said, "It was nothing to do with you, or
with your jinx, or even with poor Maclean. It was
just power politics—power politics on a world that
none of us had ever heard of until we came out here."

She whispered, "But I'm still frightened."

9

So *Lorn Lady* CAME to Grollor.

Almost everybody on that planet, a world that
makes a religion of technology, was glad to see the
ship. Even so, thought Calver, it was a dull world,
with no temptations. The Grollans look upon alcohol
as a good antiseptic, cleaning fluid and rocket fuel,
nothing more. And although they are classed as humanoid they are so grotesque in appearance,
batrachian, that their women could make no appeal
even to Pender—who, in any case, had yet to recover
from the severe fright that he had suffered on Tharn.

In terms of weight and measurement there was little cargo to discharge on Grollor—but ideas cannot
be weighed, can be measured only by results. Calver,
as he checked the manifest, found himself wondering
what those results would be. He ticked off the cases
of technical books, of scientific instruments, of precision tools. He could not help querying the wisdom
of the Rim Government's export policy. To equip an
ally may be wise; to equip a potential rival is not.

But, he told himself, Space is vast. There would be room for the Grollan ships when they ventured beyond the bounds of their own planetary system.

The cargo was discharged and other cargo—once again tools and instruments, but manufactured under license—was loaded. But *Lorn Lady* did not lift at once. Repairs had to be made before she was spaceworthy—the main propellant pump was giving trouble—and Grollor, with its machine shop facilities and relatively cheap labor—was an ideal planet upon which to make them.

Calver and Jane Arlen went ashore. They sampled meals that were stodgy and flavorless, sipped drinks that were flavorless and non-intoxicating. They wandered around art galleries exhibiting the works of artists who were competent mechanical draftsmen and who, obviously, were in love with the machines that they depicted in such loving detail. They attended the performance of an opera (Jane was able to maintain a running translation) that was all about the efforts—eventually and happily successful—of a young works manager to persuade his sweetheart, running a screw-slotting machine in his factory, to increase her output of slotted screws.

It was when they were walking back to the spaceport after this performance that they saw, in the black sky, the flaming exhaust of an inward-bound ship.

"One of the local interplanetary jobs," said Jane, not very interested.

"No," said Calver. "That exhaust's all wrong. Too ruddy. These people haven't any ships yet that can use atomic power and still expel a clean exhaust. They always use chemical propellant inside a planetary atmosphere. That's one of our ships."

"It can't be," she said. "*Rimhound*'s not due for all of a month."

"By one of *our* ships," he corrected her, "I didn't mean one of Rim Runners' palatial cargo liners. I meant a human ship."

"There are other races," she pointed out argumentatively, "with interstellar ships. The Shaara, for example . . ."

"Those communistic bumblebees have never made it out to the Rim," he said.

"There's always a first time," she told him. "And they and the Grollans would get along fine."

"The Grollans," he said, "would never approve of the Shaara drones."

After a while she panted, "Hey! Where's the fire? If we're going to run, we shall be better off taking a taxi . . ."

"I thought you wanted exercise."

"Yes. But not this strenuous. And anybody would think you'd never seen a ship before, the way you're dragging me back to the spaceport . . ."

They paused for breath, standing on the footpath, keeping a look-out for the flashing green light that was the sign of a ground taxi. One of the mono-wheeled vehicles approached them from the direction of the port. Calver waved. The vehicle executed a neat U turn, cut across the bows of a multi-wheeled heavy truck, drew up alongside them and stood there, its gyroscope softly purring.

Calver handed the girl into the passenger compartment, said to the grinning, frog-faced driver, "The port, please."

"Sure, boss."

The vehicle shot away from its standing start, skimmed along the road toward the glare of working lights.

"You've come from the port," said Calver. "What was the ship that just landed?"

"Don't know, boss. Not Rim Runner, not one of ours. Little ship. Stranger."

"Alien?"

"Yes," said the driver. Then, "Alien, like you. You alien."

"I suppose we are," admitted Calver after a pause, glaring at Jane as she giggled. "I suppose we are. It's all a matter of viewpoint, really . . ." He asked the driver, "Did you see what she was like? Did you find out her name?"

"Little ship, not big. Not like yours. Name? Can speak your language, but not read. Did hear name, but not remember too well. Something like, you know, *Star of Er*."

"*Star of Earth?*"

"No. Not Earth. *Er*."

"Er," said Jane, not very helpfully, "is next door to Oz. Didn't you know?"

"But you see now . . ."

The taxi paused briefly at the spaceport gates, then swept on, heading away from the berth at which stood *Lorn Lady*. It cruised slowly past the strange ship. She was, as the driver had said, small. The name just under her sharp stem was picked out in glowing letters—*Star Rover*.

"There's money there," said Jane, a little enviously. "There are only a handful of men in the Galaxy who can afford an interstellar yacht . . ."

"If I had that much money," said Calver, "I

shouldn't come out to the Rim."

"Things are always so much better when you pay for them," said Jane. "After all, I did hear that T. G. Clippers are going to run cruises out to this sector of the Galaxy, and their customers will be in the millionaire class."

"More money than sense," said Calver.

The taxi stopped at *Lorn Lady*'s ramp and he and the girl got out. Calver fumbled in his pocket for a handful of the plastic coinage, paid the driver and followed Jane into the ship, up the spiral companionway that led to the officers' quarters. Captain Engels' door was open and he called to them, "Mr. Calver, Mrs. Arlen! Will you see me, please?"

"You have signed the Contract, both of you," said the old man. "And as officers of a Rim World merchant vessel you are, automatically, officers of our Naval Reserve." He smiled bleakly, adding, "Not that we have a Navy. Even so . . ."

Even so what? thought Calver, sipping the drink that the Captain had poured for him.

"This ship. This *Star Rover* . . ."

"Yes, sir. We've seen her."

"Have you considered the implications of her being here, Mr. Calver?"

"Not in any great detail, sir. But it's fairly obvious. Just a rich man with his money burning holes in his pockets, coming out here to see how the poor live."

"Perhaps, Mr. Calver. Perhaps. But there are other implications."

"Such as, sir?"

"I am surprised that you have to ask, Mr. Calver. You are already aware that Federation agents have been operating out on the Rim." There was a trace of warmth in his smile. "If my memory is not at fault, did you not meet one on Faraway?"

"I was told that she was one," said Calver—expecting, and receiving, a hostile glare from Jane.

"On our own planets," said Captain Engels, "there is efficient counter-espionage machinery. On these worlds, where our people have no jurisdiction, there is not. The Grollan Government is pro Rim Worlds—but we Rim Worlders are the only humans with whom the Grollans have been in contact. In a year or so, treaties will be ratified and we shall be secure. Until such time the Federation could steal our trade and oust us from our position of influence."

"I've no desire to get mixed up in any more private wars," said Calver bluntly.

"I was not suggesting that you should," the Captain told him coldly. "Furthermore I wish to make it quite plain that we, in spite of our status as Reserve officers, are essentially merchant spacemen. Our first duty is to our ship. On the other hand, we do have a duty to find out all that we can and, if possible, to put a spoke in the Federation's wheel."

"I see," said Calver. Then, "Have you any suggestions, sir?"

"None," said the Old Man frankly. "But you're a man with a certain amount of resource and sagacity, or should it be ingenuity? It is a long time since I read Kipling . . ."

" 'The mariner'," quoted Jane, " 'was a man of infinite resource and sagacity . . .' "

"I believe that you are right, my dear. And now, if you will think over what I have told you . . ."

"We'll do that, sir," promised Calver.

Undressing in his cabin, hanging his uniform in his wardrobe, he asked Jane, "And what's tomorrow's rig of the day? False beard and dark glasses?"

"Don't worry about it," she told him. "You're just not cut out to be a spy or counter-spy. But I'll take you as you are."

The following evening Jane did not go ashore; she was fully occupied with an overdue inventory of her stores. Calver, after his offer of assistance had been spurned for the third time, left the ship by himself in rather a bad temper. He walked from the spaceport to the city and there spent an hour in a newsreel theater. Finally, dizzy and bored after watching shot after shot of machinery of various kinds in violent motion, he left the place and went in search of a small restaurant where he had been once or twice with Jane. The proprietor of this establishment endeavored to emulate Terran cuisine and his menu, now and again, produced surprises, some of them quite pleasant ones. Even though he himself could not appreciate subtle flavorings he was willing to admit that there were those who did.

Calver sat in a booth morosely toying with his food. This was one of the restaurant's off nights. Suddenly he realized that the people in the next booth were talking English.

He was grimly amused by the fact that the couple shared his low opinion of the food. And their accent was familiar, and brought with it a wave of nostalgia. *Earth . . .* he thought. *They must be off that yacht. They must be tourists. But who'd come out to the Rim for pleasure?*

He heard the man get to his feet, caught a glimpse of him as he stalked out of the restaurant. There was something vaguely familiar about him. In Calver's mind the penny started to drop.

He pushed away from his own table, got up and walked the step or so to the next booth. The girl, who was still seated, looked at Calver and grinned ruefully. She said, "Grim, isn't it? It was too much for my brother. He said that he had an important business engagement, but I think that he's rushed back to the yacht for an alcoholic gargle to wash the taste out of his mouth."

Calver grinned.

"We thought that we should be playing safe by having something simple," she went on. "*Steak Diane*. That wasn't asking too much, was it?"

"One would think not," admitted Calver.

"And did you enjoy *your* dinner?" she asked.

"It was supposed to be *Lobster Thermidor*," he told her. "But I'd just hate to meet the arthropod that was masquerading as a lobster. My guess is that it was just an oversized cockroach . . ."

Her face, even with its grimace of disgust, was attractive—and her laugh was even more so, its silvery, tinkling quality somehow matching the gleaming platinum of her hair. She said, "Will you join me for coffee? And mine host has something that he calls brandy, if you'd care to risk it . . ."

Calver smiled. "I think that this is about as far as we can go with the encore of the scene that we played at the Rimrock House on Faraway, Miss Verrill. Already we have started to deviate from the original script."

"And what happened to my Napoleon brandy that night, Mr. Calver?"

"We finished it, of course."

"*We?*"

"One of my shipmates and myself. And what happened to you, and your . . . your brother?"

"As a matter of fact," she told him, "he *is* my brother. Oh, there was a little unpleasantry with the authorities, but nothing serious, and we were given the bum's rush off the Rim Worlds. A case of mistaken identity, actually. It seems that there's a couple who're almost our doubles who specialize in selling shares in mythical enterprises on the more backward planets . . ." There was a pause while the waitress brought the coffee service and the unlabelled bottle, and the glasses. She went on, "I never expected to meet you again, Derek. I knew that your ship called here, but you should have been out and away before we dropped in."

"We should have been," he said, "but we had delays *en route*, and now we're grounded for repairs."

"What sort of repairs?"

"I wouldn't know. I'm only the Mate. What the low mechanics do to justify their existence is a mystery."

"Only the Mate?" She looked at the braid on his epaulettes. "Yes. You have riz in the world. You were Second Officer the last time I saw you."

"Yes," agreed Calver, unwilling to joke about the circumstances of his promotion.

"But it must be fascinating, being Chief Officer of a ship on this trade. The Eastern Circuit you call it, don't you? All these new worlds, unspoiled. Grollor, and . . . and . . ."

"Yes," admitted Calver. "We get around." He sipped from his glass. "This is more like brandy than the coffee is like coffee . . . But there's not much resemblance."

"No," she agreed. "There's not." She brightened.

"But there's no need for us to drink here, is there? We have a well-stocked bar aboard the yacht." Her voice fell almost to a whisper. "And there'll be nobody aboard now . . ."

"But what about your brother? And the crew?"

"My brother has a business meeting . . ."

"Business?"

"Oh, stores and such. Clearances, Inwards and Outwards. *You* should know the sort of thing . . ."

"And the crew?"

"There're only a couple of engineers. And they're sight-seeing. Somebody asked them to visit a *lasheleq* factory. What are *lasheleqs?*"

"Search me."

She got to her feet. "Come on, then. Let's get out of this dump."

Calver rose and took the bill that the waitress presented to him. It was made out in an approximation to English, and he saw that it included the meal eaten by the girl and her brother, as well as his own. He wondered if he would be able to charge it up as expenses to whatever Government department it was that handled counter-espionage. He had every intention of trying to do so. He paid, followed the girl out into the street.

A cruising taxicab stopped for them. Calver did not recognize the driver—to him all Grollans looked the same. The driver recognized him, however. (But he was in uniform, and marks of rank are a means of identification.) He grinned, showing his jagged teeth. "Goodnight, boss. New lady tonight." (But Jane Arlen was brunette and Sonya Verrill was blonde.)

"The spaceport," said Calver brusquely.

"Sure, boss. To *Star of Er?*"

"Yes."

"*Star of Er?*" queried the girl.

"That's what they're calling your ship."

"Oh." Then, "What's this about a new lady? I thought I was the only Terran female on this planet, and I can't imagine you doing a line with any of the locals."

"We have one woman aboard the ship. The Catering Officer. We take her ashore sometimes."

"What is she like?"

"Plain," lied Calver. "Dowdy. Just what you'd expect in our class of ship—a dear old duck." He added, "She's a good cook, though."

"So am I," Sonya Verrill told him. "I do all the catering aboard *Star Rover*. I've had no complaints yet."

"I'd like to try it, some time."

"Perhaps you will, Derek."

The cab swept through the spaceport gates, swung to the right and rolled towards *Star Rover*'s berth. Calver looked to the floodlit tower that was *Lorn Lady*, wondered what Jane was doing, wondered what Jane would think if she knew what he was doing. Not that he was *doing* anything. Not that he would do anything. Or if he did do anything, it would be in his honorary capacity as a Rim Worlds counter-spy, not as a private individual. And, in any case, it would be all Jane's fault. If she hadn't flared up and called upon all the odd gods of the Galaxy to deliver her from a blundering space-oaf who would insist on getting in her hair when she had a job of work that had to be done . . .

The taxi slowed to a stop by *Star Rover*'s ramp. Calver got out, handed the girl to the concrete. He paid and dismissed the driver. He looked up at the little ship—little, but large enough, carrying, as she did, only her own machinery and personnel, to circumnavigate the Galaxy. He felt envy for the people who could afford to own such a vessel, wondered where the money came from that had purchased her —from the sale, most probably, of something quite useless and, almost certainly, at least slightly injurious. *Or from the pockets of the Federation taxpayers,* he told himself.

"No gangway watch?" he asked. "This is a rather expensive hunk of iron-mongory to leave loafing around unattended."

"We've everything that opens and shuts," she told him. "Including a sonic lock on the outer door. My brother's voice will operate it, and the voices of the two engineers. And my own, of course."

"What if you're in a hard vacuum?"

"There are such things as suit radios," she said. "In any case, in such conditions, there would almost certainly be somebody inside the ship at all times."

"And the key? Or the combination? The words?"

"Go away," she told him. "Out of earshot. Oh, it's nothing personal, but I just don't know you well enough. Yet."

He retired a few paces, watched her mount the ramp and stand before the circular door. He heard her saying something, but too softly for him to distinguish the words. He saw the big valve swing open. She turned and stood there, the light in the airlock chamber striking through her thin dress. Calver found himself staring at her. He remembered in detail, quite suddenly, what he had thought on the occasion of their first meeting, how he had quoted to himself the words of an ancient poet:

> *No beauty doth she miss*
> *When all her robes are on;*
> *But beauty's self she is*
> *When all her robes are gone . . .*

"What are you waiting for?" she called. "Come on up."

Come up and see me some time, he thought. *Who was it who used to say that? Some notorious courtesan of the Eighteenth or Twenty-first Century or thereabouts? Come up and see me some time . . . I've already seen plenty, but I shouldn't mind seeing more . . .*

He climbed the ramp to the airlock.

10

CALVER HAD SERVED aboard crack liners and had expected that the yacht would be at least as luxurious as such vessels. But she was not. The keynote of her interior fittings was efficiency, with luxury conspicuous by its absence. Oh, she was comfortable enough—but a certain standard of comfort is essential if efficiency is to be maintained. (It has taken shipowners and ship designers millennia to grasp this obvious fact.) The general impression presented, Calver decided, was that of a small fighting ship, some minor unit of the Federation Survey Service. Until now he had been willing to believe that a mistake might have been made, that Sonya Verrill and her brother might just possibly be what they claimed to be—tourists with more money than sense. Now he was sure that they were not. Now was the time to demonstrate the not quite infinite resource and sagacity that Captain Engels had attributed to him.

There was no elevator—in a vessel this size such a fitting would have been the extreme of luxury—but there was the usual spiral companionway in the axial shaft. Calver followed the girl up to the living quarters, admiring the play of the muscles under the smooth, golden skin of her calves, becoming excited by the glimpses of the gleaming, lovely length of her legs.

He followed her along the short, curving alleyway, paused as she stopped to open a door.

"Come in," she said. "This is where I live, Derek."

He looked around the sitting room, obviously part of a suite. The walls were panelled with plastic in pleasant pastel shades. There were two deep chairs, and a settee. There were bookshelves and a big, all-purpose receiver and player. The only note of luxury, as opposed to solid comfort, was struck by the low coffee table, the top of which was a slab of the fabulously expensive opalwood from Fomalhaut VI.

She waved him to a chair, went to the little bar beside the player and produced a bottle and two balloon glasses. He was amused to see that the bottle contained French brandy. She poured drinks, said, "To us."

"Here's mud in your eye," he responded.

She said, "Amuse yourself while I get changed into something more comfortable."

He remained standing until she had gone through into her bedroom, then walked to the player. He looked through the records, selected a tape called *Soft Lights And Sweet Music*. He inserted it into the machine, threaded the end of it through the playing head and onto the empty spool, switched on. He sat on the soft settee, nursing his glass, settled down to enjoy the nostalgic melodies and the play of soft, abstract color patterns on the screen.

She came back into the room. She was wearing a gown of Altairian crystal silk, the material of which it is said that the wearing of it is more naked than actual nudity—provided, of course, that the right woman is wearing it. Sonya Verrill was the right woman.

She sat down beside Calver. He could feel the warmth of her through the fabric of his uniform. He could smell the heady scent that she was wearing. He was aware of her in the worst (or the best?) way.

She said, "You must be hot in here. Why don't you take off your jacket?"

He said, lying without conviction, "I'm quite comfortable, Sonya."

She said, laughing gently, "You'll not find anything like this aboard your ship."

"No," he admitted. "Not quite."

Her fingers were playing with the buttons of his jacket, loosening them one by one, were undoing the buttons of his shirt. Her hand was cool, soft yet firm, on his chest, was warmer as it slid around to his back. Her face was close to his, her lips parted. Her eyes seemed enormous. And his arms were around her, and he felt the yielding firmness of her as he pressed her to him.

She pulled away suddenly.

She said suddenly, coldly, "I'm sorry, Derek. I thought that you'd have had rather more control of yourself than this."

He said, "I may be only a simple spaceman, but I thought that I was asked up here for this."

She said, "I may not be the type of woman to which you are accustomed, Derek, but I find something impossibly sordid about these brief affairs. Before I give myself I must have some illusion of permanence . . ."

"Give yourself? I rather gained the impression that you were throwing yourself at me . . ."

She said in a hurt voice, "That was unkind, Derek. You are an attractive brute, you know. And I'm afraid that I rather lost control. You should have had more control . . ."

"Oh."

"Of course, if we got to know each other better . . . But there's so little time . . ."

"Our repairs should be finished soon," he said.

"Are you really happy in that old wreck of yours?" she asked. "A man like you, used to big, well-found, well-run ships?" She assumed a pensive attitude. "I don't suppose for one moment you'd consider the idea, but we, my brother and I, need a navigator . . . No, not exactly a navigator—Bill's quite competent in that respect. But a pilot, a pilot for this sector of the Galaxy. For the Eastern Circuit . . ." She splashed fresh brandy into their glasses. "The pay would be generous, . . ." she added, as she moved close to him again.

He laughed with genuine amusement. "By all the odd gods of the Galaxy, are you the best that the Federation can do? This corny routine . . . Beautiful blonde spy and oafish victim . . . *I'll surrender the body beautiful, darling, if you will let me have the plans of the Borgenwelfer Disintegrator Mark XIV . . .*"

Anger flared over her face and her hand—the hand that he had thought was so soft—came swinging round in a vicious smack. He caught her wrist before she could strike him again, caught her other wrist, pressed her back on the settee so that she could not use her feet.

Surprisingly, she started to laugh. "You'd be surprised," she told him, "how many times the corny old routine does work. It was worth trying . . . Anyhow, the offer still stands. Sign on her as Eastern Circuit Pilot and you'll be well paid. And when we get back to Earth there'll be a permanent commission for you in the Survey Service—perhaps in the Naval Intelligence Branch . . ."

"And the body beautiful?"

"That part of it is up to you—and me. And I may not struggle too hard."

He got to his feet, pulling her with him. He said, "Thanks for the party, darling, but I must go. I should not love thee, dear, so much, loved I not honor more. Quote and unquote."

"Not so fast, Calver," said a man's voice.

Calver let go of the girl, turned. He saw Sonya Verrill's brother standing in the doorway of her bedroom. He was in uniform, with the trappings of a Commander in the Survey Service. He was holding a heavy pistol in a negligent yet somehow competent manner.

"Not so fast," he said again. "As Sonya's not very subtle methods have failed, the time has come for more direct ones. A revival, say, of the press gang. Or would this be classed as a Shanghai?"

"Press gang," said Calver, eyeing the pistol, wondering what his chances would be if he used Sonya as a shield. "Press gang. Brute force. The Shanghai specialists were a little more subtle. They used to dope their victims' drink. I'm surprised that you never thought of that."

"One volunteer," said Verrill, "is worth ten pressed men. And we rather hoped that you might volunteer."

"There was considerable inducement," admitted

Calver, "but I have other commitments."

The girl struggled in his grasp. "So you were lying. So this Catering Officer of yours isn't the old duck you said she was."

"But she is a good cook," said Calver, tensing himself, getting ready to throw the girl at her brother.

"I shouldn't if I were you," said another voice.

Resignedly, Calver turned slowly. Standing in the doorway to the alleyway were two more men, like Verrill in Survey Service uniform. They wore the rank and branch badges of engineer officers, but it was obvious that the automatics they held were as at home in their hands as less lethal working tools would have been.

Calver sat in an acceleration chair in the yacht's control room. He was not uncomfortable—Sonya Verrill, when she had lashed his arms and legs to the piece of furniture, had done so without unnecessary brutality. He was not uncomfortable, but after experimental strainings and twistings he had been obliged to admit that he would stay where he was until released.

Verrill was in the pilot's chair, the co-pilot's seat being occupied by his sister. The two engineers were at their stations, as Calver well knew. He had felt a sudden hope as he watched the spaceport police running, with their odd hopping gait, towards *Star Rover's* berth—and who, he wondered, had instigated the raid?—had lapsed into despair as warming up blasts had sent a sheet of vicious fire rippling out over the concrete, forcing the policemen to retreat.

"All ready below, Commander," reported Sonya in an expressionless voice.

"Thank you, Lieutenant."

"You can't get away with this," said Calver.

"But we are getting away with it," Verrill told him.

"This is an act of war," said Calver, regretting the pomposity of the words as soon as he had uttered them.

"War, my dear sir? Surely you know that you Rim Worlders are still Federation citizens, and that we, of the Survey Service, are the Federation's policemen."

"Shouldn't we be getting upstairs, Commander?" asked Sonya.

"Unless they have artillery here—and they haven't —we're quite safe, Lieutenant."

"Illegal arrest, then," went on Calver doggedly.

"Illegal arrest? Rape, Mr. Calver, is a serious crime when a civilian is the victim. But when the victim is a policewoman . . ."

"I wish that there had been rape," said Calver bitterly.

He allowed his attention to stray from the mocking face of the Commander, turned to stare for the last time (but he still hoped that it would not be the last time) at *Lorn Lady*, at the old *Forlorn Bitch*. He stiffened as he saw the brightening flicker of blue flame beneath her stern. But perhaps the engineers had finished their repairs and were testing the reaction drive. Even so, somebody must have told the spaceport police—who were still standing stupidly just clear of the blast area—of his abduction. Captain Engels must know. And Jane. (And had they written him off as an impressionable fool who would fall for a pretty face and body and a head of blond hair? What would Jane be thinking?) Somebody must have given the alarm. That taxi driver . . . Could he be a Rim Worlds agent?

"Commander Verrill!" Sonya's voice was sharp. "I think that we should blast off."

"I'm glad that I never had a back seat driver for a sister," said Calver.

"Lieutenant Verrill," ordered the Commander stiffening, "give the engineers their count-down."

"Ten . . ." she said. "Nine . . . Eight . . ."

Calver glanced out of the port again. Yes, the blue exhaust flame from *Lorn Lady* was much brighter.

"Seven . . . Six . . . Five . . ."

But surely Verrill would know. Surely his ship carried a Psionic Communications Officer, a trained telepath who would warn him. But perhaps she did not. One drawback to psionic radio is its complete lack of privacy. A telepath aboard a ship on a secret mission would betray that mission to every other telepath in the area.

"Four . . . Three . . . Two . . . One . . ."

And the fools were intent on their instruments, were not looking out through their viewports, did not see the sudden blossoming of intolerable fire below *Lorn Lady*'s stern.

"Fire!"

Acceleration pressed Calver deep into his seat, thrust his chin down to his chest. Slowly, painfully, he turned his head, saw nothing of *Lorn Lady*. Even more slowly and painfully he elevated his line of sight, saw that the old ship was already well above the yacht, was streaking for the sky like a bat out of hell. He heard Sonya gasp and swear, heard her say, "You and your damn silly regulations! You and your count-down at a time like this!"

"Switch on the radio!" ordered Verrill. "Tell those fools to give us space room!"

"Star Rover to *Lorn Lady,"* said the girl coldly. "Federation Survey Ship *Star Rover* to *Lorn Lady*. Clear space. This is an order. I repeat, this is an order."

There was a pause, during which Verrill swore, "Are the swine deaf as well as daft?" Then Jane's voice came through the speaker of the receiver.

"Rim Worlds Auxiliary Cruiser *Lorn Lady* to *Star Rover*. Land at once. We cannot be responsible if you stray into our back-blast. Land at once. This is an order."

Verrill was a competent ship handler and his small ship was maneuverable. Yet, as Calver knew, *Lorn Lady* was a powerful brute and Captain Engels, as a ship handler, was more than merely competent. Verrill, as he climbed, threw his little craft from side to side, bruising her people with the sudden changes of acceleration. Hanging above *Star Rover*, *Lorn Lady* seemed to anticipate her every move, and all the time the distance between the ships decreased. In spite of the polarization of the viewports, the light in the yacht's control room was blinding. In spite of the insulation the heat level was rising rapidly.

"Take her down," sobbed Sonya Verrill, her composure broken.

"Then tell them," said Verrill tiredly.

"Star Rover to *Lorn Lady,"* she said. "We are landing."

"Lorn Lady to *Star Rover*. Return to your berth. We shall hang over the spaceport until we see all of you, all four of you and the prisoner, leave the ship and surrender yourselves to the police. If you do not comply within a reasonable time we shall drop on you,

and reduce you to a puddle of molten slag."

"And is that your girl friend?" asked Sonya Verrill.

"It is," said Calver.

"What charming people you know, darling," she said with a return to her old manner.

So they landed and, after Calver had been untied, marched out of the ship into the arms of the police. Above the spaceport hung *Lorn Lady*, a strange, ominous comet in the black sky, a thundering meteor that did not fall. And then the roaring of her was drowned by sudden, more imminent thunder. Calver turned, as did the others, and saw a column of flameshot smoke where *Star Rover* had been. Somebody, before leaving her, had actuated the time fuse of the demolition charge.

Calver let his hand fall onto Commander Verrill's shoulder, knew that the other man appreciated the comforting pressure. He did not know (yet) what it was like to lose a ship, but could imagine how it felt.

And not far from them *Lorn Lady*, slowly, carefully, somehow tiredly, settled to her berth.

11

Two days later, *Lorn Lady* lifted from Grollor.

Star Rover's people were in prison and there they would remain until, eventually, the Federation Government paid the bill for the repair of the damage to the spaceport apron caused by the destruction of the yacht. Captain Engels had promised Commander Verrill that he would see to it that a report was sent to Federation Survey Service H.Q. But, he pointed out with wry humor, the tide flows sluggishly through official channels. And Calver felt rather sorry for his late abductors. The jail was not uncomfortable but the food, good enough by Grollan standards, was deadly dull. Jane was not pleased when he visited the prisoners on his last evening ashore, leaving them a parcel of luxuries.

"I wouldn't mind so much," she flared, "if I didn't know that everything's really for that tow-haired trollop!"

But *Lorn Lady* lifted and once she was again on the Long Haul the planet-bred hostilities were forgotten.

The officers slipped back into Deep Space routine, thankful to be on their way once more. Calver and Brentano settled down to the monotony and broken sleep of watch and watch, four hours on and four hours off. The hours of duty were long—and they were the longer for the lack of anything to do whilst in the control room. It was essential that the officer of the watch stay alert—and this desirable condition was achieved and maintained largely by the ingestion of huge quantities of black coffee. And Calver— once Jane had forgiven him, although she still taunted him about his infinite resource and sagacity —was lucky. When her own duties permitted it she would share his watch with him. At first Captain Engels was inclined to frown upon the practice—and then he, himself, admitted that in view of *Lorn Lady*'s shorthandedness it was as desirable that as many officers as possible were capable of standing a control room watch. And so Brentano, to his great disgust, found himself having to put up with Pender as an apprentice watch officer.

For day after day, week after week, the old ship fell through the distorted continuum, the outer darkness on one hand, the fantastic convolutions of the Galactic Lens on the other. She dropped down the dark infinities, through the blackness that was blacker than blackness should be, through the emptiness that was, somehow, not empty, for watch after watch, day after day, week after week.

It was on one of Calver's watches that it happened.

He was sipping from the bulb of coffee that Arlen had brought him, was nibbling at the sandwich. He was saying, "I'll always love you, darling. You never forget the mustard . . ." when she interrupted him, asking sharply, "Derek, what's that?"

Sandwich in one hand, coffee bulb in the other, he looked first at her, then in the direction along which she was pointing. He saw a faint light, a light where no light should have been. It was faint but clear, too clear, hard against the vagueness, definite against the faint, far nebulosities that, with the Interstellar Drive in operation, seemed even fainter and more distant.

"Jane!" he ordered. "The radar!"

While she went to the console he unbuckled himself from his chair, pulled himself to the telescope. He swiveled the powerful instrument, adjusted the focus. The long, slim shape swam into view—the gleaming, metal hull, the big vanes at the stern, the dim light from the control room ports at the forward end. It was a ship—and that was, or should have been, impossible.

"Jane!" he snapped. "Bearing? Range?"

He heard her reply, "Nothing on the screen . . ."

"Damn it, wench," he growled. "There must be . . ."

"There's *not*."

He left the telescope, went to stand beside Jane at the radar. As she had told him, the screen was blank. But, he told himself, it had to be blank. For there to be anything showing on it, the temporal precession rate of the target would have to be synchronized with that of *Lorn Lady*—and the odds against any two ships using the Mannschenn Drive achieving temporal synchronization are astronomical. But, without temporal synchronization, how could there be direct vision?

"Go to the telescope," he said, "and tell me what you see."

Without waiting for her report he called the Captain on the telephone. "Chief Officer here," he reported. "Unidentified vessel to port . . ."

"Bearing? Range?" he heard the cracked old voice demand.

"I don't know, sir. Radar seems to be inoperable."

The Old Man, as always, was in the control room almost immediately. He went first to the radar console, wasted no time there, then to the telescope. He ordered quietly, "Mr. Calver, call out Mr. Brentano and Mr. Levine. We will try to communicate."

Calver picked up the telephone, buzzed the two communications officers. Brentano, alert in spite of his short rations of sleep, answered his call at once. Levine, typically, was far from alert, insisted that the situation be explained to him in words of one syllable —and then demanded a repetition.

When he had finished he heard Captain Engels say, "She's closer, Mr. Calver. Seems to be a converging course . . ."

"How do you know, sir?"

The old man grinned. He said, "One can manage without radar, Calver. When I first came up here the image of that ship extended over three graticules— now it extends over five . . . But what about the radio officers? Are they up?"

"Brentano is, sir. He'll be in Electronic Communications now. Levine was hard to wake . . ."

"He always is. You'd better go and make sure that he's functioning. I shall be all right here, with Mrs. Arlen. If I want you in a hurry I shall sound the General Alarm."

"But, sir . . . Could it be pirates, do you think?"

"Pirates, Mr. Calver? There are many wonders on

the Rim—but pirates have never been among them. What ship plying between these poverty-stricken planets is worth the pirating?"

The telephone buzzed. Calver picked up the instrument, heard, "Electronic Communications here. No signals audible on any frequency. Am transmitting on all frequencies."

"Brentano, sir," reported Calver. "He's trying—but there are no results."

"Drag Mr. Levine out," ordered Engels.

Calver pulled himself through the hatchway into the officers' flat, went to Levine's cabin—which was also his place of duty. He found the Psionic Radio Officer out of his bunk, strapped into the swivel chair by the table upon which was the glass globe in which lived the psionic amplifier, below which was the complexity of tanks and pumps and piping that handled nutrition and excretion. He looked with distaste at the gray, wrinkled thing in the globe, while his nostrils twitched at the imagined smell of dog. Like most spacemen, he accepted psionic radio intellectually but not emotionally. It was not the operator himself, the trained telepath, that he found revolting —although there were some who did—but the amplifier, the dog's brain tissue culture, without which it would have been impossible for human thought-waves to span interstellar distances. Revolting, too, was the way in which the majority of Psionic Radio Operators made pets of their organic equipment—rewarding it by visualization of trees and bones . . .

He said, "Levine!"

The little man opened his eyes, had trouble focusing them on the Chief Officer. He muttered, without much interest, "Oh, it's you, Calver . . ."

"What do you receive?"

"I hear the P.R.O. of *Thermopylae* . . . She's one of the T.G. clippers . . . Don't know what she's doing out here . . ."

"Could it be her within sight?"

"Oh, no. She's off Elsinore. Making arrangements for disembarkation of passengers . . ."

"Do you hear anybody close?"

"No. Why should I?"

"There's a ship," said Calver patiently. "Within sight. Her temporal precession rate is synchronized with our own. Her velocity matches. *Who is she? What is she?*"

"I don't know," replied Levine mildly. "All I can pick up at close range is the usual babble from the minds of all you people—and, as you damn well know, I never eavesdrop on my shipmates. Apart from anything else, I should be breaking my oath if I did . . ."

"Then eavesdrop," said Calver, "if it's the only way that you can do any short range listening."

"Oh, all right. But don't blame me. . ." Levine stiffened suddenly. "This is damned funny. First time I've ever struck anything like it. A sort of echo effect . . . You're thinking, *Why do we have to be at the mercy of this teacup reader,* and, at not quite the same time, you're thinking, *Why do we have to be at the mercy of this crystal gazer?*"

The telephone buzzed. Calver said, "I'll take it." He heard Captain Engels say, "That you, Mr. Calver? Has he got anything?" "No," Calver replied, "But . . ."

"Come back here," ordered the Old Man. "We're going to try visual communication."

Back in the control room Calver found that a lamp had been rigged by Brentano, a portable searchlight with a key and shutters. He gave it only a hasty glance, looked from it out through the viewports, saw that the strange ship was much closer. The Old Man had been right. She was on a converging course. A collision course? But there was no real danger. All that was necessary was for one or other of the vessels to vary her rate of temporal precession by as little as one micro-second and, thereby, to drift (although drift was far too slow a word) out of the common frame of reference.

The Captain was back at the telescope so Calver pulled a pair of powerful prismatic binoculars from their clip, focused them. He could see the shape of the stranger plainly now. He had read, somewhere, that a ship operating her interstellar drive is a source of photons; this was the first time that he had been given the opportunity of checking the validity of the hypothesis. The gleaming hull was faintly luminous —as, no doubt, was the hull of *Lorn Lady* to the observers in the other control room.

He heard a rapid, rhythmic clicking, looked around, saw that Brentano was operating his key. By ear as much as by sight he read the symbols and the letters—the AA, AA of calling up, BT, the break sign, then again AA. He heard Brentano complain, "She doesn't answer . . ."

And then there was a bright light flashing from the stem of the other, a staccato blinking, the repetition of letters and symbols that made no sense.

"Alien . . ." Calver heard Brentano mutter.

And yet the strange ship was not alien. Her design proclaimed the fact that she had been built by human, not by merely humanoid hands. There was a . . . a humanness about her. She could almost have been the sister of *Lorn Lady* . . . Could she, wondered Calver, be a mirage, an odd mirror image, produced by some freak bending of Space and Time? But the name—he could not yet quite read it—on the bows and on the big stern vanes was too long . . .

He realized that Captain Engels had left the telescope, had gone to the telephone. He heard the Old Man say, "Mr. Bendix, stand by. When I buzz twice, cut the Drive. Cut *and* brake."

He felt rather than saw Jane standing beside him, heard her whisper, "If there should be a collision . . . It would be my fault . . ."

He tried to laugh. "Don't worry about your catastrophes, Calamity Jane, until they've happened. There'll be no collision."

He wished that he felt as confident as he had sounded. He considered the advisability of reaching out to the telephone selector board, giving the two short buzzes that would be the signal for Bendix to cut the Drive, remembered that once before he had been on the verge of mutiny. He thought wryly, *Father knows best* . . .

The other ship was still closer. Calver could see the figures of those in her control room, could begin, by the intermittent flashes of Brentano's lamp, to make out details. They looked human enough. They *were* human. And they were, somehow, familiar . . . Uneasily, he shifted his regard. And the name . . . ? Could he read it now? There were two words . . .

And the letters . . . ? Terran script? *T* . . . *H* . . . *E*
. . . *"The* . . ." he said aloud. *"The Outsider* . . ." He
knew of no ship so called on the Rim—and yet it was
a name that belonged to the edge of the Galaxy.

He looked back to the control room. He could see
the people there more plainly still. He could see the
tall man in a uniform not unlike his own, but with
the four golden bars of command on his epaulettes.
He could see the woman beside him—the tall woman, also in uniform, tall and slender, with the startling streak of silver in her black, glossy hair. He
could see the small man behind the other signalling
lamp, the dark, compact, competent little man who
was still, as was Brentano, striving in vain to establish visual communication.

The shutter of Brentano's lamp jammed, the
bright beam of light shone directly into the stranger's
control room. Calver cried out aloud. The man behind the other lamp was Brentano, the tall woman
was Jane. And the other Captain was . . . himself . . .

And the distance between the two ships was diminishing rapidly, too rapidly, and Calver, turning,
saw old Captain Engels pushing himself away from
the telescope, reaching out a skinny hand for the telephone selector board. From the ports of the other
control room the white faces stared into their own.
He could see, plainly, the horror on the other Jane's
face, knew that it must be a reflection of that on the
face of his own Jane Arlen.

He tensed himself for the crash, for the scream of
tearing metal, for the shriek of explosively escaping
air. His arm went about Jane and he pressed her to
him tightly. There had been times when he would
have been willing to go out in such a disaster—but

those times, thanks to Arlen, were now past. It was ironical that disaster should come now that he had found something—someone—to live for.

He heard Engels gasp with relief—and knew that the signal could never have reached Bendix in time. He was conscious of a . . . a merging, a merging, a merging and, almost simultaneously, a separation. He tried to capture the strange memories that, briefly, had existed in his mind—utterly absurd and impossible memories of shipwreck and salvage, of the salvage money that had made possible the running of the Rim as an independent trader.

He listened to the dying whine of the Drive as the precessing gyroscopes slowed to a stop, experienced the inevitable sense of temporal disorientation. He looked out of the ports—saw on the one hand the too familiar nothingness, on the other the Galactic Lens. Of the strange ship there was no sign.

Engels said tiredly, "Tell Bendix to restart the Drive."

"But, Captain, what was it?"

"I've heard of them," whispered the old man. "I've heard of them, but I've never quite believed in them. Until now . . ."

"But what was it?"

"You can ask our friends on Stree that question," said Captain Engels. "They might be able to tell you. But we, on the Rim, know such apparitions as Rim Ghosts . . ."

12

SLOWLY, CAUTIOUSLY, through an overcast sky, *Lorn Lady* dropped down to Stree. With tired, bored efficiency she drifted in to the clearing in the jungle that was the spaceport, fell through the clouds of steam of her own generating until her big stern vanes touched the ground (mud before her coming, now baked hard) and the Reaction Drive was cut. Calver looked out through the drizzle-dimmed viewports, through the slowly thinning steam, to the towering trees, the trees that marched on all sides to the limit of vision, whose ranks faded into the gray mists.

He heard Captain Engels say, "Mr. Calver, please go down to the airlock to receive the Agent . . ."

"The Agent . . ." he echoed, looking at the green form that lumbered lazily into the clearing, at the great lizard that walked, kangaroo-like (or dinosaur-like) on its two hind legs. The Commission's trade was limited to planets with human or humanoid dominant races; Calver felt somewhat shocked at the prospects of having to extend the usual courtesies to a reptile. He knew, too, that Captain Engels did not like lizards; it was a phobia with him. He had been told that Engels, whenever possible, left any and all dealings with the natives of Stree to his Chief Officer.

He found Jane Arlen waiting for him at the airlock. She said, "I know the drill, Derek—and Treeth is quite a good fellow once you get used to him."

"Treeth? That dinosaur outside?"

"Yes. That's his name."

"I suppose he can speak English."

"Of course. He speaks and reads English, as you should know. After all, when the bulk of our cargo for here is books . . . And he likes tea. Be sure to ask him up to partake of a pot of the horrid brew with us."

Calver operated the manual controls of the airlock. Both doors sighed open. The warm air that billowed in, that mingled with the stale ship's atmosphere, was too humid to be refreshing, but the scent of it was far from unpleasant. Calver looked out, pressed the button that controlled the ramp. Like a tongue of metal it extended itself from the hull, quivering slightly, sought and found the ground.

Treeth came slowly up the inclined surface, smiling horridly, displaying rows of needle-sharp teeth. He said—and the hissing undertones were hardly noticeable—"Mrs. Arlen. Salutations. And to you, sir, salutations."

"Salutations," replied Calver.

"Treeth," said Jane, "this is Mr. Calver, our new Chief Officer."

"And where is my old friend, Mr. Maclean?"

"Dead," said Jane briefly.

"I am sad—as, no doubt, you are. But remember that nothing dies, that the Past still exists, must exist.

You people, with the ingenuity of your Interstellar Drive, have come so close to a solution of these problems—and yet, somehow, you are incapable of taking the final step. But that final step is a matter for the mind, not for the machine. You have bound yourselves to your machines, to your intricacies of glass and metal, magnetic fields and electron streams. You . . ."

"Some tea, Treeth?" asked Jane brightly.

"But of course. It is a matter of great regret to us that the climate of our planet is unsuitable for the planting of tea, and that shipping space is so severely limited. No doubt, in the future, more tonnage will be available and then, perhaps, greater imports of the herb will become possible . . ."

He was inside the ship now—and Calver was not, as he had feared that he would be, repelled. Treeth was a lizard, and a fearsome looking lizard—but about him was an aura of amiability. He was a lizard —and, as are representatives of his breed on most other worlds, he was a clean lizard. There was a very faint muskiness hanging about him—but a dog coming in out of the wet would have smelled far worse.

Jane led the way up to the messroom. Treeth followed. Behind the native Calver marvelled at the skill with which he negotiated the spiral stairway—and at his ability to maintain a non-stop conversation during the entire ascent. He stopped only when, seated on the messroom deck, his legs and tail a stable tripod, he took the cup of tea that Jane had poured him between his two claws, sipped appreciatively. Calver took the opportunity to talk business.

He said, "We have the usual consignment of books —some on microfilm, some bound. There are the latest treatises on philosophy, also the latest contemporary novels. There are also music tapes. And, of course, tea . . ."

Treeth extended his cup to Jane for a refill. He said, "Good. And we, Mr. Calver, can offer you the usual cargo in exchange. The *sissari* jewels. There are three dozen cut to your requirements. Fourteen rolls of parchment, upon which is the translation of Sessor's philosophical works . . ."

Calver remembered what Engels had said— "Their jewels—they're diamonds, actually, but the lizards have a fantastic way of cutting them—are fabulously valuable; but those parchments of theirs may hold all the secrets of the Universe . . ." He wondered what questions would be answered by Sessor's philosophy—then recalled something else that Engels had said: "You can ask our friends on Stree that question. They might be able to tell you . . ."

He said, abruptly, "We had an odd experience *en route* from Grollor."

"Indeed, Mr. Calver? And what was it?"

Calver told him—and told him of Captain Engel's reference to Rim Ghosts.

Treeth was silent as he sipped his tea, then held out the cup for yet another refill. He said then, "It is as I remarked when I first boarded, when you told me of poor Mr. Maclean's death. The Past, I said, is still living—and that applies to all the Pasts, not only to the immediate Past. We, on this planet, have lived for ages on the Rim—you, on your four colonized worlds, are only newcomers. Even so—you have known for centuries that the Universe is expanding, have suspected that new matter is in the process of continual creation, fills always the void left by the expansion of the old.

"Once—and was it in the Galaxy before this one, or the Galaxy before that, or before that?—there was an Earth that was almost the exact duplicate of your Earth, an Earth whose culture spread out among the stars, as yours has done. Once there was another Derek Calver, another Jane Arlen, another Louis Brentano—and they ran the Rim in a ship not called *Lorn Lady*, but *The Outsider* . . . And we, on our Rim, are expanding through the space once occupied by that long ago Rim, and there was empathy between yourselves and your other, earlier selves . . ."

"But we found it impossible," said Calver, "to establish communication. Levine, our Psionic Radio Officer, did say that he picked up telepathic transmissions that were, as near as dammit, echoes of our own thoughts, but that was all. And we rigged a signal lamp and tried to flash a message—just as they did. But all we received was gibberish."

"That earlier Earth could not have been quite identical," said Treeth. "Perhaps it was not Samuel Morse who invented the telegraph and the code that bears his name. Perhaps it was somebody called, say, Taylor, who decided that A in the Taylor Code would be one dot, not dot dash . . ."

"H'm," grunted Calver. "That's possible, I suppose. But my predecessor was luckier than me. I have memories of the memories I . . . shared when the two ships merged briefly. The other Calver was Master—Master *and* Owner. He'd got the money to buy his ship as a reward for some piece of salvage . . ."

"You might yet do the same," said Treeth.

"Not bloody likely," laughed Jane. "There's not a

one of the rustbuckets running the Rim that would be worth salvaging." Her face darkened. "Too—if there ever were any salvage operations at which I was present, I should be in the ship requiring salvage . . ."

The Agent made the fearsome grimace that passed for a smile. He said, "Mrs. Arlen, I have told you before that a losing sequence cannot last forever, that the tide must turn some time . . ."

"Sure," she said. "I just stick around and wait for the Galaxy after this one, or the one after that, and the luck will change . . ." She paused, went on bitterly, "I thought that it had changed—and then too many people were killed on Tharn . . ."

Calver broke the silence, spread manifest and cargo plan on the table.

He said briskly, "How soon can you commence discharge? The chests of tea will be first out, then the books . . ."

Calver, to his regret, had no further opportunities for conversation with Treeth. Captain Engels did not like Stree. He liked neither the climate nor the inhabitants. He enjoined upon his Mate the necessity for a quick discharge, a speedy loading and an undelayed blast-off. The local lizards could not be hurried—but the handful of cargo could be, and was, slung out by ship's personnel with ship's gear and covered with tarpaulins against the drizzle. Treeth, bribed by the gift of a small chest of tea from Jane Arlen's stores, saw to it that the outward cargo—the jewels and the parchments—was down before discharge of the inward consignment was finished.

Mellise was the next planet of call.

Mellise is a watery world, fully four-fifths of its surface being covered by the shallow seas. Mellise, with its absence of great land masses and, in consequence, of the conditions producing steep barometric gradients, should not be a stormy world. Normally it is not. Normally the only winds experienced are the steady, predictable Trades and Anti-Trades. But there is a long, straggling archipelago almost coincident with the Equator, and at the changes of the Equinox conditions obtain, although briefly, favorable to the breeding of hurricanes.

Mellise is a watery world—and, in the main, a very pleasant one.

Calver let the slight surf carry him in to the white beach, feeling the pleasant heat of the sun on his bare skin. He grounded gently, got to his feet, stood with the water lapping around his ankles, watched Jane making for the shore with long, easy strokes. He thought, irreverently, *Venus on the half shell*, as she stood erect, the droplets of water sparkling on her smooth, tanned skin. He thought, *But that Venus was a carroty cat, and her feet were ugly . . . Why is it that so few artists who paint from the nude seem to have been able to afford or find a model with straight feet? Why is it that so many artists seem to favor that ugly, bunion-like bend at the big toe?*

She came to him, walking gracefully through the shallow water. She smiled and said, "Why so serious, darling? What are you thinking about?"

"Your feet," he said.

"My *feet*? Derek! Don't tell me that I've got myself a fetishist!"

"I worship everything of yours," he told her. *"Everything."*

"The ship . . ." she murmured, pushing away from him.

"Damn the ship," he swore—but he glanced inland, saw the blunt, gleaming spire that was the stem of *Lorn Lady*, just visible above the feathery, purple foliage of the trees. There was little likelihood that there would be anybody in the control room, but it was just possible. And Pender, should he be there, would be quite capable of using the telescope.

Calver walked slowly inland towards the sheltering trees. As he walked he felt again his gratitude for the breakdown of the pumps that had caused the delay in departure, the grounding that had given to him and the girl what was almost a honeymoon, that had enabled him to convince her that she was loved and wanted, and that her jinx—if there ever had been such a malign influence in her life—was dead.

The unexpected holiday had been good—coming, as it had, after a period of intense activity. There had been little leisure during the discharge—nets and cordage and harpoon guns—and little during the loading, although the great, lustrous pearls that were their homeward cargo had offered few problems in stowage, had been put with the Streean diamonds in the ship's strongroom.

Behind them there was a muffled snorting sound. Arlen turned, looked back towards the sea. She swore, pointed, said, "Company . . ."

Calver looked, saw the black blob that had broken the surface of the water. He echoed the girl's curse.

She shrugged, led the way to the tree under which they had left their clothing. He watched her appreciatively as she pulled on her shirt, climbed into her shorts. Reluctantly he put on his own tropical uniform. It was not prudery that had caused them to dress; it was the knowledge that to the natives, who themselves always went naked, all Terrans looked alike, could be distinguished only by badges of rank.

The Mellisan waddled through the shallows, his sleek, black hide gleaming in the sunlight. The necklace of gaudy shells around his long, sinuous neck proclaimed him a person of some consequence. Calver thought that he was the Chief who had supervised the discharge and loading from the shore end, but could not be sure.

"Meelongee," said the native, his voice like that of a Siamese cat.

"Meelongee," replied Arlen.

The word meant, Calver knew, "greetings." It was about the only word of which he did know the meaning.

The Mellisan shifted from one webbed foot to the other. He gesticulated with his stubby arms. It was impossible for Calver to read the expression on the black, long-muzzled face—but he guessed that it was one of grave concern. There was anxiety in the yelping voice.

Worry shadowed Arlen's features.

"Derek," she asked. "When shall we be ready for Space?"

"At least another twenty-four hours," he said. "Why?"

"That will be too late. Our friend here tells me that there will be a big blow before tomorrow morning—a gale, or a hurricane . . ."

"Not a cloud in the sky," said Calver, looking upwards.

"Isn't there an old saying," she asked quietly,

"about the calm before the storm? Hadn't we better get back and warn the Old Man?"

"Yes," he agreed.

Arlen thanked the native in his own tongue. He bowed clumsily, backed into the water, turned suddenly and was gone with hardly a splash. The two Terrans walked along the rough path from the beach to the clearing that was dignified with the name of spaceport. Once Arlen stopped, saying nothing, and pointed. Calver stared at the little furry animals, not unlike squirrels, that normally lived in the trees. Whole tribes of them had come down from their arboreal homes, were industriously digging burrows in the soil.

Arlen and Calver came into the clearing, hurried to the ramp. They ran up the spiral staircase from the airlock to the control room. The Chief Officer went directly to the aneroid barometer. It had, he recalled, registered 1020 millibars that morning. The 1010 noon reading he had ascribed to diurnal range. Since noon it had dropped to 930 millibars. He tapped the face of the instrument with his forefinger. The needle dropped sharply.

He went to the telephone, pressed the selector button for the Reaction Drive Room. It was Bendix who answered, "Yes? What do you want?"

"How long will Renault be on those pumps of his?"

"It'd be a ten-minute job if this lousy outfit carried spares!" snapped Bendix. "But when we have to make impellers by hand . . ."

"How long will you be?"

"Until this time tomorrow."

"Not good enough." He turned, said to the girl,

"Arlen, wake the Old Man, will you? You know what to tell him." Then, into the telephone, "Can't Renault fake up some sort of jury rig to get us upstairs in a hurry? We've been warned that there's the father and mother of all storms brewing, and our own observations confirm the warning."

Renault came to the other end of the line. He said, "We're doing our best, Calver. You know that. The best I can promise is tomorrow noon. Now leave us alone, will you?"

Arlen came back into the control room, followed by Captain Engels.

The Old Man, thought Calver, looked an old man in fact as well as in name. He always had looked old —but, until recently, there had been an air of wiry indestructability about him. That now was gone.

He walked slowly, a little unsteadily, to the aneroid. He studied it for a few moments.

He said, "I have heard about these storms, Mr. Calver. I always hoped that it would be my good luck never to experience one. A grounded spaceship is, perhaps, the most helpless of all Man's creations." He paused. "I am older than you, Mr. Calver, much older, but all my spacefaring experience has been on the Rim—and, until very recently, only on the Ultimo, Lorn, Thule and Faraway run. Perhaps you . . ."

"Perhaps . . ." echoed Calver. He said, "On my way out from Earth to the Rim I was obliged, at times, to do jobs outside the usual run of a spaceman's experience. Once, for a few months, I was Second Mate of a tops'l schooner on Atlantia. I was no good as a seaman—it was as a navigator that they wanted me—but I did my best to learn . . ."

"Speaking as a seaman," said Engels, "where do

you think lies the danger?"

"The trees," said Calver slowly, considering his words, "will break the force of the wind at ground level, but the upper portion of the ship will be exposed to its full fury. The situation is analogous to that of a surface ship, a sailing ship, caught in a blow before she has time to shorten sail. A surface ship, in such a predicament, will be driven over on to her beam ends—unless she is first dismasted . . ."

"Spare us the nautical technicalities," said Engels dryly.

"Sorry, sir. What I mean is this: The danger is that we shall be blown over, on to our side—and once that happens we just sit here until the next ship comes in. *Lorn Lady* will be a total loss." He gestured towards the barometer. "And, sir, there's real dirt coming . . ."

"Never mind the prognostications, Mr. Calver. I believe you. The question is this: What are we doing about it?"

"There's something I read once . . ." began Arlen hesitantly.

"Yes, Mrs. Arlen?" asked Engels. "What was it?"

"It was in a historical novel. It was about the early days of space flight, the first explorations of Mars and Venus . . ."

"Mars and Venus?"

"Two planets in Earth's solar system," she told the Captain. "Venus is a world very like this, but much closer to its primary. Fierce storms are of very frequent occurrence. Anyhow, in the book, the crew of one of the rockets had to set up stays—I think that's the right word—to prevent their ship from being blown over . . ."

"Stays . . ." muttered Calver thoughtfully. "Of

course . . . There are the towing lugs forward, and there are the towing wires . . . We have shackles, and bottle screws . . ."

"And to what do you propose to anchor your . . . stays?" asked the Captain.

"To the roots of the stoutest trees," replied Calver.

"It could work . . ." murmured the Old Man.

"It will have to work," said Arlen.

"Shall I go ahead with it, sir?" asked Calver.

Captain Engels tapped the face of the aneroid barometer. Its needle fell another few millibars. He walked to the nearest port and looked out at the sky. All the brilliance had gone from the westering sun, which now presented a dull, smudgy appearance. Overhead the long mares' tails had appeared in what had been a cloudless sky. Faintly audible in the control room was a distant, sighing rumble, rhythmic and ominous. Engels asked, "What is that noise?"

"The surf," said Calver. "There was almost a flat calm, but the swell's getting up."

"Rig your stays, Mr. Calver," ordered the Captain.

13

By NIGHTFALL the job was done. Calver, aided by Arlen, Levine, Pender and old Doc Malone, had broken out the towing wires, the shackles and the bottle screws from the spare gear store. He had shackled the four wires to the towing lugs just abaft *Lorn Lady*'s stem. These wires had been brought down to the boles of convenient, stout trees and had been again shackled to the powerful bottle screws—themselves shackled to the heavy wire strops around the trunks. They had been set up tight—but not too tight. Calver was haunted by a vision of the frail old ship crumpling down upon herself if too much weight were put on the stays.

Sunset had been a dismal, gray end to the day, and with it had come the wind, fitful at first, uncertain, bringing with it occasional vicious squalls of rain and hail. The swell was heavy now, breaking high on the beach. The sea had lost its usual phosphorescence and every roaring comber was black and ominous. The sky was black, and the sea was black, and the frequent, dazzling lightning brought even deeper darkness after every frightening flash.

Calver, his last inspection made, entered the ship and climbed wearily up to Control. His light uniform was sweat-soaked and every muscle was aching and trembling. He reported to Captain Engels, "All secure, sir." He sank gratefully into one of the acceleration chairs.

"Thank you, Mr. Calver." The Old Man tapped the aneroid. "Still falling, still falling," he murmured.

"How are the engineers getting on?" asked Calver.

"They are still working, still working. But there's no hope, now, of our getting away before the blow hits us."

Arlen appeared with a tray upon which there was a plate of sandwiches, a can of cold beer. She put it on one arm of the chair, disposed herself gracefully on the other. She had been working, Calver well knew, as hard as any of the men, but had still found the time to attend to their needs.

"Thanks, Arlen," said Calver. He took a satisfying swallow of the beer, bit deeply into one of the sandwiches.

He ate and drank slowly, carefully, displaying an outward calmness that he did not feel, trying to ignore the growing tumult outside. The rain was heavy now, torrential, cascading down the weather ports, drumming upon the hull like a swarm of micrometeorites. The old ship trembled as the gusts hit her, trembled and groaned. Something crashed into her—the branch of a tree? the tree itself?—and she seemed to sag under the blow, to sag and to recover. Calver looked around at the others. Arlen's face was pale, but calm. Levine's thin features had, somehow, assumed an almost ludicrous expression of polite interest. Fat little Pender was terrified and didn't care who knew it. Old Doc Malone looked like a Buddha with Neanderthal Man somewhere in his ancestry. Captain Engels' eyes were the only part of him that seemed alive, and they were fixed anxiously on the aneroid with its plunging needle.

"I wish that you'd use more mustard when you make sandwiches, Arlen," complained Calver, his voice deliberately casual.

"Mustard with *lamb*?" she demanded scornfully.

"*I* like it," he said.

"*You* would," she told him.

"Will this wind get any worse?" asked Pender anxiously.

"Probably," said Calver.

"Mightn't we be safer outside?"

"We might be—if we were amphibians, like the natives. This island will be under water when the storm's at its height."

"Oh," muttered Pender. "Oh . . ."

The wind was steady now, but stronger than any of the gusts had been. *Lorn Lady* seemed to shift and settle. Calver wished that he could see out of the ports to inspect his stay wires. He got to his feet and, ignoring Pender's protests, switched off the control room lights, switched on the external floods. The ports to leeward were clear enough, and through them he could see the two lee stays, silvery threads against the darkness, hanging in graceful catenaries. It must be, he realized, the weather stays that now had all the weight, that must have stretched. They were still tight, bar taut, he knew, although they could not be seen through the streaming ports to windward. Their thrumming could be felt rather than heard. Walking to inspect the inclinometer, Calver was not surprised to find that the ship was all of three degrees from the vertical.

He tried not to think of what the consequences would be should a stay carry away, should one of the tail fins to leeward crumple under the strain. By the unsteady glare of the lightning he made his way back to his chair, sat down again.

"There's nothing further that we can do," said Arlen.

"Not yet," he said. "But there will be."

"What?" she asked. "When?"

"I don't know. We just have to wait."

"Can we have the lights on again?" asked Pender plaintively.

"Switch them on, then," Calver told him.

It was a little more cheerful with normal lighting in the control room. The wind and the rain, the thunder and the lightning, were still there but, somehow, more distant. There was a sense of security—of false security Calver knew full well. There was the sense of false security that comes from familiar surroundings, no matter what hell is raging outside.

Now and again Calver would get up to walk to the aneroid, to stand with Captain Engels to stare at the instrument. He knew what had to be done when the needle stopped falling, and hoped that there would be enough time for it to be done. He thought how ironical it was that spacemen should be confronted with a situation that must have been all too familiar to the seamen of the long-dead days of sail on Earth's seas, that was still familiar to the seamen of worlds upon which wind-driven ships were still employed. How fantastic it was that *Lorn Lady* might well be wrecked by the same forces as had destroyed many a proud windjammer.

As they waited, the air of the control room became heavy with smoke. The fumes of burning tobacco eased the strain on taut nerves, helped to dull the apprehensions even of Pender. Arlen got up from the arm of Calver's chair and went to make coffee, taking some to the Engineers who, with Brentano, were still working on the pumps. Doc Malone went to his cabin and returned with a bottle of the raw liquor of his own manufacture, insisted on tipping a stiff tot into each coffee cup.

Then—"It's stopped falling!" cried Captain Engels.

"The trough," said Calver. "The eye of the storm. Sir, we must go outside again. There will be a shift of wind at any moment and when it comes, unless we have taken up the slack on the lee stays, we shall be caught aback."

"By all means, Mr. Calver. Do as you see fit." He sighed. "I am afraid that I can be of no help to you."

"Your place is here, sir," said Calver gently.

He led the way to the axial shaft, clattered down the ladder to the airlock. Th tools that he had used before were still there, the spanners and the heavy spikes. He satisfied himself that nothing was missing. With the others standing well back, waiting, he opened the outer airlock door a crack. Save for a distant moaning and the splashing of water, all was quiet. He opened the door to its full extent, saw in the light of the floods that the sea had covered the island. The ramp, of course, had been retracted, but the rungs of the ladder, part of the ship's permanent structure, were still there. He counted the number of rungs visible above the surface, estimated that the water would not be too deep.

He clambered down the ladder, dropped. The water was not cold; it came to his waist. He called to the others. Arlen followed, then Levine, then Doc Malone. Pender stayed in the airlock to pass the tools to them, at last came down himself with obvious reluctance.

They splashed clumsily through the flood to the trees—the trees to which what had been the two lee stays were anchored. It was heavy going; they could not see what was underfoot and floating debris impeded their progress. Once Arlen screamed faintly as she blundered into the battered body of one of the natives.

Calver left Malone, Pender and Levine at the nearer of the two slack stays, carried on with Arlen to the farther one. He and the girl worked well together, she holding the bar that prevented the bottle screw from rotating bodily, he turning with his spike the threaded sleeve. He realized that the other party was having trouble. He could hear Doc Malone's picturesque curses and Pender's petulant whine.

Calver gave the sleeve a last half turn, grasped the tight wire with his free hand to test it. It was taut, but not too taut.

"Come on," he said to Arlen. "We'll give the others a hand. They . . ."

The wind tore the words from his mouth, tossed them into the suddenly howling darkness. He caught Arlen by the ballooning slack of her shirt, felt the fabric rip in his hand. He flung himself after her as she staggered helplessly downwind, caught her but could not halt either her or himself, fell with her. They fell, and threshed and floundered for long seconds under the water. Calver regained his footing at last, struggled to his feet, dragged Arlen with him. He stood there his back to the wind and the almost solid rain, holding her tightly to him, gasping for breath, feeling, against his side, her own tortured gasps. He stood there, and at last was able to look at the tall, shining tower that was the ship. He thought that he saw her shudder, begin to shift.

He turned slowly, supported by Arlen as well as supporting her, fighting to retain his balance, to look at the stays. The one that he had tightened was still taut; the other hung in a bight. Two figures at the bole of the tree—he knew that they would be Malone and Levine—were fighting yet with the refractory bottle screw.

Let the stay hold, he thought intensely. *Let the stay hold.*

Then, before his eyes, the tree to which it was made fast lifted, was pulled up and clear of the water by the whiplash of the wire. It looked, with its sprawling roots, like some huge, octopoidal monster at the end of a giant's fishing line. At the other end of the line was *Lorn Lady,* and she was toppling, as she must topple with that dreadful pressure against her, the weight of the wind suddenly unchecked. Over she went, and over. . .

. . . and stopped.

The second stay, the slack stay, miraculously had held. By the bole of the tree old Doc Malone raised his pudgy arms slowly against the fury of the wind, made the thumbs up sign.

And thumbs up it is, thought Calver. *We've licked the storm.* In his relief he failed to notice the suddenly-rising water level until the wave hit him, knocked him off his feet. The force of the sea was broken by the trees but was still not to be underestimated. Calver struggled vainly, managed only to keep his head above the surface. He saw the sheer, steel cliff against which he was being driven, one of the ship's vanes, and flung out his hands to take the impact. And then a swirling eddy pulled him to one side, but not far enough, and his head struck the edge of the vane a grazing blow.

He remembered little thereafter, only the columns of the trees past which he was swept, the trunks at which he grasped feebly, only the floating debris by which he was jostled. He realized dimly that he had been washed off the island, was being carried out to sea. He was still in the lee of the land and the water was relatively calm, and he knew that unless he made some effort to swim back it would soon be too late. But it was too much trouble. Everything was too much trouble.

Then there was somebody beside him, somebody whose body gleamed whitely in the dark water, almost luminous, suddenly bright in the renewed, intermittent flaring of the lightning. There were the strong hands clasped under his chin and the pressure, the feel of firm breasts against the skin of his back, the strenuously kicking legs that sometimes brushed his own, inertly dangling ones. There was the voice saying, gasping, "Wake up, damn you! Help yourself! Don't give up!"

He tried to answer, spluttered as the brackish water filled his mouth. Abruptly he decided that breath was too precious to waste on speech. He broke free of the other's hands, turned over, began to swim— weakly at first, then more strongly. She kept beside him, matching his pace, murmuring encouragement. But they were too far from the beach and the off- shore set was strong—and he was too weak, too tired.

"Jane," he gasped. "Don't . . . wait . . . Go in . . . Don't . . . worry about . . . me . . ."

"Both of . . . us . . ." she replied, "will make . . . it. Both or . . . neither . . ."

Suddenly realization came, the bitter knowledge that if he ceased to struggle, if he let himself sink into the warm water, she should share this last, ir- redeemable failure. And suddenly he did not want to fail. There was so much that he had done, so much that there was still to do. Automatically his arms and legs moved—and then, consciously, he was making the little extra effort (little, but so much) that enabled him (them?) to move closer, by such pitifully slow degrees, to the beach.

Lightning flared and crackled through the sky but, between the flashes, through the curtain of rain, he could see the floodlit ship, the tower that still stood, raised against the fury of the night. Most of the trees must be down, he thought, for him to be able to see *Lorn Lady* so clearly. Most of the trees must be down, but those that he had selected as anchors for his stays must be, with the exception of the one pulled up by the roots, still standing.

He could see the floodlit ship, still distant, still, in spite of all his efforts, no closer. He called upon the last reserves of his strength, drove aching arms and legs through water that seemed to have the consisten- cy of molasses. Jane was still at his side, still keeping pace—but the sight of her white, strained face in a lightning flash told him that she, too, was tiring.

Then, bobbing just ahead of him, there was a little light and his right hand, in its forward sweep, struck something solid. It was a floating tree branch, and he cursed this obstacle, the necessity for a detour. Then he saw that there was an electric torch lashed to the branch and that from it, to the beach, snaked a long line. Treading water, he helped Jane until she was able to pull herself up onto it, to lie across it. He followed suit, was relieved to find that it supported the weight of both of them. He felt the roughness of bark under his chest, the knotty clump of twigs under his left hand, the wet smoothness of Jane's back under his right arm. He shouted, knowing that his voice could never carry against the wind.

Even so, the floating branch began to move, jerkily at first, then steadily, toward the island. Calver could see lights flashing there, moving figures. They were close now. They were close—and suddenly they were all around him, splashing in the shallow water, shouting. There was Malone and there was Levine, and Bendix, and Renault and Brentano, and they lifted him and Jane from the log to which they were still clinging, their kindly hands loosening the stiff, clutching fingers from their desperate grasp on bark and twigs. They supported Jane and Calver, holding them up against the still considerable weight of the wind, half carried them towards the ship.

Calver knew that thanks were unasked for, would, in any case, be inadequate. But he was curious. "How . . .?" he began, gasping, trying to make himself heard above the storm. "How did you . . .?"

"It was Levine!" shouted Brentano. "It was

Levine! I'd never have dreamed it possible to get a telepathic fix—but he did! Psionic radar, no less!''

Calver wanted them to help Jane into the ship first, but they refused, insisted that he take precedence. A suspicion crept into his mind—a suspicion that was confirmed when he had climbed the long stairway to the control room, when he stood there, looked at the body of Captain Engels sprawled on the deck beneath one of the ports. He hardly listened to Malone's explanation, knew what must have happened, could feel the shock that must have stopped the old man's heart when he saw the first of the stays carry away, when the ship began to tilt.

He looked around him at the others.

"And Pender?" he asked.

"He ran, so he did," said Malone. "At the first sign of trouble he ran . . ."

"And . . .?"

"When we knew that the stay would hold," said Levine, "I . . . searched. Just as I searched for you later. But there was . . . nothing. The wind must have caught him, battered him against a tree, carried him out to sea . . ."

Calver walked to the ports, looked out. The remaining three stays were holding. The wind was moderating. Overhead the clouds were breaking and the lightness of the sky told him that dawn was not far away.

He said—remembering what his first duty as Chief Officer had been—"Mr. Brentano, will you have the Captain's body taken down to the cold chambers? And then you can all of you stand down unless required. I shall stay up here."

"If it's all the same to you, Captain," said Renault, "we'll carry on with our repairs."

"If you so wish," said Calver.

When the others were gone, taking the body of the old man with them, he collapsed tiredly into a chair, the Captain's chair. So he had his command, he thought. So he had his command—but this was never the way that he would have wished to gain it. So he—naked, bruised, battered—had his command, the captaincy over an old, tired, worn-out rust-bucket . . .

He heard Jane coming into the control room. She was dressed, but not in uniform, was wearing a robe that accentuated her femininity. She carried a tray, with coffee, and towels and clothing.

She put the tray and the other things down, knelt beside his chair.

"Derek," she said, "Derek, I'm . . . I'm frightened . . . My jinx . . ."

"What jinx?" he asked. "We saved the ship, didn't we?"

"But this was the second thing," she whispered. "First the trouble on Tharn, now this . . . Disasters always come in threes . . ."

"Calamity Jane," he said softly. "Calamity Jane . . . Please don't talk up any more calamities . . ."

And he closed her mouth in the most effective way of all.

14

THE REPAIRS were completed—there was minor damage to the hull as well as the original malfunction of the pumps—and *Lorn Lady* lifted from Mellise. Calver was Master and Brentano, orginally Electronic Radio Officer and Jack of all trades, was his Mate. Arlen was Second Mate. Levine would have liked to have helped out, but he was one of those unfortunate people to whom machines of any kind are an insoluble mystery, to whom the language of mathematics is utter gibberish.

But Levine—as they all well knew—pulled his weight. It was Levine who came into the control room where Calver, to give Arlen a chance to prepare a meal, was standing part of her watch. (Old Doc Malone was, in the opinion of all hands, the worst cook in the Universe.)

"Captain," he said, "we have company."

"Company?" asked Calver. "*Faraway Queen*'s not due to make the Eastern Circuit for another month."

"It's that T.G. Clipper," said Levine, "the one

that I heard when she was off Elsinore, in the Shakespearian System. *Thermopylae*. I've been yarning with her P.R.O. He wanted the names of the officers here."

"Trans-Galactic Clippers? That's Bendix's old company, isn't it? Anyhow, what the hell is she doing on the Rim?"

"A Galactic cruise, Captain," said Levine, grinning. "See the romantic Rim Worlds, Man's last frontier. Breathe the balmy air of Lorn, redolent of sulphur dioxide and old socks . . ."

"And we're getting paid for being out here!" marveled Calver. "What world is she visiting first?"

"None of the colonized ones. She's showing her passengers that weird planet, Eblis. She's going to hang off it in closed orbit until they've all had a bellyful of spouting volcanoes and lava lakes and the like on the viewscreens, then she's making for Lorn . . ." He stiffened. "Hello! Something's wrong somewhere . . ."

Although no telepath himself, Calver felt a thrill of apprehension. Psionic Radio had always made him feel uneasy. He could imagine the psionic amplifier, the tissue culture from the brain of a living dog, hanging in its nutrient solution and probing the gulfs between the stars with its tendrils of thought, sounding an alarm in the brain of its master at the first hint of some danger imperceptible to the common run of humanity.

Levine's thin face was expressionless, his eyes glazed. He picked up the stylus from its clip on the desk before Calver, began to write in his neat script on the scribbling pad. Calver read the words as they were set down.

S.O.S. S.O.S. S.O.S. Thermopylae, *off Eblis.*
Tube linings burned out. Falling in spiral orbit towards
planet. Cannot use Mannschenn Drive to break free from
orbit, ship losing mass due to leakage from after compart-
ments. Require immediate assistance. S.O.S. S.O.S. S.O.S.

"Can he hear you? asked Calver. He repeated the
words more loudly, "Can he hear you?"

"Of course," muttered Levine.

"Then tell him," Calver said, "that we're on our
way."

He went to the chart tank, studied it, projected a
hypothetical trajectory from the spot of light that was
Lorn Lady's estimated position to the brighter, bigger
spark that was the Eblis sun. He studied the picture
briefly, read distances off the scales. He knew that
Bendix was in the Interstellar Drive Room, went to
the telephone, called him. "Mr. Bendix," he said, "I
shall want you to push the Drive as hard as you can
without throwing us back to last Thursday. One of
your old ships is in trouble off Eblis. Yes,
Thermopylae. Have everything ready. I'll give you the
word as soon as we're about to change trajectory."
He switched to the Reaction Drive Engineer's cabin.
"Mr. Renault, stand by rockets and gyroscopes.
We're going to the assistance of *Thermopylae* off
Eblis." He switched to Public Address. "This is the
Captain speaking. Will all off-duty personnel report
at once to Control?"

Levine was writing on the pad again.

Thermopylae to *Lorn Lady. I hear you,* Lorn Lady.
Hurry, please. Estimated first contact with atmosphere in
thirty-six hours, Terran standard . . .

Arlen and Brentano, followed by old Doc Malone,
hurried into the control room. Calver pointed to the

pad before the silent Levine, then busied himself setting up the tri-di chart on large scale. It showed the ball of light that was the Eblis sun, the far smaller ball that was Eblis itself and, just inside the verge glass, the tiny spark that was *Lorn Lady*. He read off co-ordinates, threw the problem to the computer and tried not to show his impatience while the machine quietly murmured to itself. He looked at the figures on the screen.

"Thirty-five hours . . ." he said. "Thirty-five hours —assuming that our D.R. isn't all to hell. But Bendix should be able to cut that . . ."

"And Renault can give her an extra boost," said Brentano.

"We daren't throw away too much reaction mass," said Calver. "We may need every ounce for maneuvering . . ." He ordered sharply, "Cut Interstellar Drive!"

The familiar whine faltered and died. There was the nausea, the brief loss of temporal orientation, the subtly distorted perspective. And then, outside the ports, the Galactic Lens resolved itself from what had been, as poor Maclean had once put it, a Klein Flask blown by a drunken glassblower. There was the hum of the big, directional gyroscope starting up.

"Mr. Brentano," ordered Calver, "a position, if you please. You've the Eblis Sun, and Kinsolving's Star, and the Pointers . . ." He turned to the others. "Doc, you'd better secure for acceleration. And you, Jane. Mr. Levine, is your amplifier secure?"

"All secure," said Levine, emerging briefly from his trance.

"Then you'd better stay here. Tell *Thermopylae* that we're hurrying."

As he spoke he was bringing the Eblis Sun right ahead, centering the ruddy star in the cartwheel sight that was the forward port of the control room. He gave Renault the Stand By signal, then braked the directional gyroscope to a stop. He glanced behind him, saw that Brentano had taken his observations, was feeding the data into the computer. An accurate position now was not necessary for him to determine the line of *Lorn Lady's* flight, but it would be required to help him to estimate time of arrival off Eblis. But that could wait. At his command the rockets burst into roaring life, building up acceleration. Calver watched his meters and gauges carefully. Too high an initial speed would be as wasteful of time as too low a one. Deceleration had still to be carried out. Too, there would be the question of reserves of reaction mass.

He said, as much to himself as anybody, his fingers tense on the controls set in the arm of the chair, "That will do. Cut Reaction Drive."

He cut the Drive.

He reached for the telephone. "Mr. Bendix, resume Interstellar Drive." He added, "It's up to you, Mr. Bendix."

It was a short voyage and, paradoxically, a long one. Bendix drove his machine close to the critical limit, too close, so close that *Lorn Lady* became almost a timeship rather than a spaceship. Time Travel is impossible—in theory. Time Travel is impossible—but everybody aboard the old ship knew that it was all too possible.

Calver went once to the Mannschenn Drive Room. He stood in the doorway, almost choking on the fumes of hot lubricating oil, looking into the compartment, watching the engineer who, his face worried and intent, was making minor adjustments to the controls. He felt rather than heard the thin, high whine of the precessing gyroscopes, hardly dared look at the tumbling, precessing wheels, the gleaming wheels that whirled in the glittering haze, that seemed always to be on the point of falling down the dark infinities, always on the point of vanishing and yet, somehow, were always there, always there to pull eye and mind after them down the dimensions, back and back to the primal Chaos.

He wrenched his regard away from the main body of the machine, realized suddenly that something was missing. It was the governor, that comfortingly stable rotor at which he always looked after too long a time spent staring at the precessing gyroscopes. The governor was gone, removed by Bendix, who was controlling the Drive unit by hand.

Calver shrugged. Bendix knew what he was doing. He hoped.

The engineer straightened, looked around. "Captain . . ." he said vaguely. Then, more alertly, "How're we doing?"

"Fine," said Calver.

"Any more word from *Thermopylae?*"

"Yes. They're hanging on. They're all ready to abandon ship, but hope that they won't have to."

"And I . . ."

"Watch your controls!" shouted Calver.

Bendix stooped again. Calver saw his face pale beneath the grime, saw the long hands flash to the verniers. The high, thin keening deepened in tone ever so slightly, steadied. Bendix mumbled, not looking up, "That was close . . ."

"What was?"

"We were almost caught in a Time Cycle . . ."

"But all the text books," said Calver, "say that that's impossible."

"You know it's not," said Bendix. "I know it's not . . ."

"Better put that governor back," said Calver.

"It will mean stopping the Drive," Bendix told him.

"Then . . ." Calver paused. "Mr. Bendix, will you be able to last out? Remember that we shan't be able to help *Thermopylae's* people if we're thrown back into the remote Past."

"I'll last out," said Bendix stubbornly. "I'll last out. See that I get plenty of coffee and cigarettes, and I'll manage . . ."

Calver went back to Control. He was learning the hardest lesson that a shipmaster ever has to learn—the lesson that teaches him not to interfere. He had told Bendix that he wanted maximum objective speed made to Eblis—and Bendix was obeying his orders. So doing, he was hazarding the ship—but this would not be the first time in her long career that she had been hazarded. Calver was conscious that her safety hung upon the ability of one man to keep awake, to stay alert. But how many times had she been at the mercy of a single fuse, a single transistor? What was the difference, if any?

He went back to Control, told Jane to see to it that Bendix had all that he required to keep him functioning efficiently. He stood over the chart tank, looking into the sphere of blackness in which swam the little lights that were suns and worlds and ships, the glowing filament that was *Lorn Lady's* trajectory. He saw that Brentano, working from data supplied by the crippled *Thermopylae*, had set up the liner's orbit around Eblis. The effect was like that of the rings of Saturn—but this ring was dreadfully lopsided.

He strapped himself in his chair, tried to ignore the ever-recurrent feeling of *deja vu*, the loss of temporal orientation, tried to push all thoughts of the crazy, fantastic machine, with its almost as crazy keeper, out of his mind. He tried to decide what gear he would require, what his procedure would be. It would have to be a tow. *Lorn Lady* was too small, too ill-found, to accommodate all the people, crew and passengers, from the big ship. It would have to be a tow ... And then he found himself remembering those memories that were not his, the memories that he had shared when *Lorn Lady*, briefly, had merged with the Rim Ghost.

A tow, he thought.

A tow, all the way from Eblis to Lorn. Propellant will be no problem. Thermopylae *won't be able to use any, so I'll be able to take hers. There'll be the problem, of course, of synchronizing Manneschenn Drive Units—but if Bendix can do what he's doing now, he shouldn't find that beyond him ...*

A tow, and the standard Lloyd's Agreement ...

A shipmaster is businessman as well as spaceman and, whilst ever ready to save life and property, keeps always in mind the interests of his Owners—and of himself.

"A penny for them," said Jane brightly, bringing in coffee.

He said, "They're worth rather more than a penny. They're worth a few million dollars."

Below the two ships hung the burning world of

Eblis, a glowing, crimson affront to the dark. *Lorn Lady* had made the run in less than thirty-three hours, Terran Standard, but there was little enough time to spare. Already *Thermopylae* had grazed the outermost, most tenuous layers of the Eblis atmosphere, already the elements of her elliptical orbit were such as to make it obvious, without calculation, that the final plunge could not long be delayed.

Calver, on his arrival off the baleful planet, had been pleasantly surprised to find much in readiness. Before *Lorn Lady* had flickered into sight in normal Space, *Thermopylae*'s tow lines had been broken out and shackled to the lugs just abaft her needle prow. Before *Lorn Lady* had ceased to decelerate, while she had yet to match orbits, spacesuited crewmen were leaping the gulf between the ships, trailing the light lines that would be used to pull the heavy wires across.

Orbits matched, Calver put on his spacesuit and went outside. He found *Thermopylae*'s people already busy about his stern vanes, already heaving in the first of the heavy wires. He found the liner's Chief Officer, recognizing him by the three gold bars inset into the plastic of his helmet, touched helmets with him, talked briefly and to the point. He realized that the other man knew his job; if he had not, he would not have been second-in-command of a great liner. He realized that the other man knew his job—and knew that the other man was far from realizing the fragility of *Lorn Lady*. He stopped the spaceman who was trying to hammer the pin of a shackle through the towing lug—it was too neat a fit—made the strangers wait until he had brought out shackles from his own stores.

This took time, just as it took time for Calver, now back in his control room, to jockey his vessel into the best position, to be sure that none of the lines would be cut by his back-blast and then—carefully, carefully—to take the weight. Velocity, mass, thrust, inertia —all had to be considered, all had to be juggled.

Calver juggled them, coming ahead slowly, slowly, his attention fixed on the periscope rigged by Brentano, on the trailing lines, on the blowtorch of the exhaust, all the brighter for the strontium salts added to the propellant. He juggled them, taking the weight gently until all four lines were taut, building up acceleration slowly until the main venturi was delivering its maximum thrust. *Lorn Lady* was doing her best —and the radar readings, checked and rechecked by Brentano, made it dreadfully obvious that her best was not good enough.

It was Arlen who looked at the atmospheric pressure gauge, who saw that the needle was falling rapidly. She signalled to Brentano, who left the radar to look at the dial.

The little man swore, then whispered fiercely, "She's rotten. She's coming apart at the seams, leaking like a colander . . ."

"Spacesuits?" she asked.

"Of course. I'll tell Doc and the engineers. You look after the Old Man."

Arlen nudged Levine, who was sitting on the other side of her. She snapped, "Get into your suit," and saw him open his eyes wide in comprehension, go to the rack on which the suits were kept. She turned to watch Calver, hesitating to disturb him in his tricky work, waited until she saw the tense lines of his jaw momentarily relax. "Derek! We're losing air, fast.

You'll have to get back into your spacesuit!"

He did not answer but glanced hastily at the pressure gauge, realized the seriousness of the situation. He pondered briefly the advisability of turning the controls over to Brentano for a minute or so, then rejected the idea. Brentano was a good officer, an outstanding officer, but he had no experience of ship handling.

"Derek!" Arlen's voice was sharp. "Your suit!"

"It will have to wait."

He thought, *That pound or so of extra thrust . . . Renault's giving her all he's got . . . But . . .*

"Your suit!"

Reluctantly he looked away from the controls, saw that the others, with the exception of Arlen, were already wearing the bulky, pressurized garments, the transparent helmets. He glared at the woman.

"Put yours on!" he snapped. "That's an order!"

Thrust . . . he thought. *Thrust . . .*

And for lack of thrust the needle peaks of the hell world beneath them were reaching up through the crimson, glowing clouds, reaching up to rip the belly of the huge Trans-Galactic Clipper with her fifteen hundred passengers and three hundred of a crew, to rip her belly and to spill her screaming people into the lava lakes below.

He should have used his boats, thought Calver. Thermopylae's *skipper should have used his boats and put his passengers into the relative safety of a closed orbit around the planet while there was yet time . . . He would have used his boats,* thought Calver bitterly, *either to attempt a tow, or for lifesaving, if I hadn't come bumbling along in this decrepit old barge with my futile promises of assistance . . .*

He chanced another sidewise glance, saw that

Brentano and Levine were forcing Arlen into her suit. That, he told himself, was one worry the less.

Thrust . . . he thought. *Thrust* . . . *The auxiliary jets? But the tow wires? How long will they last in the blast of the auxiliaries?*

The speaker of the short range receiver crackled and an emotionless voice, the voice of the liner's Master, said, *"Thermopylae to Lorn Lady.* Thank you, *Lorn Lady.* It was a good try, but it wasn't quite good enough. Stand by to cast off. I intend to abandon ship while there is time."

"Wait!" shouted Calver. "Wait!" He was shocked at the thin quality of his voice in the thinning air. "Wait . . ." he whispered.

His hand dropped to the firing keys of the auxiliary jets. He felt the sudden surge of additional power that pressed him down into the padding of his chair. He saw, on the periscope screen, the sudden blossoming of fire around *Lorn Lady*'s stern but forward of the main venturi, the vanes, the towing lugs.

Turning, he saw Brentano look up and away from the radar, his dark face behind the transparency one big grin.

Then he felt, rather than heard, the dreadful splintering and grinding, the rending, of old, crystallized metal. On the screen he saw the coruscation of blinding sparks from the severed parts of one of the wires, saw the whole stern of the ship tilting at an impossible angle relative to the rest of her. As he looked, hardly comprehending, the air was gone from the control room in one explosive gasp and he was choking on nothingness, suffocating. Somebody was bending over him, trying to do something to him. *Let me alone!* he thought. He realized that it was Jane,

Calamity Jane. With a flash of empathy he read her thoughts. *It's not your fault,* he was trying to say. *Jane, it's not your fault.* But his lungs were empty and no sound came.

She got the helmet over his head and opened the valve, pulled up his jacket to make a rough, temporary seal around the neck of the transparent bowl. Calver heard the sharp hissing of the air, had barely enough sense to take a deep breath, and another. He was dimly aware that the others were pulling him out of his seat, forcing his clumsy limbs into the arms and legs of the suit, tugging and sealing it around him.

For what seemed a long time, to be able to breathe was all he asked. Then, partly recovered, he put his helmet against Brentano's, asked, "What happened?"

"She broke in two, Captain. After that first wire parted. The uneven, unbalanced strain . . . She broke in two. Everybody's safe, but she's a total loss."

"And *Thermopylae?*"

"In a closed orbit. A stable orbit."

Calver should have felt triumphant, but he did not. He had lost his ship.

15

THROUGH THE control room ports they could see the
crimson globe of Eblis and, hanging to one side of it,
the incredibly long, slim shape of the Trans-Galactic
Clipper. They could see, too, the after section of *Lorn
Lady* and the busy, spacesuited figures working
around the rent and battered stern. Calver watched
with a numb feeling. The responsibilities of a shipmaster do not cease with the loss of his ship, but after
all that can be done has been done, when the safety
of personnel and of valuable cargo has been assured,
there is an end to responsibility.

Little now remained to be done.

The old ship was dead, but some of her would live
on for a while. Her cannibalized tube linings would
provide *Thermopylae* with the jury rig that would
enable her to reach Port Forlorn.

Calver watched the bright, electric sparks of the
cutting torches, the brief stars against the blackness
that had never known a star. Somehow, this final dis-

memberment of *Lorn Lady* hurt him more than the actual wreck had done.

Jane Arlen put her gloved hands on his space-suited shoulders, touched her helmet to his. "Derek," she said, her voice strange, remote. "Derek, I think that this had better be goodbye. I always bring bad luck with me, wherever I go. Perhaps you'll believe me now."

He shook himself out of his apathetic mood. He said, a little too loudly, "Rubbish! *Lorn Lady* was due for the breakers years ago. And by the time that the lawyers have finished arguing, Rim Runners will be getting a fine new ship out of the deal and—who knows?—I may be Master of her . . ."

She said, ignoring his sudden optimism, "I hate to leave her. The poor old *Forlorn Lady* . . ."

"We must go," he said gently. "They are waiting for us aboard *Thermopylae*."

Together they left the old, broken ship. Together, using their suit reaction units, they jetted across the emptiness to the huge liner, to the circle of light that was the airlock door. In the little compartment, when the outer door had closed, they divested themselves of their suits, felt pride in rather than embarrassment for the shabby uniforms so revealed. They stepped through the inner door, the magnetic soles of their shoes silent on the carpeted deck. Steel lay beneath it —but, as they had known when they had served in vessels of this class, passengers must be shielded from the harsh realities of Space.

The junior officer waiting to receive them saluted smartly.

"Glad to have you aboard, Captain Calver," he said. "May I take you to Captain Hendriks?"

"Thank you," said Calver.

They followed their guide along alleyways, through public rooms. The passengers—the plump, sleek men, the expensive women—stared at the man who had lost his ship to save their lives. More than once there were the beginnings of a demonstration, spontaneous outbursts of clapping and cheering. Calver was thankful when they entered the privacy of the axial shaft. Hand over hand, he and Arlen pulled themselves swiftly along the guide rail behind *Thermopylae*'s officer.

The Captain of the liner—an old man, a man who had aged many years in the last few hours—was seated in his day room, behind his big, polished desk. He unsnapped the buckle of his seat belt as they entered his cabin, advanced to meet them.

He said simply, "Captain Calver, my thanks are inadequate."

"I did what I could," said Calver.

"I shall do what I can," said Hendriks. "Sometimes, too often, in wrangles over salvage, the owners of the ships involved are remembered and their crews, who have done the work, taken the risks, are forgotten. But I am not without influence . . ."

"That aspect of the matter had never occurred to me," said Calver.

"Have you been Master long?" asked Hendriks.

"No. Only a dog watch."

"There's more to the game than navigation, than ship handling," said the big ship man.

"I guess so."

Hendriks busied himself at his liquor cabinet, brought out drinking bulbs. He apologized. "The best I have isn't good enough . . . This Samian wine?

The Altairian Angels' Tears?"

"Anything will do," said Calver.

"Perhaps the Angels' Tears," said Arlen.

"As you wish." Hendriks looked at her, at Calver. He said, "You must hate it out here. But you'll be able to return now, perhaps, to the warmth and the light of the Center . . . ."

"So we shall," said Calver, with a mild amazement. "So we shall." His hand sought and found Jane Arlen's, closed upon it, felt the answering warmth and pressure.

"But I belong on the Rim," he said. "We belong on the Rim."

THE SHIP FROM OUTSIDE

A. BERTRAM CHANDLER

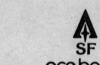

SF
ace books
A Division of Charter Communications Inc.
A GROSSET & DUNLAP COMPANY
51 Madison Avenue
New York, New York 10010

THE SHIP FROM OUTSIDE

Copyright © 1963 by Ace Books, Inc.

THE SHIP FROM OUTSIDE

1

I<small>T WAS ON</small> Stree that Calver, Master of the star-tramp *Rimfire,* received the news. He was in his day cabin at the time and he and Jane Calver, who was both his wife and his Catering Officer, were trying to entertain the large, not unhandsome lizard who acted as Rim Runners' local agent. It had been heavy going; the saurians of Stree are avid for new knowledge and delight in long-winded and woolly philosophical discussions. Both Jane and Calver tried hard not to show their relief when there was a sharp rapping at the cabin door.

"Excuse me, Treeth," Calver said.

"Most certainly, Captain," replied the agent. "Doubtless one of your officers bears tidings of great import."

"I doubt it," said Jane Calver, with a slight shrug of her shapely shoulders. "It'll be no more than some minor problem of stowage, or something."

"Or something," agreed her husband. He raised his voice. "Come in."

The agent, who had been sitting on the deck, rose gracefully to his feet, his long tail skimming the afternoon tea crockery on the low coffee table with a scant millimeter of clearance. Jane, when the expected crash failed to eventuate, heaved an audible sigh of relief. Treeth looked at Calver and grinned, showing all his needle teeth. Calver said nothing but wished that a childish sense of humor did not, as it so often and too often does, go hand in hand with super intelligence.

Levine, the little Psionic Radio Officer, bounced into the cabin. For a moment Calver thought that the man had been drinking, then rejected the idea; Levine was well known for his abstemious ways. But there are other euphoriacs than alcohol.

"Captain," he babbled, "I've picked up a message. An important one. Really important. Donaldson, the P.R.O. at Port Farewell, must have hooked up every telepath and every dog's brain amplifier on the whole damn planet to punch it through at this range."

"And what is this news?" asked Calver.

"The *Thermopylae* salvage case," cried Levine. "It's been settled at last."

"So Rim Runners get their new ship," said Calver. "So what?"

"To hell with Rim Runners!" exploded Levine. *We* get *our* whack—all of us who were in the poor old *Lorn Lady* at the time."

Treeth sat down again. He showed that he was interested by forgetting to repeat his infantile joke with his tail and the tea things. He said, in the well-modulated voice that held only the suggestion of a croak, the merest hint of a hiss, "I trust that you will forgive my curiosity, Captain. But we, as you know, were utterly ignorant of commercial matters until your Commodore Grimes made his first landing on our planet. What *is* salvage?"

"Putting it briefly," Calver told him, "roughly and briefly, it's this. If you come across another ship in distress you do all that you can to save life and property. The lifesaving is, after all, it's own reward. It's when property—the other vessel, or her cargo, or both—is saved that the legal complications creep in. There are so many interested parties—the owners of the ships involved, the owners of the cargo and, last but not least, Lloyds of London, who carry the insurance. . . ."

"Last but not least," corrected Jane, "the crew of the ship that carries out the act of salvage, the people who've done all the work."

"Anyhow," went on Calver, "the whole mess is dumped on the lap of an Admiralty court. The court decides who gets paid how much for doing what."

"And this *Thermopylae?*" asked Treeth. "We heard something about her from Captain Vickery, of the *Sundowner*. It happened shortly after *Lorn Lady*'s last visit here, if I remember rightly. I shall be obliged if you will apprise me of the relevant facts."

"All right," said Calver. "*Thermopylae* was—and, so far as I know, still is—one of the Trans-Galactic Clippers, a large passenger liner. She was making a cruising voyage out along the Rim. She got into trouble off Eblis. . . ."

"A most unpleasant world," said Treeth. "I have seen pictures of it."

"As you say, a most unpleasant world. Anyhow, *Thermopylae* was putting herself into orbit around

Eblis so that her passengers could admire the scenery and—things always seem to happen at the worst possible times—she blew her tube linings. As a result of this she was doomed to make a series of grazing ellipses until such time as she crashed to the surface. We, in *Lorn Lady,* picked up her distress calls and just about busted a gut getting there in time. We tried to tow her into a stable orbit. We succeeded—but wrecked our own ship in the process. Then *Thermopylae* used our tube linings to make temporary repairs to her own reaction drive units. As you can see, it was the sort of case that brings joy to the hearts of the lawyers and large wads of folding money into their pockets; in addition to the straightforward salvage there was the sacrifice of one ship to save the other."

"And you have, at last, been rewarded by the owners of *Thermopylae?*" asked Treeth.

"So it would appear," answered Calver.

"And how!" cried Levine, who had been waiting for a chance to get a word in. "*And* by Lloyds! A cool three quarters of a million to *Lorn Lady's* crew! I haven't got the individual figures yet, but . . ."

"This," said Jane, "calls for a celebration. Luckily we're well stocked with liquor. . . ."

The agent got to his feet again. "And now I must depart," he said gently. "For me, a stranger, an outsider, to be present at your thanksgiving would not be fitting. But there is one thing about you beings that never ceases to mystify me—the need that you feel to deaden the effects of the exhilaration that comes with good news by the ingestion of alcohol. . . ." He paused. "Good afternoon to you, Captain and Captain's lady, and to you, Mr. Levine.

I am sufficiently familiar with your vessel to be able to find my own way ashore.

"Good afternoon—and my sincere congratulations."

There was Calver, tall and gangling, and there was Jane Calver who, as "Calamity Jane" Arlen, had been Catering Officer of the lost *Lorn Lady*. Calver sat at the head of the table in *Rimfire*'s saloon and Jane, tall and slim, and with the silver streak in her glossy dark hair gleaming like a slender coronet, sat at his right hand. Very much Captain and Captain's lady they had been when the other officers had been with them, the officers who had not served in *Lorn Lady*. But now these others had retired to their several cabins and the party was for *Lorn Lady*'s people only.

There was the painfully thin Bendix, with the few remaining strands of black hair brushed carefully over his shining scalp, who had been Interstellar Drive Engineer in T.G. Clippers before coming out to the Rim for reasons known only to himself. There was Renault, the Rocket King, swarthy, always in need of depilation, Reaction Drive Engineer—he, like Jane and Calver, was out of the Interstellar Transport Commission's ships. There was little Brentano, in charge of Electronic Radio Communications, highly competent and capable of standing a watch in the control room or in either of the two engine rooms should the need arise. There was Levine, another small man and also competent—extremely so—but only in his own field. There was old Doc Malone, looking like a jovial monk who had, somehow, put on a uniform in mistake for his habit.

The decanter was passed around the table.

"A toast," said Bendix harshly. "A toast. We'll drink to you, Calver. It's thanks to you that this good fortune has come our way."

"No," demurred the Captain. "No. We'll drink to us, to all of us. We were all in it together, and we all of us did our best." He raised his glass. "To us," he repeated quietly.

"And to hell with the Rim!" Brentano almost shouted. "To hell with Lorn and Faraway, Ultimo and Thule and the whole damned Eastern Circuit!"

"And are you going home, Brentano?" asked Doc Malone. "And are you going home? To the warm Cluster Worlds, to the swarming suns and their attendant planets? Won't you feel confined, shut in? Won't you miss the empty sky, the call of it, the mystery of it? Won't you miss this freemasonry of ours?"

"And what about you, Doc?" countered Brentano. "Aren't you going home?"

The old man was silent for what could have been only seconds, but it seemed longer. He said at last, very softly, ". . . and home there's no returning."

"I'm afraid he's right," murmured Bendix, breaking the sudden silence.

"He is right," Renault said.

And Calver remembered how he and Jane had stood in the Captain's cabin aboard *Thermopylae,* and how her hand had found his, and how he had said, "But we belong on the Rim."

He said it again.

"So we belong on the Rim," said Jane briskly. "We seem to be in complete agreement on that point, with the exception of friend Brentano. . . ."

"Why make an exception of me?" demanded the Radio Officer plaintively. "I'm as much a Rim Runner as any of you."

"But you said—." began Jane.

"What I say isn't always what I think, or feel." His face clouded. "Old Doc put it in a nutshell. *And home there's no returning*—not unless we want to face what we ran away from, not unless we want to reopen old wounds. All the same, there must be more in life than running the Eastern Circuit."

"What if we ran it on our own behalf?" asked Calver.

"You mean . . .?" queried Renault.

"What I said. With what we've got we shall be able to buy an obsolescent *Epsilon* Class tramp and have enough left over for the refit. We know the trade, and there's quite a deal of goodwill on the Eastern Circuit planets that's ours rather than the Company's."

"The Sundown Line didn't last long," quibbled Levine.

"Perhaps not," said Bendix, "but they didn't lose any money when Rim Runners bought them out."

"It was never in my thoughts," said old Doc Malone, "that I should be a shipowner in the evening of my days."

"You aren't one yet," remarked Brentano.

"Perhaps not. But the idea is not without its charm. Now, just supposing that we do buy ourselves a ship, what do we call ourselves?"

"The Outsiders," said Calver.

2

CALVER WAS relieved that it was not necessary to make a voyage all the way to Terra to pick up a suitable ship. The return to Terra would have brought back too many memories—for Jane as well as for himself. When he had come out to the Rim he had said goodbye to Earth, and he liked his farewells to be permanent.

It was Levine who, spending his watches gossiping with his opposite numbers in ships within telepathic range, learned that the Commission's *Epsilon Aurigae* had been delivered to Nova Caledon for sale to a small local company, and that the sale had broken down. It was Levine who succeeded in getting in touch with the P.R.O. at Port Caledon and persuading him to pass word to the Commission's agent there that buyers would shortly be on the way.

The stickiest part of it all, of course, was the mass resignation of all *Rimfire*'s senior officers when she set down at Port Faraway. Commodore Grimes—back in harness as Astronautical Superintendent after his exploratory jaunts—stormed and blustered, threatened to sue Calver and the others for breach of contract. Then, when he saw that it was hopeless, he softened.

"You're all good men," he said. "Yes—and one good woman. I don't like to see you go. But, with all that money coming to you, you'd be fools to stay on the Rim."

"But we are staying on the Rim, sir," said Calver quietly.

"What? If you intend to live on the interest of your salvage money, Captain, there are far better places to do it."

"Commodore," said Calver, "you're an astronaut, not a businessman. I'm talking to you now as one spaceman to another, and I'll be grateful if you respect the confidence. We intend to set up shop as shipowners. You've often said yourself that there's a grave shortage of tonnage on the Eastern Circuit."

Grimes laughed. "You know, Calver, if I were in your shoes I'd probably be doing the same myself. But I warn you, there won't always be a shortage of ships, Rim Runner ships, out here."

"But there is now," said Calver.

"There is now. We may be willing to charter you. But when there's no longer a shortage. . . ."

"You'll run us out of space," finished Calver.

"Too right," promised Grims. "We will. . . Meanwhile, Calver, the best of luck. Let me know when you're due back out here and I'll see what I can do for you—provided that it doesn't conflict with Rim Runners' interests, of course."

"Thank you, sir," said Calver, shaking hands.

* * *

So they booked passage for Nova Caledon, all of them, making the lengthy, roundabout voyage that was inevitable in this poorly serviced sector of the Galaxy. From Faraway to Elsinore they traveled in the Shakespearean Lines' *Miranda,* and from Elsinore to van Diemen's Planet in the Commission's *Delta Sagittarius.* On van Diemen's Planet they were lucky enough to find that the Waverley Royal Mail's *Countess of Arran* had been delayed by engineroom repairs, otherwise they would have been obliged to wait a month on that world for the next connection.

At last they dropped down through the inevitable misty drizzle to Port Caledon. Calver, as a shipmaster, could have enjoyed the freedom of the *Countess*'s control room, but he preferred to stay in the observation lounge with his own officers and, of course, with Jane.

There was, they saw, only one other ship in the port—obviously an *Epsilon* Class vessel.

"Ours," Jane murmured.

"Ours," repeated Bendix.

"She looks a mess," said Brentano glumly.

"No more a mess than the poor old *Lorn Lady* was," said Bendix.

"She's a ship," said Calver. "She'll do. She'll have to do."

"She's *our* ship," stated Jane firmly. "Of course she'll do."

Conversation lapsed as they settled down into the acceleration chairs, adjusting their seat belts. Calver felt the apprehension that he always felt when he was traveling as passenger, knew that the others were feeling it too. It was not that he was a better ship handler than *Countess of Arran*'s Captain, it was just that unless he knew what was happening he was acutely unhappy.

There was the usual slight jar and quiver, the subdued creaking and whispering of the shock absorbing springs and cylinders. There was the usual spate of instruction and information from the bulkhead speakers. And, shortly thereafter, there were the dragging customs and immigration formalities, the filling in of forms and the answering of questions. And then, when this was finished, there was the problem of the disposal of their not inconsiderable baggage. The Master of the *Countess* was very helpful and introduced Calver to the Deputy Port Captain who, in his turn, arranged temporary stowage in the spaceport's gear store and also put through a call to the Commission's agent.

When the agent arrived, Calver and his people were already aboard the ship and had commenced their inspection of her instruments and machinery. And she was, Calver had decided, a good ship. She was overage, and obsolescent, but the Commission looks after its vessels well. After the weeks of neglect at Port Caledon there was much to be done before she would be habitable, but there was no doubt as to her spaceworthiness.

Finally Calver stood with the agent and Jane in the control room.

"You're getting a good ship here, Captain," said the agent. "It was lucky for you that Caledonian Spaceships folded before they ever got off the ground."

"I know," said Calver.

"There's one thing that I don't like about her," said Jane.

"And what is that, Mrs. Calver?"

"Her name. As you know, most ships have fancy names and their crews are able to twist them round into something amusing and affectionate. But *Epsilon Aurigae* . . ."

"Don't listen to her," said Calver. "In any case, we shall be changing the name."

"Of course," agreed the agent. "And what are you calling her?"

"*The Outsider*," said Jane.

"And how in the galaxy can you twist *that* into something affectionate and amusing?" asked the puzzled agent.

So *The Outsider* she was:

When the new, shining, golden letters of her new name had been welded to the sharp prow—a romanticizing of the drab legalities involved in changing name and port of registry—Jane went up in the cage to the top of the scaffolding and there, with the others watching from below—smashed a bottle of champagne over the gleaming characters. And then, with this last ritual performed, *The Outsider* was ready for space. She was fueled and provisioned. Hydroponic tanks and yeast and tissue culture vats were functioning perfectly. She had, even, already begun to earn her keep. Her cargo compartments were tightly stowed with casks of whisky and bales of tweed for the Rim Worlds.

Manning the ship had been the biggest problem.

There is no shortage of spacemen at the Centre; neither, oddly enough, is the shortage really acute out on the Rim. It is on halfway worlds such as Nova Caledon that it is hard to find qualified personnel. In the end, however, Calver was able to engage a Chief

Officer of sorts, a drunken derelict who had missed his ship on Nova Caledon. He found a Second Officer —a Nova Caledonian who, tired of space, had come ashore to raise sheep and who now, tired of sheep, was willing to make the voyage out to the Rim provided that repatriation was guaranteed. Then there were two junior professors—one of physics and the other of mathematics—from the University of Nova Caledon who wanted to see something of the Galaxy and who were willing to sign on as junior engineers. There were no pursers available—but Jane and the two communications officers would be able to cope with that side of things quite easily.

After the brief christening ceremony Jane returned to ground level and the scaffolding was wheeled away. Slowly, with dignity, a parade in miniature, *The Outsider*'s people marched up the ramp to the airlock, Calver in the lead. Once inside the ship, they dispersed to their stations. Spaceport Control gave the final clearance, the conventional good wishes. Renault's rockets coughed and sighed gently, then gave tongue to the familiar screaming roar. *The Outsider* lifted, slowly at first, delicately balanced atop the lengthening column of her incandescent exhaust. Faster and faster she climbed through the misty skies of Nova Caledon until the pearly overcast was beneath her and ahead of her was the star-spangled blackness of space.

Once she was well clear of the atmosphere Calver put her through her paces. She was a good ship and responded sweetly to her controls. She was a good ship and, with one exception, she had a good crew to serve her. The two scientists made up in intelligence and enthusiasm for what they lacked in practical en-

gineering experience. The ex-sheepman demon-
strated that he had forgotten very little about ships in
his years ashore. Of the capabilities of the old crew of
Lorn Lady there was, of course, no doubt. The Mate
was the weak link in the chain; his reactions were
painfully slow and he seemed to have no interest
whatever in his duties. Calver decided to have Brentano rig up duplicate, tell-tale instruments in the
Master's cabin at the first opportunity. There is little
risk of mishap to a well-found, well-organized ship in
deep space—but on the rare occasions that mishaps
do occur they are liable to be disastrous unless the
officer of the watch is alert. Calver also made up his
mind to instruct Jane to keep Maudsley's liquor ra-
tion to the bare minimum and to impress upon old
Doc Malone not to give the Mate any of his home-
made Irish whisky. Furthermore, he would read the
Riot Act to the Mate on the first suitable occasion.

The first thing to be done, however, was to set
course for the Rim. Her rocket drive silent, *The Outsider* rotated around her humming gyroscopes to the
correct heading, checked and steadied. For the last
time the rockets flared and she pushed off into the
black infinity, the pale-gleaming sphere that was
Nova Caledon dwindling astern of her. There was
free fall again as the Reaction Drive was cut, there
was the familiar—yet never familiar—gut-and-mind-
wrenching twist, the uncanny feeling of *deja vu* as the
Mannschenn Drive built up its temporal precession
fields.

And then, outside the control room ports, the
hard, brilliant stars flickered and faded, and were replaced by the hypnotically coiling whorls of lumi-
nosity, the shifting colors known only to those who

have made the Long Drop, who have ridden to the stars on a crazy contraption of precessing gyroscopes through the warped fabric of the continuum.

3

TIME—objective and subjective—passed.

It passed fast and not unpleasantly for most of *The Outsider*'s people. There was much to do, many things that were not quite right and that could be, and were tinkered with until they were brought to the state of perfection that gladdens the heart of an efficient officer—especially an efficient officer who is also an owner. Cappell, the Second Mate, and Lloyd and Ritter, the two junior engineers, had no shares in the ship but were infected, nonetheless, by the general enthusiasm. Maudsley was the odd man out, the malcontent. He refused to mix with the others, bolting his meals in silence and then retiring immediately to his own cabin.

Calver discussed him with Jane. He said. "I'm

sorry that we had to ship that unsociable bastard. Unluckily, Cappell has only a Second Pilot's ticket, and Maudsley's a Master Astronaut. Even so. . . ."

"We were stuck on Nova Caledon until we could find two certificated officers," said Jane. "We had to take what we could get. In any case, Maudsley's improving."

"Is he?" asked Calver. "Is he? I can't say that I've noticed it. He's as much a mournful bloodhound walking on two legs as he was when we signed him on. More so, in fact. Then he was able to maintain the normal alcoholic blood content, and it did give him a little sparkle."

"But he *is* improving," insisted Jane. "He's looking healthier. He's putting on weight."

"All right, all right. We know that you're a good cook. It's his manner that I don't like."

"And I didn't like yours when I first met *you*. Remember? There you were, an ex-Chief Officer out of the Commission's big ships, joining a scruffy little Rim Runners' tramp as Second Mate and hating every moment of it. After all, Derek, Maudsley has come down in the world too. He *has* sailed as Master. . . ."

"And he lost his ship, and was very lucky not to lose his Certificate."

"You lost your ship."

"In rather different circumstances, my dear. And nobody—neither Rim Runners nor ourselves—lost out on the deal."

"What about Lloyds' and Trans-Galactic Clippers?" quibbled Jane.

"They can afford it," Calver told her. He carefully filled and lit his pipe. "Anyhow, we shall be getting rid of our Mr. Maudsley as soon as we make Port Faraway."

"Even though you are Master and part owner," she flared, "there's no need to be so hard. With the exception of Cappell and Lloyd and Ritter—and, I suppose, Levine—we're all of us outsiders here, throw-outs from the Centre and the big ships, outsiders on the Rim. Maudsley's like us—or, if you prefer it, like what we used to be. He's had his troubles, and he's running away from them, and he's just about hit rock bottom. This is his chance of rehabilitation. Would you deny it to him?"

"This," said Calver evenly, "happens to be a shipping company—even though it is only a one ship company—not a charitable organization. When and if Mr. Maudsley stops behaving like a first trip cadet with a bad fit of the sulks and starts behaving like a Chief Officer, I'll consider keeping him on. Until then. . ."

"I still think that you're far too harsh," she told him.

"And I still think," he said, "that I have the best interests of the ship and her owners at heart."

That was all that was said then—but more, much more, was said later. That was when Maudsley—who possessed other attributes of the bloodhound beside the appearance—discovered old Doc Malone's secret cache of whisky and drank himself into insensibility. Calver's first reaction was annoyance, his second was disgust. He did not start to get worried until Malone came to see him in the control room where, because of the incapacitation of the Chief Officer, Calver was keeping a watch.

"Captain," said Malone, "we've a very sick man on our hands."

"Doctor," said Calver coldly, "we have a drunken, irresponsible wastrel on our hands and I, personally, shall see to it that he is first out of the airlock when we reach port."

"He'll be first out of the airlock all right," said Malone, "but it'll be long before we reach port."

"What do you mean?"

"I mean that he's dying. He was as weak as a kitten when we pushed off from Port Caledon and this last bout, coming as it did after a period of enforced abstinence, has been too much for his system."

"In this day and age?" scoffed Calver.

"Yes. In this day and age. In any day and age all that the physician has ever done has been to help the patient to recover. When there's no will to live, what can any doctor do? Jane's with him now, but I think that you'd better come along yourself."

"Wait till I call Brentano up to Control," said Calver, reaching for the telephone. And then, when the indispensable little Radio Officer was in charge of the watch, he followed Malone to the officers' flat.

Maudsley's cabin reeked of vomit and decay and stale liquor. Maudsley was strapped in his bunk and Jane, quietly and efficiently, was cleaning the air of the disgusting globules of fluid with an absorbent cloth. She looked around as her husband and the doctor entered. She said, "He's unconscious again." She grimaced. "Just as well—although I'm sure that there's nothing left in his stomach now."

Calver looked at Maudsley. The man no longer resembled a bloodhound. He no longer resembled anything living. His head was a skull over which dirty white parchment had been stretched. The rise and fall of his chest was barely perceptible.

"He talked," said Jane briefly. "He had a lucid moment, and he talked. He told me that he was running away. But—and this was the odd part—he said that he was running *from* the Rim."

Calver saw Maudsley's eyes flicker open, saw the dry lips twitch, heard the creaking, almost inaudible whisper. "Yes, damn you all. From the Rim, and from the Outsiders. If I'd been sober, I'd never have signed on aboard your stinking ship. You're taking me back, you bastard, but I'll not go." His voice rose to a shriek. "I'll not go! You can't force me." He laughed then, wildly and frighteningly, and his voice dropped again, to a low, confidential whisper. "There's wealth there, and power and knowledge, and it was almost in my grasp, but I was afraid. I'm still afraid. If you take me back to the Rim I shall know, all the time, that it's out there, waiting for me, and I'll be afraid to go and find it again, and that will be the worst of all, knowing that it's there. . ." He looked at Calver and Jane and Malone with burning, pleading eyes. "You must see that. Even you must see that. . ."

"What is it that's out there?" asked Calver quietly.

A cunning expression flickered over Maudsley's ravaged face. "I'll see you in hell before I tell you. It's mine, *mine!* If I told you, you might get past the Outsiders and then it would be yours. It wouldn't be fair. I lost my ship, and I lost my commission. I lost the *Polar Queen* and that was the price I paid. Yes I paid, and I paid too much, and I'm still paying. But I shall go back to the Rim when I'm ready, and not before, and I'll go back Outside to find again what I've paid for, but I shan't go until *I* want to go. You can't carry me back against my will. You can't. Doctor, tell him that he can't. Tell him!"

"You'd better leave him to me," said Malone to Calver. "He's frightened of you, and he hates you."

"What about getting Levine in here?" whispered Calver.

"I'd like to, but the little man's too bloody ethical. He takes his oath too seriously. He'd never enter the mind of a non-telepath unless invited. . . ." He took Maudsley's limp wrist in his hand. "And now you'd better leave him to me. Both of you."

4

THEY SAT IN *The Outsider*'s saloon, their seat belts giving the not very convincing illusion of gravity. Calver
was there, and Jane, and Doc Malone. And Renault,
who kept no watch in deep space, and Bendix, who
had no qualms about leaving his Mannschenn Drive
in the competent hands of a Doctor of Physics. And
little Brentano was there, and Levine.

Calver waited until pipes and cigars and cigarettes
were under way and was amused to note that the
ever efficient Brentano watched the drifting eddies of
smoke until satisfied that the air circulation system
was working properly.

He said, "As you all know, we have made a deviation from our trajectory. The doctor advises me that
only by landing Mr. Maudsley at the first convenient

port can we save his life, that his psychological condition will grow progressively worse as we near the Rim. So we shall put him ashore at Dunsinane in the Shakespearean Sector.

"However, let us forget the technicalities of navigation, let us forget that we are spacemen and regard this as a shareholders' meeting. We don't own this ship just for the fun of it—well, I suppose that in a way we do, but skip that—but to make money. Our present intention is to run the Eastern Circuit on Time Charter to Rim Runners and then, eventually, to compete with our late employers on the same trade. I don't think that any of us are really happy about the prospects of competing with a company that is, after all, as near as, dammit, government owned. Some trade of which we should have the monopoly would be the ideal set-up."

"That," said Bendix, "is a blinding glimpse of the obvious. But what trade?"

"*Outside,*" suggested Calver quietly.

"But there's nothing Outside," objected Bendix. "Nothing. Not until some genius comes up with an intergalactic drive."

"There's *something,*" said Calver. "There's something. There're the odd artifacts that drift in from time to time. You've seen the one in the museum at Port Farewell. A ship's boat—or it could be a ship's boat, or a life raft. Whatever it is, or was, it could have been made by none of the spacefaring races in this galaxy. We've got intelligent fluorine breathers —but none with the physical characteristics of an oversized flatworm. . ."

"And so what?" asked Bendix. "There's bound to be intelligent life in the next galaxy, and in the one after that, and in the one after that. If we could make contact with 'em, we'd trade with 'em. But it's one helluva big if."

"It is that," agreed Calver. "However," he went on, "let's start at the beginning. As we all know, our Chief Officer was dead drunk when we signed him on at Port Caledon, so much so that he could hardly have cared less where the ship was bound. He did sober up, after a fashion, but something was eating him. And then he managed to find old Doc's private stock of what he calls Irish whisky. . . ."

"And ye'd never tell the difference!" interjected Malone.

"That's a matter of opinion. Anyhow, our Mr. Maudsley hit the bottle again to drown his fears, and the more he tried to drown them the worse they got. What he's frightened of is something, or *somebody* called the Outsiders. When we picked him up he was running away—just as we all have done. But he was running *from* the Rim, not towards it."

"Something threw a scare into him," agreed the doctor. "It's likely that I'll have to keep him under sedation all the way to Dunsinane."

"Jane?" said Calver.

"I've been nursing him," she said. "I felt sorry for him from the very start. I feel even sorrier for him now. I've listened to his ramblings, his ravings. His ship was the *Polar Queen,* one of those odd tramps that drifts out to the Rim from time to time. He was Master of her. He lost her, smashed her up when making an incredibly bad landing at Port Farewell. Then he was with Rim Runners for a while; the Court of Enquiry suspended his Master's Certificate for six months but granted him a First Pilot's one for that period. When the six months were up he reclaimed his Certificate, left Rim Runners and has been trying to make his way back to the Centre Worlds ever since."

"I've heard of him," said Bendix. "He was Second Mate of the *Rimstar*. They called him Windy Maudsley. He used to be in a state of near panic from blast-off to touch-down. Everybody thought that it was the aftermath of the loss of the *Polar Queen*."

"And what about the rest of *Polar Queen*'s crew?" asked Brentano.

"It was a bad crash," said Bendix. "I remember old Captain Engels telling me about it. He was in Port Farewell in *Lorn Lady* when it happened. It seems that Maudsley was in the Control Room and escaped with only slight injuries. His Chief and Second Officers weren't so lucky. They weren't killed outright but they died in the hospital without recovering consciousness. The rest of the crowd were . . . mashed."

"Can you remember anything else, Bendix?" asked Calver.

"No. After all, I only got the story at second hand."

"I was just a kid when it happened," contributed Levine. "But I was crazy to get into space, and anything about spaceships or spacemen in the news I just lapped up. As I remember the reports, Maudsley's breath stank of whisky when they dragged him out of the wreckage. Luckily for him, the investigation proved that a tube lining had burned out, otherwise he'd have lost his ticket instead of getting away with a six months' suspension."

"And you've managed to get in touch with Port Farewell?" asked Calver.

"Yes, Captain. There are ways and means of stepping up the psionic amplifier, you know, although I fear that I shall have to indent for a new dog's brain when we arrive. Anyhow, I got in touch with Donaldson. He looked up the records for us. He tells me that *Polar Queen* was making a relatively short hop between Ultimo and Thule, and that at the time of her arrival at Port Farewell she was well overdue. Maudsley said at the Enquiry that the Mannschenn Drive had been giving him trouble. He was, of course, the only witness from the ship. . ."

"And now, Levine, what do *you* know of the Outsiders?"

"You know as much as I do, Captain . . ." The telepath paused and grinned. "Sorry, you don't. Even if we leave my . . . talent out of it, I was born and brought up on the Rim, and none of you were. So I'll just assume that you know nothing.

"Well, they've always been a sort of legend out on the Rim, these Outsiders. Some say that they're supernatural beings, even that they're the old gods of mankind, and of other intelligent races, driven outside the galaxy and waiting there to come back when, at last, faith and belief return. And others say that they're intelligent beings, not unlike ourselves, that have made the voyage across the gulf from some other galaxy. There are the wild tales about strange ships in the sky—and there have been the strange artifacts found on some of the Rim worlds and in our sector of space. . .

"But I haven't heard the Outsiders as much as mentioned for years now."

"Just suppose . . ." murmured Calver. "Just suppose . . . Just suppose that there's a big ship hanging out there, somewhere. . . A ship that made the crossing. . . Just suppose that her crew discovered intelligent life on the Rim worlds—but discovered that life in the anti-matter systems. . . Or, perhaps, our systems are anti-matter to them. . . Just suppose that they've assumed that our entire galaxy is composed of anti-matter. . ."

"People with enough curiosity and know-how to make the crossing wouldn't give up that easily," said Jane sharply.

"I don't suppose they would, my dear. I was just playing with ideas, feeding them into the computer to see if two pairs of them made four. But I've this strong hunch that there *is* something out there, and that Maudsley stumbled on it. I've got this hunch that it, whatever it is, is worth finding again."

"There *is* something out there," said Jane. "Maudsley found it, and it drove him to drink, ruined his career. Whatever it is, it's dangerous."

"Not necessarily. As far as we know, Maudsley's ship was undamaged until the crash. All his crew were accounted for, and they were all alive until the smash-up killed them. I grant you this—there is something out there that's frightening. But . . . How shall I put it?

"I was raised on Earth, a country boy, in a farming district. Earth, as you know, is very old-fashioned and doesn't believe in using tanks of chemical nutrient to grow food when there's good, honest dirt on hand. So there were the crops out in the open, cereals, and there were the birds that regarded the fields as huge free lunch counters. And there were the scarecrows . . ."

"What are they?" asked Levine.

"A rough figure of a man, mansized, made of old clothing stuffed with rags or straw, held erect by a post. If it's so constructed that the arms will wave in the wind, so much the better. The birds take it for a man and sheer off. Oh, some of the smarter ones spot the deception after a while and dig in, but the majority stay clear.

"Well, I'll get back to this hypothetical ship of mine. For some reason she's been abandoned. Her owners, however, have set up some sort of scarecrow that was good enough to scare off poor Maudsley, but not good enough—or bad enough—to do any actual physical damage to *Polar Queen* and her people. But we, expecting a scarecrow and, furthermore, possessing the right psychological and emotional make-up for life on the Rim, are far less liable to be scared off and just might find something worthwhile.

"This, then, is my proposal. We pump Maudsley of all he knows about the Outsiders, using every means of persuasion short of actual torture. We pay him well for what he tells us. Then, when our present cargo is discharged, we go hunting Outside to find whatever it was that Maudsley found."

"Derek," said Jane firmly, "you may be Master, but you are also no more than one of the shareholders. In all matters pertaining to the actual running of the ship your word is law—but in all matters pertaining to her future employment *we,* all of us, the owners, decide."

"Then," asked Calver stiffly, "what do you propose?"

"That we put the matter to the vote. I move that we do not set off on any wild goose chases and that we put the ship on the Eastern Circuit on the Rim

Runners time charter. We've been into all this before, and we all agreed that, the way things are at present, we shall need Rim Runners' repair, office and agency facilities. *When* we're well enough established we can set up our own shoreside organization."

"I second that," said Brentano.

"A show of hands," said Bendix.

"As you please," said Calver. "A show of hands. All in favor of Jane's motion?"

His own hand was the only one not raised. He looked rather ruefully at the others around the table.

"Derek," said Jane, "we must be sensible. We've all rehabilitated ourselves to an extent that, not so long ago, would have seemed impossible. Are we to throw it all away for a wild dream?"

Calver filled his pipe again carefully, used one of the old-fashioned matches that he affected to light it. He said slowly, "Even so ... how shall I put it? I came out to the Rim as all of us did—because of the mess I'd made of my life in the Centre. But there was more to it than that, much more. After all, you can drink yourself to death anywhere in the Galaxy where there are human vices—even those communistic bumble bees, the Shaara, make and use alcohol. I came out to the Rim because it was, I thought, the last frontier. Now I've learned that it's not, that there's still another one beyond it."

Bendix puffed a cigarette into glowing life. He said, "I see what you mean, Calver. And I think that it applies, to a greater or lesser degree, to all of us. But Jane is right. We must consolidate. We must make the ship pay for herself before we think of anything else. But," he turned to Jane, "we must face the fact that Rim Runners will just be making a convenience of us until such time as their own fleet is built up, and then they'll lose no time in running us off the Eastern Circuit and the Shakespearean Sector trade. But if we have some sort of ace up our sleeve."

"If you can call it an ace," grumbled Brentano. "Old legends, with no basis of fact, the ravings of a drunken derelict."

"There's *something* out there," said old Doc Malone. "And I, for one, would like to find out what it is before I'm dragged off the stage. But there's no rush, no hurry at all, at all. It, whatever it is, will keep. After the ship has paid for herself, after the Time Charter's expired and we're on our own, will be time enough."

"All right," said Calver. "So that would seem to be that. Meanwhile, we must find out all that we can from Maudsley. I don't suppose that you could help, Levine?"

"I could, Captain," said the telepath, "but I won't. My oath . . ."

"If you'd agreed," said Jane, "I'd have lost the rather great respect that I hold for you."

"Bless you, my children," murmured Calver sardonically. "So it's up to you, Doc."

"Yes," said Malone, "it's time that I had another look at the patient."

He left the saloon with the peculiar, unhurried grace of a fat man in free fall. He returned with more speed than grace. He reported that Maudsley must have more or less recovered, had left his cabin and found, somewhere, a bottle of cleaning alcohol. Drifting in the air of his cabin were mingled globules of

the crude intoxicant—what was left of it—and blood
from his slashed throat.

5

So, on charter to Rim Runners, they ran the Eastern Circuit—Tharn, Grollor, Mellise and Stree, with occasional side trips to the Shakespearean Sector. Cappell—the spaceman turned sheep herder turned spaceman—stayed with them, and, after intensive coaching by Calver, managed to scrape through the examination for his First Pilot's Certificate and was promoted to Chief Officer, replacing in that rank yet another drunken derelict whom Calver had been obliged to sign on in Dunsinane. And both Lloyd and Ritter liked the life and, with their already high academic qualifications found no trouble in adding engineers' Certificates of Competency to them. Bendix, to everybody's surprise, married, and Julia, his wife, was a highly efficient secretary who became, in a very short time indeed, a highly efficient Purser. And Brentano married—a biochemist who was able to take over the care of the hydroponic tanks, the yeast and algae vats and the tissue cultures from Doc Malone. Tanya Brentano was of Slavic stock and, in the opinion of everybody but the doctor, her vodka was far superior to Malone's "Irish" whisky. Brentano, as well as changing his marital status, changed his rank, sitting for and passing, without any trouble, the examination for his Second Pilot's Certificate, thus making room for Elise Renault, who was a qualified radio technician.

They ran the Eastern Circuit for two years, for twenty-four busy, happy months. *The Outsider* was a home rather than a ship, her people a family rather than a crew. Maudsley had been forgotten, Calver often thought, by everybody but himself. He had not forgotten. He still felt the lure of Outside, the magnetism of the unsolved mystery out there in the darkness. He tried to tell himself that this was romantic foolishness, that when the Time Charter expired *The Outsider* could make a stab at running in competition with Rim Runners and, should this be unsuccessful, could go tramping through the galaxy. He tried to tell himself this, but failed to convince himself. Every voyage he brought with him old books and records, and carefully went through them all to try to find some sort of a clue.

So, for two years, they ran the Eastern Circuit, and then the Charter expired. For six months they tried to function as a private company and learned, the hard way, that good will is all very nice as long as there is no financial loss involved. Calver's friends on Tharn would have liked to have shipped their cargoes in *The Outsider*—but, with Rim Runners' freights only sixty percent of those asked by Calver they did not feel justified in spending money on carriage that would be better spent on imports. The drably efficient humanoids of Grollor were without sentiment. They had worked out for themselves the principle of buying in the cheapest market and selling in the dearest long before Commodore Grimes' survey expedition had landed on their planet. For a little while there was trade to be done with both Mellise and Stree—but even the happy amphibians and the philosophical lizards had begun to acquire, from contact with humanity, a sordid commercialism.

At the end of six months of independent trading— the ship was at Port Forlorn, discharging a pitifully small consignment of Mellisan dried fish and a smaller one of parchment rolls from Stree—there was a shareholders' meeting. All hands were present. (Cappell, Lloyd and Ritter had been offered, and had taken, the opportunity of receiving some of their pay in shares, and the new wives had been given shares as wedding presents.)

"Julia?" said Calver from his seat at the head of the saloon table.

The Purser rose to her feet.

"You all know how things have been going lately," she reported in her cool, pleasant voice. "You'll not be surprised when I tell you that we're in the red. I have the figures for the last half year. . ."

"You needn't bother with them, dear," said Bendix. "Even I can see that running costs have been far in excess of income."

"I take it," said Calver, "that we're all in agreement on that point. Thank you, Julia." The Purser resumed her seat. "As I see it, we have little control over what happens next, as long as we stay on the Rim. I have a letter here from Commodore Grimes.

It seems that Rim Runners are prepared to buy the ship from us, the price to be determined after a survey. Alternatively, they'd offer us a one way charter to Nova Caledon, the implication being that it's as good a way of getting us out of their hair.

"Of course, if we sell the ship we shall do more than break even."

"But we don't want to sell," stated Jane firmly.

"Then there's the old business of Maudsley and his Outsider," went on Calver.

"No," said Jane. "No. We're shipowners, not explorers. I propose that we accept the Nova Caledon charter and play by ear from then on."

"Let me finish," Calver told her. "This Outsiders business has stuck in my mind, if not in yours. I've been doing a deal of research on it. I managed to get hold of a pile of back numbers of the *Port Farewell Argus* covering the *Polar Queen* disaster and the subsequent enquiry. At last I found what I was looking for. It was a typical Sunday Supplement article, written with his tongue in his cheek by some journalist who'd passed a few hours getting drunk with Maudsley. It was mainly a rehash of all the old legends about the Outsiders and it contained the statement, alleged to have been made by Maudsley, which I'll quote: 'Put Macbeth and Kinsolvings' Sun in line, and keep them so. That's the way that we came back. Fifty light years, and all hands choking on the stink of frying oil from the Mannschenn Drive . . .'

"It's a lead."

"Is it?" queried Jane. "And, if so, to what? But tell me, why didn't Grimes follow it when he made his last survey voyage in *Faraway Quest?*"

"Because Grimes, as I shouldn't have to tell you, is

apt to be pigheaded. He's made up his mind that there's nothing—and I mean *nothing*—Outside. He was one of the assessors at the Court of Enquiry before which Maudsley appeared, and said that in his opinion all Maudsley's talk of the Outsiders was no more than *delirium tremens*."

"As it probably was," said Jane.

"I don't think so," said Doc Malone.

"And neither do I," said Calver. He paused. "Well, ladies and gentlemen, we own a ship. The ship is temporarily out of employment. We can sell her, and show a good profit on our venture. We can accept the one-way charter and then go tramping— and, as you know, quite a few tramps still get by on the leavings of the big lines and the various government-owned services. Or we can push off from Port Forlorn as soon as the cargo's out and the stores are aboard, and run west until we have Macbeth and Kinsolving's Sun in line, and then. . ."

"The Nova Caledon charter," said Jane. "Show hands."

And Calver's hand was the only one not raised.

6

"WHERE ARE you going?" asked Jane.

"Ashore," said Calver.

"If you'll wait a few minutes it won't take me long to get ready."

"I'm sorry," he told her. "But I'd rather go by myself."

"Sulking?" she demanded.

He favored her with a wry grin. "Sort of. But I want to get off the ship, by myself, to have a few drinks and think things out."

"Things," she told him, "have already been decided."

"Not everything," he said.

"Derek," said Jane quietly, "listen to me. Please. I know that this Outsider business has become something of an obsession with you, and I can, to a certain extent, appreciate the lure of it all. To a certain extent. But remember that women are different from men—and, after all, it was the women's vote that decided in favor of the Nova Caledon charter. Bendix

203

and Renault and Brentano voted along with their wives."

"And the others? Doc Malone and Cappell and Lloyd and Ritter?"

She shrugged. "They're realists, I suppose. Just as we women are realists. Even though we're accepted in space, even though we take the same risks as you, we have that basic longing for security. We'd hate to see the security that we've achieved thrown away on a wild goose chase."

"Security . . ." repeated Calver. "What security is there in tramping from star to star, hungry for the crumbs that fall from the tables of the rich corporations?"

"And what security," she countered, "is there in blasting off into the utterly unknown, into that illimitable expanse of sweet damn all?"

He said, "There's something there."

"Is there?"

"Yes. Maudsley found it. And he managed to convince you at the time."

"A Rim ghost," she said. "That's what it must have been. Remember the one that we saw, in *Lorn Lady,* all those years ago?"

"I do," he agreed. "But . . ."

"Oh, go ashore," she told him. "Go ashore and have a few drinks, or too many drinks if you like. It will do you good, help you to get over your sulks."

He said, "All right. I'll do that."

He kissed Jane perfunctorily, then took his cap and his uniform cloak from their hooks. He left his quarters and clattered down the spiral staircase in the axial shaft, feeling a little better after the physical exercise. Outside the airlock it was cold, with a bitter breeze that stirred the gritty dust that lay, as always, on the fire-scarred apron, and drove before it a rustling flurry of dead leaves and old newspapers.

Calver tried to wipe a speck of grit from his eye, then looked around him with distaste at the untidiness and decrepitude revealed by the glare of the spaceport floodlights. He thought, *After all, I shan't be sorry to leave the Rim worlds for good.*

He asked himself: *But shall I?*

He shrugged, pulling his cloak more tightly about his body, then walked rapidly to the main entrance. As he approached the edge of the field, away from the bright lights, he could see the sky—the black emptiness, with the faint, far and few nebulosities that made it seem so much emptier and, low in the west, the pale-glowing arc of the Galactic lens. But it was the distant nebulae that caught and held his attention. From which one had the Outsiders come?

If there were any Outsiders.

"Shall I call you a cab, Captain?" asked the gatekeeper.

"No, thank you," Calver told him. "It's not far into town, and the walk will do me good."

"I hear that you'll be leaving the Rim shortly," said the man.

"Yes," said Calver.

He walked on briskly, along the shabby street with the tall warehouses on either side. He went into the first tavern—*The Jolly Rocketeer*—sat at the bar and ordered a pink gin. There were a few spacemen— from *Rim Galleon* and *Rim Caravel*, as both vessels were in port—in the place, but nobody whom Calver knew. There was the foreman stevedore who was in charge of the loading of *The Outsider*'s cargo for Nova

Caledon. Calver bought him a drink and had another one himself. He decided after the second gin that he was hungry, and decided, too, that nothing on display in the tavern's snack bar looked very tempting. He said goodnight to the stevedore and went out.

He had heard that the food at the newly opened Rimrock Hilton was good and decided to put it to the test. He doubted if the hotel's chef would be as good as Jane, but a change, after all, would be refreshing. And he did not want to return to his ship for a while yet.

Twenty minutes' brisk walk brought him to the floodlit tower of the hotel. He returned the salute of a doorman whose stylish livery made his own uniform look like that of an Apprentice Spaceman Third Class. In the foyer another obsequious Galactic Admiral asked his pleasure. Calver said that he would like a meal. The Galactic Admiral recommended the Captain's Cabin. Calver said that he had come ashore to get away from ships and that he would prefer to eat in surroundings that some ingenious interior decorator had not tried to make as much like a ship as possible.

"Then, sir," said the functionary, "might I suggest the Chop House?"

"The Chop House?" queried Calver. "Chinese?"

"No sir. Strictly period. Nineteenth Century Anglo-Terran Sawdust on the floor, rough wooden tables and benches . . ."

"Real sawdust?" asked Calver sardonically.

"Of course, sir . . . Confidentially, for reasons of hygiene, we did use synthetic sawdust, but it hasn't the aroma."

"You could have used a synthetic aroma too," said Calver.

He allowed himself to be guided to an elevator whose pilot, a mere Commodore, delivered him to the correct floor. He went into the Chop House. It looked, as far as he could judge, authentic enough. There was the sawdust, as promised. There were the rough tables and benches and, overhead, genuine seemingly oaken rafters. On the walls were ancient sporting prints and from the walls protruded flaring gas jets.

A waiter in a rusty black dress suit, over which he wore a stained, once-white apron, guided Calver to a table. Calver wondered if the man's mutton chop whiskers were synthetic or genuine, almost asked and then thought better of it. He sat down and studied the menu which, in keeping with the decor, was scrawled on a slate.

He made his decision, ordered his meal.

It was not a good one.

"I thought that I should be playing safe by having something simple," murmured a hauntingly familiar voice. *"Steak Diane* . . . that wasn't asking too much, was it?"

"One would think not," admitted Calver, turning to look at the woman at the neighboring table.

"I saw you making faces over your dinner," she said.

"Mixed grill," he told her. "My guess is that the various animals contributing their bits and pieces to it must have died of old age."

"Last time," she said, "it was *Lobster Thermidor,* wasn't it? Perhaps this breaking of the pattern is a good omen."

"For what?" he countered.

He thought, *She hasn't changed. Except that she's dyed*

her platinum hair green. But she's still damned attractive. Too attractive.

She shrugged. "Well, the last two times we met were rather disastrous, weren't they? The first time was on Faraway, wasn't it? And your girlfriend turned the local cops on to me. And the second time was on Grollor, and there was that most unfortunate clash between the Federation Survey Service, Intelligence Branch, and the Rim Worlds Naval Reserve. . ."

Calver got up and joined the girl at her table.

"Still playing Olga Popovsky, the Beautiful Spy?" he asked.

"And are you still playing Lieutenant Commander Calver, R.W.N.R.?" she countered.

"I had to resign my commission," he told her.

"Were you a naughty boy, or something?" she asked lightly. "No, don't tell me. After all, I'm still in Intelligence, so I may as well use some." She started to tick off points on her slim fingers. "One: You've risen in the world. You're a big, fat Captain. Two: Those buttons on your uniform aren't Rim Runner buttons. Three: That pretty badge on your cap isn't the Rim Runner badge. Intriguing design, isn't it? A gold ring with silver stars inside it, and a conventional silver rocket outside. May I ask which company's uniform it is?"

"M.O.B.C.," said Calver.

"M.O.B.C.?"

"My own bloody company."

She laughed, and there was still that tinkling quality to it. "All right, Derek, I'll come clean. I know about *The Outsider,* and what you've been doing and how you've been doing. As a matter of fact I was going to call on you, officially, tomorrow."

"Were you, now? Wouldn't that be rather risky?"

"Not this time. I wouldn't say that your local cops are wildly in love with me, but they've nothing against me. The Federation has bowed to the inevitable and has recognized the right of the Rim Worlds Confederacy to go its own sweet way. As far as we're concerned you can make whatever alliances and treaties you please. I'm here by permission of your government—who, also, has promised to help me in my investigations."

"And what," asked Calver, "are you investigating this time?"

"To begin with," she told him, "the psychological breakdown and eventual suicide of one of our people."

"Did it happen here?" he asked. "On the Rim?"

"No," she said, "in deep space. Between Nova Caledon and Dunsinane."

"Between Nova Caledon and Dunsinane," echoed Calver, shivering slightly with a premonitory chill.

"Yes. His name was Maudsley. Commander Maudsley."

7

THEY ADJOURNED to Sonya Verrill's suite where the girl, producing her own percolator, brewed coffee. There was brandy too, the authentic product of far away France, in fragile inhalers. There were soft lights and, after Sonya had adjusted the controls of the hotel's playmaster, sweet music. But the atmosphere was not one of seduction, despite the fact that Sonya Verrill had, in her own words, changed into "something more comfortable." Calver realized, with something of a shock, that the flimsy semi-transparency that did little to hide her lovely body was failing to register.

He thought, *Blast the Outsiders. When I'm more interested in them than in a beautiful woman, there's something wrong with me.*

He said, "So Maudsley was one of your people."

"He was," said the girl. "He was a good man. He found that being a tramp Master was an excellent cover for his real activities. Frankly, he was running a sort of economic and political survey of your Rim

Worlds Federation when he became interested in the Outsider legends."

"He found something," said Calver. "I'm convinced of that. He found something—and it ruined him."

"He wasn't a coward," said the girl. "He'd never have risen to the rank of Commander in Intelligence if he had been. But did he give you any clues? Did he drop any hints at all as to what it was that he'd found?"

"Hints," said Calver. "Hints—but that was all. There was something out there. Something that could make its discoverer rich, or powerful, or both. Something that terrified him."

"But why didn't he report?" asked Sonya, as much of herself as of Calver. "Why didn't he report to H.Q.? God knows we've enough specialists loafing around to be able to handle anything."

"How loyal was Maudsley to your Service?" asked Calver. "I could be wrong, but my own analysis is this: He found this thing—and he wanted it for himself. It was too big for him to handle—but he clung to the hope that sooner or later he'd be big enough to handle it. Of course, the way that he was going he never would be—but, after all, many men allow completely illogical hopes to dominate their lives."

"And what about you, Derek?" she asked. "Do you think that you could handle it?"

"I don't know," he told her. "I don't know. If I knew what it was, I'd be able to give you an answer. But I just don't know."

"But would you want to try?"

He said, "Sonya that's been my ambition ever since I first heard of Maudsley's Outsiders. As you know, I'm a shipowner—but, unluckily, I don't own the ship outright. When our Time Charter expired I wanted to go exploring, wanted to find whatever it was that Maudsley found. But the others voted me down. Now, as you've probably learned already, we're loading a cargo for Nova Caledon and it's unlikely that we shall ever return to the Rim. . . ." He sipped his brandy. "But it would be so easy to find . . . *it*. Macbeth and Kinsolving's Sun in line, and push out for fifty light years. . . . But I shall never do it now. And I suppose that your people will have a survey vessel out here shortly, and they'll find the Outsiders while I'm tramping from system to system, picking up cargoes when and where I can."

He realized that she was sitting on the arm of his chair, felt the warmth of her lightly clad body. Her fingers were gently stroking his head, disarranging his hair.

She said, "At the moment we can't spare any ships. They're all tied up in Wilkinson's Cluster."

"What's happening there?" he asked.

"There's a dispute between our colonies and the Shaara ones. It's very complicated. The humans are objecting to the subjection of a native humanoid race by, I quote, a bunch of communistic bumble bees. And the Shaara Regent has been trying to stamp out alcoholism in the worlds under her control and is objecting, not unreasonably, to the large scale bootlegging being carried out by certain humans. There's been shooting, and one or two minor invasions. Both the Survey Service and the Royal Shaaran Navy are trying to sort things out before they develop into a large scale war."

"Interesting," he said.

"Yes. And rather dangerous. Although we've always gotten along reasonably well with the Shaara Empire, there's still the hostility that must always exist between the mammal and the anthropod."

"We mammals must stick together," said Calver —and wondered if it were the brandy or himself talking. Not that it mattered.

"Not so fast, spaceman, not so fast," admonished Sonya Verrill. She disengaged herself, was back in her own chair before Calver realized what was happening. She went on, "I admit that there's unfinished business between us—and this time, now that politics aren't in the way, we may just get around to finishing it. But there's other business as well."

"Such as?" asked Calver.

"The future employment of your ship. You have the one way charter out to Nova Caledon, and then you're on your own. Isn't that so? Well, I can offer you a charter."

"Go on."

"It would mean that you and your people would have to accept temporary commissions in the Survey Service, and that one of our people—possibly myself —would have to travel aboard. You would have to sign an agreement to the effect that anything found— any artifacts, any new knowledge—would be Survey Service property."

"I'm sorry," said Calver, "but I'm still a Rim Worlder, and I think that this . . . this *thing* is Rim World property."

"But your own government isn't interested. They know what I'm out here for. I've even tried to persuade your Commodore Grimes to recommission his *Faraway Quest*, but he regards the Outsider legend as just a legend, and nothing more. He regards poor Maudsley as no more than a hopelessly unreliable alcoholic who's better off dead."

"Thanks for the offer," said Calver. "I appreciate it. Perhaps I'm selfish, but I want the discovery, when it's made, to be my discovery, or *our* discovery . . ."

"You mean . . .?" she murmured.

"I'm sorry, Sonya. I don't. When I said *our*, I meant *our* in the sense of belonging to *The Outsider* and her people."

"It seems to me," she said, "that I'm the outsider as far as you're concerned. I must be slipping. Where's the fatal charm before which Admirals, Generals, Prime Ministers and Dictators have fallen?" Her wry grin sat oddly on her perfect features, but was far from unattractive. "And now here's a mere tramp Captain turning me down."

"I'm not turning *you* down," said Calver, "only your kind offer of a charter."

She said, "Then all is not lost."

She was standing now, facing him, and her hands were fluttering at the fastenings of her robe. It fell from her, slowly, a lacy froth that slipped down her golden body, exposing breasts and gently rounded belly and full thighs, collapsing at last to a gossamer foam about her slender ankles.

She said simply, "There are no strings, Derek. This is just us, the two of us, and nothing to do with your ship on the Survey Service. . ."

His jacket was off, thrown carelessly to the floor, but he was having trouble with his necktie.

"Let me," she said, helping him.

*   *   *

Jane stirred uneasily in the double bunk in the darkened cabin.

"So you're back," she muttered.

"Yes."

"Have a nice evening?"

"Yes, thank you. I ran into an old shipmate," he said, not too untruthfully, "and we had dinner and a few drinks together."

"What is that smell?" she asked sharply.

"What smell?" he countered.

Fleur de floosie. A somewhat expensive version, I admit . . ."

He said, "Sydney—Sydney Small, that is, he's in *Rim Galleon* now—was showing me a bottle of perfume that he'd picked up from the Captain of some tramp whom he met at Port Fortinbras. Some got spilled."

"Oh," she said. "Oh. It reminded me, somehow, of that little tow-haired trollop that you got entangled with years ago. That spy wench, whatever her name was."

"Odd," said Calver.

He went through to his bathroom and showered carefully and thoroughly.

8

The Outsider, her holds stowed to capacity, lifted from Port Forlorn, climbed slowly through the cloud strata and, clear of the atmosphere, turned on her humming gyroscopes until the cartwheel sight built into the transparency of her stem was centered on that portion of the Galactic Lens in which lay the Empire of Waverley.

"Goodbye to the Rim," said Brentano, a little glumly.

"We shall be back," Calver told him.

"Perhaps," admitted the Second Mate. "Perhaps. I suppose that there'll be the odd charter or so to bring us out this way."

"Goodbye to the Rim," said Jane. "And goodbye to . . ."

"To what?" asked Calver.

"Or to whom?" she countered.

"Well, then, to whom?" he demanded.

"To your dear shipmate Sydney Small," she sneered. "The one with the expensive but somewhat vulgar taste in perfume. Remember?"

Calver ignored this. He gave the necessary orders, saw to it that with no waste of time his ship was falling down her long trajectory, her Mannschenn Drive unit whining softly, the Galactic Lens ahead distorted like a Klein flask produced by a drunken glass blower in a moment of extreme mental aberration. Then, when there was nothing further that he could do, he went down to his quarters, leaving the watch to Brentano.

Jane was not there, but he thought nothing of this. She would be in the galley, probably, preparing the next meal, or in the pantry making a fresh brew of coffee in the percolator. And then, with more than a slight shock, he noticed a certain bareness about the cabin. The little clock—its case a beautiful example of the Aldebaranian metal workers' art—was gone from its usual position on the bulkhead. And the sphere of transparent crystal in which was embedded a Vegan moonflower was missing from the desk, as was the elaborate little silver mobile from Tharn. Calver slid open the wardrobe doors. All of Jane's clothes were gone from their stretchers.

"Jane!" he called irritably. "Jane!"

Her reply came faintly from somewhere outside. "There's no need to shout."

He went into the alleyway. He was not surprised to find that his wife had moved into the spare cabin. He followed her inside, shut the door firmly.

"What's the big idea?" he demanded.

"In the circumstances," she told him coldly, "I thought that I'd like to sleep alone."

"What circumstances?"

She said, "I suppose you thought that you were

quite safe when you told me about the mythical Sydney Small, especially since *Rim Galleon* blasted off the same morning that you came back reeking like a whore's garret. But, when I had occasion to go to the shipping office on some business of my own, I saw the copy of *Rim Galleon's* Articles lying on the desk. I browsed through it. I need hardly tell you that there's nobody by the name of Sydney Small in the crew."

"So?"

"So. So I decided to make a few more investigations. I rang the Rimrock Hilton. (I was going to ring all the hotels but, knowing the style in which these Federation spies seem to live, I thought I'd save time by ringing the most expensive ones first.) The girl at the desk was most obliging. "Yes there was a Miss Verrill staying there. A Miss Sonya Verrill. A Terran citizen."

"But . . ." began Calver.

"No, Derek. It's no use trying to explain—and it's certainly no use trying to lie again. You know that I'm not possessive and that I've never tried to keep you in a cage. If you'd spent the night with some little casual pick-up it wouldn't have mattered, it wouldn't have really mattered. But Sonya Verrill, of all people. Are you incapable of learning? The first time that she got her claws into you, you almost fell foul of the police, and that would have been the end of your career in Rim Runners. The second time, on Grollor, was even worse, and Captain Engels had to risk his ship and all our lives to get you out of the stupid jam you were in. Can't you learn, won't you learn that as far as you're concerned, that woman is poison."

"Even so," said Calver.

"Even so my left foot. You're behaving like some spottyfaced adolescent who's got his ideas about women from the most meretricious so-called stars of the most inanely juvenile tri-do shows."

"Even so," said Calver coldly, "Miss Verrill and I talked business. She made me an offer, and I turned it down."

"Like hell you did!"

"I did," stated Calver virtuously. "But I can change my mind. And I'm sure that the other shareholders will back me up, even though it will mean having Miss Verrill along as an observer." He added unkindly, "That will mean, of course, that she'll have to bunk in the spare cabin, unless she cares to . . ."

"And what was this famous offer?" she sneered. "I don't mean the one that you so obviously didn't turn down, but the other."

Calver pulled himself into a chair and adjusted the belt. He filled and lit his pipe, said nothing until it was drawing to his satisfaction. He watched the play of emotions on Jane's face—hurt anger, wounded pride and, finally, curiosity. He could not help but feel that he had behaved and was still behaving shabbily. But he could see, now, a way whereby he could get what he wanted.

He said, "Miss Verrill and I enjoyed a very interesting conversation."

She flared, "I'm sure you did!"

Calver fiddled with his pipe and relit it.

She said, "Go on, damn you. Go on."

"It seems," said Calver slowly, "that our Mr. Maudsley was really the Survey Service's Commander Maudsley. Intelligence, of course.''

"Where in the galaxy do they get their officers from?'' marvelled Jane. ''Nymphomaniacs, alcoholics . . .''

Calver played with his pipe again.

"Well?'' she demanded.

"Maudsley wasn't an alcoholic until after he'd found the Outsiders. It seems that he wanted to keep the knowledge to himself; in any case, he made no reports back to his H.Q. Understandably, his superiors want to know just what's been happening. So they sent Miss Verrill . . .''

"They must think a lot of her. All the ships and people at their disposal, and they send her.''

"There's a spot of bother in Wilkinson's Cluster—practically a state of war between human and Shaara colonists.''

"That accounts for it,'' said Jane. ''There'll be no demand for her peculiar talents there. She wouldn't get far trying to seduce a Shaara drone.''

"Will you shut up,'' exploded Calver, ''and let me finish? The Survey Service is convinced that there's something in the legends about the Outsiders. They can't spare any ships to make an immediate investigation. But they'd like to charter a ship, no doubt on very advantageous terms to the owners concerned, and I've had the offer. I've no doubt that if and when I tell the other shareholders they'll be all in favor of accepting the charter. It won't matter to them that there'll be a Survey Service observer travelling with us. And I've already told you who the observer will be.''

"No,'' said Jane. Her face was white. ''No.''

"But why not? A charter's a charter.''

"No," she said again.

"Then can you suggest any future profitable employment, my dear?"

"Can you?" she countered.

"Perhaps," he said. "Perhaps. It will be a risk, a gamble. We might lose everything, the ship and our lives. But we might be rich beyond the dreams of avarice."

She said, "I admire this melodramatic line of speech. You must have caught it off some of the charming people you know—these cloak-and-dagger types."

"Melodrama," he said, "is often much more true to life than understatement. Anyhow, this is my proposal—that we carry out my original plan of trying to find the Outsiders, for ourselves and not for the Survey Service."

"And how do you propose to persuade the others?"

He said, "That's where you will help. You'll have to talk the women into going."

"And if I don't?"

"Then I tell them about the offer of the Survey Service charter."

She looked at him with cold hostility.

She said softly, "You bastard."

9

CALVER NEVER found out how his wife talked the other women around to the idea of a private expedition in search of the Outsiders—but talk them into it she did. Her manner with him remained cold, hostile—and he knew that this hostility was as much the consequence of his blackmail as of his brief affair with Sonya Verrill. But he did not care, he told himself. He hoped that he would soon be in a position to achieve his real ambition, would soon be able to lead his crew out and away from the galaxy, to fame (perhaps) and fortune (possibly). But it was neither fame nor fortune that was the real lure. He would repeat to himself two lines of archaic poetry that, somehow, had stuck in his memory, that somehow, during these last few days had come to the surface!

For lust of knowing what should not be known
We take the Golden Road to Samarkand . . .

But the voyage, he knew, would be no golden journey. It would be a long, sickening drop into the Ultimate Nothingness, a protracted fall through the Night, away from warmth and light and humanity. It would be a weary search for the unknown, possibly the unknowable. And when it—whatever *it* was—was found, would anybody be the better off? Maudsley had found it—and it had destroyed him.

But Maudsley, thought Calver, was a weakling. . .

But Maudsley, Calver told himself, daring at last to admit doubt, was not a weakling. The Survey Service does not promote weaklings to Commander's rank.

But Maudsley, Calver insisted, must have been a weakling. Not overtly, but in some subtle way. There must have been some fatal flaw in his character.

And what guarantee, Calver asked himself, *have I that there is not some fatal flaw in my character?*

But his doubts were passing ones and his determination to see the thing through remained. While Jane, whom he rarely saw now, did her work with the women, he worked on the men. He did not tell them about the offer of the Survey Service charter, but he did hint that he had learned that the Survey Service was interested, and that it would be a feather in *The Outsider*'s cap if her people beat the Survey Service to the discovery. Old Doc Malone was his first convert, and an easy one. Said the old man, "Believe it or not, Calver, I've never been a one for tossing my bonnet over the windmill. But I'd like to be doing it just once."

"Now's your chance, Doc," Calver told him.

"Could be, could be. But the rest of you . . . You're young, all of you, and you run the risk of losing both the ship and your lives."

"And don't we," countered Calver, "every time that we push off into deep space, every time that we make a landing?"

"Yes, but . . ." Then the doctor grinned. "As far as the ship's concerned, she's covered by Lloyds."

"And as far as our lives are concerned," said Calver, "we shall be doing something useful with them."

"You hope," said Malone. "We hope."

"We hope," agreed Calver.

"But the others," persisted the Doctor.

"Lloyd and Ritter are both scientists. They're coming round to my way of thinking. Levine will follow the majority."

"And Renault and Brentano and Bendix?"

"I think they'll vote the way their wives tell them."

"And just what the hell is going on, Calver?" demanded the doctor. "I always thought that I had my fingers on the pulse of this ship, but now I'm not so sure. There's some sort of trouble between you and Jane—but then, all marriages pass through the My-God-how-the-hell-did-I-ever-get-shackled-to-this? stage. And yet this same Jane is doing her damnedest to persuade the other wives that we should drop everything and push off for Outside."

"I am not without influence," said Calver carefully.

"It seems not. And Cappell?"

Calver's face clouded. "Now that we're nearing his home planet he's feeling the call of the land again. He's already worked out that with his back pay and the resale of his shares to us he'll be able to buy and stock a sheep run. This was before the Outsider business was mentioned. I'm afraid that we shall have to let him go."

"H'm. And Brentano has only a Second Pilot's ticket and hasn't got his time in yet to sit for First. And the Port Authorities on any of the Empire of Waverley planets are sticklers for regulations. Whatever we do after Nova Caledon—tramping or our own private venture—we shall strike a snag there."

"There's bound to be somebody," said Calver, "with either a Master's or a First Pilot's Certificate."

"Is there? And if there were, would you ship another one like Maudsley on what could well be a hazardous voyage?"

"If I have to, yes. As long as we have the minimum number of tickets shown on the Articles we shall be able to blast off, and after that I can stand a watch myself if I have to."

"We shall see," said the Doctor. "We shall see. And it's not beyond the bounds of possibility that we shall be able to get a permit, in any case."

Calver looked at the doctor, and the doctor looked at Calver. Both men knew what was wrong. Both men, now, could hear the irregularity in the whining note of the Mannschenn Drive and knew that the temporal precession fields were fluctuating wildly. And then, to confirm their fears, the alarm bells started to ring.

Slowly, carefully, Calver unbuckled his seat belt and rose to his feet. It would not be wise to try to hurry. On such occasions in the past he had, now and again, tried to move fast and, as he put it later, finished up not knowing if it were breakfast time or last Thursday. Slowly, carefully, he left his cabin and went out into the alleyway and carefully, slowly, climbed the short ladder to the control room.

Brentano was on watch. There was nothing that he could do but sit there and watch the unreliable instruments. He saw Calver and said, his words coming at carefully spaced intervals, "This does not make sense."

"And what does not?" queried the Master.

"Interference effect. No other ship should have passed closely enough to us to cause it. But one has."

"Opposite trajectory?" asked Calver.

"No."

Bendix's voice came over the intercom speaker. "Captain, we must shut down. We must shut down and restart."

"Then shut down," ordered Calver. He said to Brentano, "It's a good thing that we aren't in a hurry."

Two objective weeks overdue. *The Outsider* dropped through the drizzle to Port Caledon. She fell gently through the steam generated by her flaring exhausts and grounded with a faint jar on the apron. Calver rang *Finished With Engines* then stared out through the big viewport and watched the beetle-like groundcar, from the bonnet of which fluttered the Port Administration flag, making its way over the wet concrete to the ship. Cappell unbuckled himself from his chair and went down to the airlock to receive the officials.

Calver left Brentano to make all secure and then followed his Chief Officer from the control room. In his own day cabin he found that Jane—although she was no longer in evidence—had laid out all that would be required, the decanters and glasses, the box of cigarettes and the box of cigars, the folder containing Manifest, Bill of Health and the clearance from the last port, and the crew list.

Calver sat down at his desk, filled and lit his pipe. He got to his feet again when Cappell ushered in the Customs and Immigration boarding officers and motioned them to chairs after shaking hands with them.

'Ye're late, Captain,'' said the Customs official. "Ye should ha' been here afore *Rim Caravel*. She's a'ready discharged an' loaded an' oot again.''

"Mannschenn Drive trouble," said Calver. "But I'm sorry that *Rim Caravel*'s away. I'd have liked a word or two with her Master.''

"An' whyfor, Captain?''

"The Drive trouble was due to interference. It's stretching the long arm of coincidence rather much when two ships pass closely enough for interference effect.'' He paused. "In any case, I didn't think that *Rim Caravel* was all fast, although she was *Delta* Class when she was under the Commission's flag.''

"She's no' a' that fast,'' admitted the Customs man. "But her Captain—a verry pleasant wee man —was sayin' that there was some urrgency . . .''

"And how was it that he didn't have to shut his Drive down?''

"Ah'm no' an engineer, Captain an' ah ken little aboot such matters. But mebbe his Drive's a later model, or mebbe his engineers were a' ready to adjust their controls. . . . But ah'm no' a technician.''

Grimes, thought Calver. *The old bastard. He must have given* Rim Caravel's *Master instructions. It wouldn't be all that hard for his navigator to work out our trajectory and to follow it, although it must have been rather risky to push the*

Drive to the limits of safety. . . . But what the hell has he gained by it? He's inconvenienced us, but it's done no good to either Rim Runners or himself.

Remembering his hostly duties, he poured drinks and offered cigarettes.

10

"THE MEETING," said Calver, "is called to order."

The buzz of conversation around the saloon table ceased and his officers—and fellow shareholders—turned to look at him. Jane's regard was cold, but the others, he could see, were all prepared to be friendly.

He said, "I have no need to tell you that discharge will be completed at about noon tomorrow. Mr. Bendix and Mr. Renault have assured me that their machinery is in perfect working order. There is the question of stores."

"What little we require in the way of preserved provisions can be loaded tomorrow before noon. As you know, we have not found it necessary to touch our present stocks," reported Jane.

"Thank you. Well, once again we are faced with the problem of future employment. I have made enquiries, but there are no cargoes offering out of Port Caledon in any direction. And as far as Rim Runners are concerned we're just a nuisance."

Julia Bendix removed the spectacles from her high

bridged nose and used them as a signal to attract and hold his attention. She said, "I understand that the Skoda Corporation on Carinthia is chartering tonnage to lift ore from the Sokolsky System to their smelters at New Prague."

"That is correct," confirmed Levine.

"I have given the matter some thought," said Calver, "but have come to the conclusion that every tramp with a halfway efficient psionic radio officer will already be homing on New Prague."

"And that is correct, too," said Levine.

"Carinthia is quite a way from here," went on Calver. "And we're liable to be making a long voyage and getting nothing for our pains at the end of it." He said, after a pause, "And I don't think that that's sound economics."

"It is not," agreed Julia, "but I thought it right that all of us here should be informed of the only faint hope of possible employment."

"Thank you, Julia," said Calver. "Now, all of you have been thinking me rather a monomaniac on the subject of the Outsiders. But I think you will agree that our late Mr. Maudsley did find something out there—something with which he was unable to cope. But I have faith in you, and myself, and am quite sure that we shall be able to handle it. And knowledge is not only power, it is also money."

"And knowledge," said Lloyd, "is worth acquiring for its own sake."

"Definitely," grunted Ritter.

"But how can you be sure that there is something?" quibbled Elise Renault. "Oh, I know that Jane's made it all very convincing—she nursed Mr. Maudsley during his final illness and had to listen to his ravings. But hallucinations are not unknown."

"Especially after too much alcohol," added her husband.

"I think that I can recognize the truth when I hear it, Elise," said Jane coldly.

"Yes, Jane. But an hallucination is real to the person concerned."

"Let's put it this way," said Calver. "We have two choices—a wild goose chase to Carinthia, where we shall find a traffic jam of star tramps scrambling for charters by the time we get there. Or, even more probably, the scramble will already be over and we shall just have thrown away time and fuel for sweet damn all. The second choice is another wild goose chase to Outside—but at least there'll be no cutthroat competition."

"And that's rather strange," said Renault. "Maudsley's story must be well circulated by now. How is it that nobody else has thought of investigating it? Why hasn't Grimes recommissioned *Faraway Quest* and pushed off on another of his wild goose chases?"

"As far as I can gather," Calver said, "the Commodore has some sort of a bee in his bonnet about the Outsiders. He's made up his mind that there ain't no such animals—so, as far as he's concerned, there just ain't no such animals. But I've kept my ear to the ground and, while exploring every avenue have left no stone unturned."

"I'm sure that you've explored some fascinating avenues, Derek," commented his wife, rather too sweetly.

He favored her with a forced grin. "Anyhow, I've kept my ears flapping. I know for a fact that the Survey Service people are very interested in Maudsley's story."

"Then why don't they send a ship?" demanded Renault.

"Because, at the moment, they have no ships to spare. Their entire force, except for vessels required for essential guard duties elsewhere, is tied up in Wilkinson's Cluster. There's some sort of a squabble between the Federation and the Shaara Empire. No doubt, when things simmer down, they will be sending a ship. But it would be rather nice if we got there first."

"Agreed," said Lloyd. "Speaking as scientist, I have often deplored the way in which the Survey Service classifies practically every discovery made by its own people as Top Secret, To Be Destroyed By Fire Before Reading."

"You can say that again," grunted Ritter.

"So I can take it that nobody has any real objections to the search for the Outsiders?"

"It's a wild goose chase," said old Doc Malone. "Ye're all of you callin' it that, an' ye're all of you right. But that's what I like about it."

"I suppose we have to go somewhere," contributed Bendix. "I just supply the motive power."

"I thought that I did," argued Renault. "You just put the clocks back."

"Brentano?" said Calver.

"Frankly, Captain, the idea appeals to me. We shall, at least, be getting off the tramlines."

"But the tramlines give at least an illusion of security," his wife objected, although not very strongly.

The little man grinned, "But our tramlines have been torn up, now, anyhow."

Julia Bendix went through heliographing motions with her spectacles again. She said, "We may as well put the matter to the vote, although I don't think there's much need. We've all of us talked it over among ourselves, and I think I'm right in saying that we've all agreed to let Derek have his own way for this once. After all, we can afford it. It's a gamble—but we have to be in to win. But . . ."

"But . . .?" echoed Calver.

"There's this small matter of a replacement for Cappell."

"All part of the gamble," said Calver airily. "I think it will be a calculated risk if we just lift without clearance. We shall be breaking all manner of laws, both local and galactic, but if we find what we hope to find, what will it matter? After all, we've done our best. We've tried to find an officer with the right qualifications, but there are none available. We've tried to get a permit to sail shorthanded, and if the local Shipping Master won't play, that's not our fault. After all, this is our ship and we're quite capable of taking her anywhere with the people we have."

"Up the rebels!" cried Doc Malone.

"I'm sure that I like it," said Julia.

Somebody was rapping sharply on the saloon door. "Come in!" called Calver irritably, expecting that the intruder would be a stevedore or a port official. But it was not. It was a kilted giant who strode into the compartment with a certain arrogance, the three gleaming chevrons of a Sergeant of Police prominent on his sleeve. He was followed by four constables and by two men in blue overalls.

He said, "Captain, ye'll excuse me for breakin' up this meetin', but ah've a job o' work tae dae."

"Indeed?" said Calver coldly.

"There's rumors, Captain, an' Rumoour's a lyin' jade, although she could be speakin' the truth the no. Yon Port Captain's been told that ye're thinkin' o' liftin' ship wi'oot clearance. An' that, on this planet, is classed as a crime."

"Indeed?" said Calver.

"Indeed, Captain. But we, the Police Force o' this world, tak' pride in the way in which we can prevent crime afore its commission. An' that is what we are here for."

"Indeed?" said Calver.

"Ay. An' so if yer Chief Interstellar Drive Engineer will lead the way, yon laddies . . ." he waved a huge hand towards the boiler-suited men, "will removed the governor from yer Mannschenn Drive Unit."

Calver looked at the policemen. They were armed, and his people were not. They were trained in unarmed combat, and his people were not. Furthermore, there were probably reinforcements outside the ship.

He said tiredly, "All right, Mr. Bendix."

11

CALVER STORMED into the Port Captain's office, ignoring the nervous receptionist who tried to ask him his business.

"Captain MacLaren," he demanded, "what is the meaning of your high-handed action?"

MacLaren looked both embarrassed and apologetic. He said, "Sit down, Captain. Just listen to me long enough for me to tell you that it was no action of mine. I'm a spaceman, and I'm quite sure that your ship would be better off with her present crew than with some stranger, probably an incompetent soak, added to make up the number. If it rested with me, I'd give you clearance with my blessings."

"So you're a little woolly lamb," sneered Calver, "and there's someone else behind it."

"Calver," said MacLaren, "regulations are regulations. You and I, as practical spacemen, know that they're made to be broken. But you and I both know that there are certain people connected with the shipping industry who, while they are able to quote regulations by the yard, know no more about ships than that fire comes out of one end."

"The Shipping Master," suggested Calver.

"Yes. Old Paul."

"But the way he was talking earlier I thought that I should have no trouble in getting a permit."

"And then," went on the Port Captain, "there are Mr. Paul's superiors."

"What? You mean the Department of Navigation?"

"Yes. Paul and myself may be big frogs in a small puddle in Port Caledon, but as far as the Department's concerned we're very small frogs in a big puddle. When Ministers of the Crown say, 'jump,' we jump."

"But all these bloody policemen clumping in their big boots all over my ship. . . . And immobilizing the ship."

MacLaren smiled thinly. "Come, now, Captain, would you have paid any attention to a writ tacked to the tail fin? For all I know, you have some venture in mind that would enable you to pay, without feeling it, the fine imposed for unauthorized departure—if you ever return to this or any other Empire of Waverley planet, that is. And both Mr. Paul and I were instructed—instructed, not requested—to make sure that you did not make an unauthorized departure."

"Or any other sort of departure?" asked Calver suddenly. "There was that funny business of *Rim Caravel*. We didn't see her—she wasn't in phase with us—but she overtook us and passed so close that our Drive was thrown out of kilter. Who wanted to make sure that we were delayed?"

"I know nothing about that, Captain," said MacLaren.

"And what sort of pull has Grimes got out here? I didn't think that the Rim Confederacy was on more than speaking terms with your Empire, but I must have been wrong. Why does Grimes want us delayed still further?"

"Grimes?"

"Commodore Grimes, then."

"Oh, yes. Your Astronautical Superintendent and commanding officer of your Naval Reserve. . . . But I can assure you, Calver, that Grimes has no standing here. I don't know much about politics, but our Government has always leaned more towards the Federation than to your Confederacy and, furthermore, recognized the Rim Confederacy only with extreme reluctance."

"Something stinks," said Calver.

"Yes. I admit that. As far as I'm concerned you could have blasted off from here, with my blessings, as soon as your port dues were paid. I'm sorry, Calver, but I tell you again that this is none of my doing."

Calver was ready to clutch at straws. "Your assistants," he said. "They all possess qualifications. Would either of them be willing to ship with us as Mate? I'd pay well, considerably above regular rates."

"Not a hope," MacLaren told him. "Not a hope. As a matter of fact I've already sounded them on the subject, but they're newly married, both of them, and prefer all night at home in bed to watchkeeping aboard an interstellar tramp."

"I could," said Calver, "even go so far as to sign on

an extra woman in some capacity."

"A pregnant woman?" countered the Port Captain.

"Oh." Calver got to his feet. "Well, thanks for what you've told me. I think I'll go and have a word with Mr. Paul."

"He doesn't bully easily," MacLaren told him. "The more you bully him, the less likely you are to get your permit."

Perhaps a small monetary gift, tactfully offered, thought Calver, but he did not say it. He said goodbye to MacLaren and went out into the passage. The Shipping Office was in the same building as the Port Captain's office, but at a lower level. A fast and smoothly running escalator carried him to his destination.

There were the usual clerks behind the long counter doing nothing in particular. One of them looked up. "Oh, it's Captain Calver, isn't it? Mr. Paul would like tae see ye, sir. He'll be in his office."

Calver went into the Shipping Master's little cubicle.

"Sit ye doon, Captain," said Paul jovially. He raised a warning hand. "No, afore ye lose what little temper ye have I'll tell ye that I've guid news for ye. Ay. Verra guid news."

"You're letting me have my permit?" asked Calver.

"Permit, Captain. 'Tis better news than that. Ye'll no be wantin' a permit the no."

"Indeed? So you've found a Mate for me?" He added, "Some drunken bum, I suppose, but as long as he holds at least a First Pilot's license he'll do."

"No, not a drunken bum, Captain—but a maist

effeecient officer. Some captains wouldna approve, but the way that ye a'ready ha' the ship manned it'll mak' nae deefference."

"You mean . . .?" asked Calver.

"Ay. A wumman. She came oot here as passenger in *Rim Caravel* on her way back to the Centre Worlds. But she's in nae hurry, an' when she heard ye were held up wi' crew shortage she volunteered."

"A woman," repeated Calver.

"Ye've plenty a'ready. What's yin mair? An' she holds the qualifications. No' a certificate pairhaps, but she has her Commission as Lieutenant Commander in the Survey Service, Executive Branch . . ."

"And her name," said Calver coldly, "is Sonya Verrill."

"Ye a'ready ken the lass, Captain? That makes things easier."

"Doesn't it?" said Calver.

He was waiting for her in the Shipping Office when she arrived from her hotel. She was wearing a severe business suit that accentuated rather than hid her femininity. She smiled enticingly at Paul and his clerks and even more seductively at Calver. She murmured, "Aren't you going to say, 'Welcome aboard,' Derek?"

He said, "You aren't aboard yet."

"But I shall be—otherwise you don't lift ship."

He said, "I'd like to see this commission of yours."

"But of course." She pulled out the document from her handbag. "Here."

"I thought you were Intelligence," he said.

"I am— but all of us hold commissions in the Executive Branch. We have to be able to handle ships should the need arise."

"I see." He handed the paper back to her.

Mr. Paul had the ship's Articles open on the counter. He coughed to attract attention. "If ye'll let me have some details, Miss Verrill . . . Year o' birth." She told him, adding, "Earth Standard." Calver tried to work out her age but failed. He had been so long on the Rim that he had lost touch with Terran measurements of time. Paul's stylus scratched busily. "Address of next of kin?"

"Still your brother?" asked Calver before she could answer.

"Yes, Derek. I'll give him your regards when next I write." She gave Paul the full details.

"Rank or rating . . .? Pay . . .?" These questions Calver answered. "Number and grade of certificate or commission?"

Then it was over and Calver was looking at his new Chief Officer with something short of enthusiasm. He said, "There's a bar on the next deck down. Could you use a drink?"

"I'd rather like to get myself and my gear on board, sir."

"I'm in no hurry," said Calver, with a short, apprehensive laugh. "Come on. A drink first. That's an order."

"And will it be poisoned?" she asked.

"Unfortunately," he said, "it's all at rather short notice. Had I been warned I might have arranged it." He laughed again. "I'd better warn you, while we're on the subject of poisoning, that my wife's the Catering Officer."

Old Mr. Paul chuckled tolerantly. "Anyone can

see that ye're old shipmates," he said.

"Yes," admitted Calver. "We were once. Briefly."

He remembered his kidnaping on Grollor by Sonya Verrill and her brother, and the subsequent destruction of the space yacht *Star Rover*. That had been a sticky situation—but not one half so sticky as this one promised to be.

12

"Name your poison," he said, as though the words were to be taken literally.

"Scotch on the rocks," she said. "The local variety isn't too bad."

He said, "I'll have the same," and gave the order to the barman.

When the drinks had been placed before them he raised his glass but was at a loss for a suitable toast. Finally he muttered, "Mud in your eye."

"And in yours," she responded.

They sipped in silence.

She said, "You don't like me, Derek."

He looked at her, finally admitting, "That's not altogether true, Sonya, but . . ."

"But you like to keep your wives and your popsies in airtight compartments."

"Too right," he admitted. "And furthermore . . ."

"Furthermore?"

"I certainly don't like what you've been doing."

"What have I been doing?" she asked sweetly.

"What haven't you been doing?" he exploded. "You traveled out here in *Rim Caravel*. You persuaded her Master to calculate our trajectory and to follow it, knowing that interference effect would throw our Drive out of kilter and knowing, too, that his engineers, being ready for it, would be able to make the necessary adjustments to their own Mannschenn Drive Unit. So *Rim Caravel* beat us to Port Caledon by a handsome margin, leaving you to make all your arrangements. Come to that, I suppose that you got at Cappell before we shoved off from Port Faraway."

"No," she told him. "I didn't. Although I must confess that I considered Cappell the weak link in your chain."

"And the rest?" he persisted.

"Could be." She shrugged. "Could be not. I'm not saying."

"It doesn't much matter." He shrugged in his turn. "I know that you were behind it all. What I do object to is being used as a cat's paw by your blasted Survey Service."

She said, "I suppose that it does rankle more than somewhat. But try to look at it sensibly, Derek. Oh, I know damn well that your ship is staffed by a team of exceptionally competent spacemen and spacewomen, but none of you have Survey experience. I have."

"Yes, that's all very well. But if—when—we find the Outsiders, for whom will you be working? For the ship, or for the Federation? Will you be Miss Sonya Verrill, Chief Officer of *The Outsider,* or will you be Lieutenant Commander Verrill, Federation Survey Service, Intelligence Branch? That's what I want to know. That, both as Master and as Chairman of the Board, I have every right to know."

"You have," she admitted. "You have, Derek. And it's only right that all this should be ironed out before I set foot inside your airlock."

"It should have been ironed out before I let you sign," he growled.

"It should," she grinned. "You slipped up there. But if I hadn't been allowed to sign you'd have had a long, long wait for either a Chief Officer or a permit to sail shorthanded. However, I'm prepared to be quite honest with you. Cards on the table and all that. And if you aren't satisfied we'll go back to Mr. Paul and I'll tell him that I've changed my mind and that you've agreed to pay me off by mutual consent. I shan't even claim the day's pay to which I shall be entitled. And I promise you, too, that you'll be getting your permit within a couple of days at the outside."

"Fair enough," he grunted. "Fair enough. All right, Sonya, go ahead and satisfy me."

"I've already raised the point," she said, "about my being experienced in exploration and survey work."

"It's a good one," he conceded.

"It is. But I think that what really worries you is my ambiguous status. In more ways than one."

"You can say that again," he told her.

"Let's skip the personal side of it," she said. "For the time being, anyhow. . . All right—I'm a commissioned officer of the Federation's armed forces. As such, I'm bound by oath to make a full report on anything discovered. But, as you already know, it will be some little time before we, the Survey Service, are able to release any ships for exploration, and whatever claim you may make on whatever is found out there will be valid. The Service has always honored the old principle of finders are keepers. But they like to know just what has been found, and it will be up to me to keep them informed."

"H'm," he grunted.

"And always bear in mind, Derek, that I'm bound just as much by my signature on your Articles as by my oath to the Service. I'm on your books as Chief Officer, and I'll do the job to the best of my ability. Should I be required to draw upon my experience as a Survey Service officer on your behalf, I shall do so cheerfully. I'll earn my keep. Have no doubts about that."

"I haven't," he said. "But . . ."

"All right." She gestured as though throwing playing cards down to the polished surface of the bar. "Here's the rest of my hand, such as it is. This business is personally important to me. Very important."

"That," he said glumly, "is what I was most afraid of."

She laughed rather bitterly. "Men!" she flared. "The supreme egotists! And you, my dear, are no exception to the rule. Oh, I like you, Derek, make no mistake about that. But please give me credit for enough intelligence to be able to refrain from throwing your beloved ship into a state of turmoil. You can tell your everloving wife that, as far as I'm concerned, the policy will be strictly hands off." Her face clouded. "But this is a personal matter. Rather more years ago than I care to remember, Bill Maudsley and I were lovers. We broke up, but we shouldn't have done it. There were faults on both sides—as aren't there always—but we . . . matched. And it was in the cards that we'd be coming together again; there was no hurry, but the first feelers had already been put out. And then the reports came in about his disgrace—I wanted to come out here then, but I couldn't be spared—and then, eventually, about his death. . .

"And I want to find out what killed him."

He killed himself, thought Calver. *But did he? But doesn't any man, no matter how he dies, kill himself?*

"You can't blame me," Sonya Verrill was saying. "You can't blame me for wanting to know."

"I can't," he said.

As they approached the ship, following the truck upon which Sonya's baggage was loaded, they saw that it was almost ready for space. Gantries and conveyor belts had been withdrawn, and on its slender mast, an extension of the needle-pointed stem, the intensely brilliant red light, the so-called Blue Peter, was blinking. The only side port remaining open was that at the airlock.

"You have good officers," commented Sonya.

"We have good officers," he corrected her.

"So you've accepted me," she said.

"What choice had I?" he countered, grinning.

There was somebody standing in the airlock. Calver could see who it was, and his brief mood of cheerfulness abruptly departed. At first, when he had seen the state of readiness of his ship, he had berated himself for indulging in two stiff drinks almost immediately prior to blast-off, now he was sorry that he hadn't taken three.

"So you're back," said Jane coldly. "We're all ready for space."

"Formalities can't be hurried," he replied, with equal coldness.

"But I thought that you'd found and signed on a Chief Officer," she said.

"I did," he said.

"Where is he?" she demanded.

"Jane," he said, "meet Miss Sonya Verrill—or Lieutenant Commander Sonya Verrill—who'll be shipping with us as Mate."

"The word 'Mate'," she said, "is capable of several interpretations."

"Mrs. Calver," said Sonya, "I assure you that I'm qualified for the job."

"Which job?" asked Jane.

"Miss Verrill," ordered Calver, "will you get aboard, please?" He saw the Second Officer fidgeting behind Jane. "Mr. Brentano, will you please attend to the Chief Officer's baggage and show her to her cabin? And Mrs. Calver, I shall be obliged if you will go to your blast-off station."

"Is this how you keep your word, Derek?" she asked quietly.

"Circumstances beyond my control . . ." he began.

"You should learn to control yourself," she told him.

"Jane," he said, "go to your station. Please. I'll explain everything as soon as we've got this bitch upstairs."

"I hope that you can," she said.

Inside the ship intercom speakers had come to life. It was Sonya's voice, crisp, authoritative with a real Survey Service crackle to it. "Secure all! Secure all for space! Secure all!"

"Doesn't waste much time, does she?" asked Jane bitterly.

13

So *THE OUTSIDER* fell through the twisted blackness, the warped infinity, out from the Empire of Waverley towards the Rim. But it was not only the continuum that was warped and twisted. There was warping and twisting in the personalities of her people, hostilities and jealousies and frustrations. There was Calver, leading a lonelier life than he had ever led before as Master, keeping to himself, living alone and not liking it. There was Sonya Verrill, given the respect that was due to her by virtue of her rank, no less but no more. There was Jane, discharging her duties with a certain bored efficiency but determined not to mingle socially.

There was the rest of the crew, all of whom knew, by now, how things stood and all of whom were determined, even old Doc Malone, to keep their own yardarms clear. They resented Sonya's presence

aboard the ship and resented still more that machin-
ations that had resulted in her being signed on as
Chief Officer—but, as Malone put it, they would give
her a fair crack of the whip. She was Mate and she
was doing her job as such. And Calver was Master,
and he was doing his job. And Jane was the Catering
Officer, and nobody was going hungry. As long as
things did not blow up between the three of them, the
ship would run, would arrive, in the fullness of time,
at her destination. Malone said cynically, "I don't
give a damn who does what to whom as long as I
don't have to pay."

But nobody was doing anything to anybody.
Calver kept himself to himself, and Sonya Verrill
kept herself to herself, and Jane, in her off-duty hours
was unapproachable. And the ship functioned as
well as she had ever functioned, watch succeeding
watch in control room and engine room, seemingly independent of the tangled lives of her senior
officers.

Until . . .

It was Sonya Verrill's watch and Calver had occasion to visit the control room to make a routine check
of the ship's position. The girl watched him as he
stood before the big chart tank, as he set up the ex-
trapolation of the trajectory from the latest fix.

She said, "Derek, this can't go on."

Calver adjusted the controls until the luminescent
filament had firmed, looking like a fine, incandescent
wire in the blackness of the tank. Then he looked up
and around. He asked, "What can't go on?"

"This," she said. "This situation. Damn it all, I
shouldn't mind all the disapproval so much if we
were doing something. But we aren't. You're leading

the life of a monk, and I might as well be in a nunnery. So, come to that, might your wife." She grinned wryly. "There's nothing so annoying as being punished for uncommitted crimes."

"But we aren't being punished," he said.

"Aren't we? I've sailed in taut ships, Derek, really taut ships, commanded by the more notorious martinets of the Survey Service. But none of them could hold a candle to this one. Everybody growled, but, compared to this set-up, everybody was happy. The game's crooked and you know it."

"So the game's crooked," he agreed. "But what can we do about it?"

"You're Master," she told him.

"So I'm Master. And you, my dear, are Mate—and, as such, responsible for the smooth running of the vessel."

She said, "But she is running smoothly. That's the worst part of it all. She's running too smoothly. I'd welcome some sort of a blow-up."

"No ship can run too smoothly," he said stiffly.

"But too much is being bottled up," she said. "The longer it's bottled up the worse it will be."

"And what do you expect me to do?" he asked. "Give the order, 'All hands unbottle'? What was the orthodox technique in the Survey Service in situations such as this?"

"In the Survey Service," she told him, "such situations would never be allowed to arise."

"No? Well, I suppose when you have a large pool of officers you can make sure that incompatibles aren't allowed to ship together. But you, my dear, made sure that we had no large pool of officers to pick and choose from."

She said, "I suppose that we, you and I, are incompatible."

He said, "That's just the trouble. We aren't, and everybody knows it."

She said, "Why the hell can't you and Jane make it up?"

"Jane doesn't like you," he told her. "She never has, not from the very start. And that was when she and I were just getting acquainted."

"Spare me the details. She didn't like me when you and she were no more than casual shipmates. She dislikes me still more now."

"She has her reasons," said Calver.

"All right, she has reasons. But I, as you know, have my reasons for being aboard this rustbucket of yours. I'm not here for love of you."

"Thank you. And I never asked to have you here. All I wanted was a permit so that I could get the hell off Nova Caledon without delay."

"But I am here," she said.

"Too right you are," he agreed. "Too bloody right."

"Well," she demanded, "what are you doing about it?"

"I suppose," he said slowly, "that I could push Jane out through the airlock without a spacesuit—although I doubt if the others would back me up. Or I could do the same to you. Or, better still, to both of you."

She told him, "You are a sadistic bastard, you know."

He said, "That's the way that I feel just now."

"Then why don't you do something about it?"

"About what?"

"About this bloody absurd situation, you fool."

He said, "I just might, at that."

"What, master mind?"

"We can, at least, take the strain off ourselves. To hell with everybody else."

"Including Jane?"

"Including Jane."

She said, "I'm a woman, and what you suggest runs counter to the rules of the lodge to which all women belong. But if she won't see reason . . ."

"She won't," said Calver.

"All right."

"You come off watch at twenty-hundred hours," said Calver, "and there's no reason why the Chief Officer shouldn't have a quiet drink with the Master in her watch below."

"There's not," agreed Sonya. "But . . ." She went on after a pause, "Oh, damn the stinking atmosphere aboard this ship! There are so many people, interesting people, charming people, whom I'd love to meet and to talk with. But all of them treat me as though I were an ambulatory case of Venusian Purple Rot. And I know whose fault that is."

"Not altogether," objected Calver, trying hard to be fair. "After all, just bear in mind that everybody is scared of getting involved in a nasty mess. They just refuse to take sides."

"Could be. But that's all the more reason why we untouchables should stick together."

"Twenty-hundred hours, then," said Calver, leaving the control room.

It was good, thought Calver, to be able to enjoy female company in his cabin once more, even though it was not Jane. He looked at Sonya as she sat in her chair, as she contrived to convey the impression of graceful relaxation even though she was, perforce, strapped into the piece of furniture by her seat belt. He handed her another bulb of his prized *lacrissa* brandy and took another for himself from his wine locker.

"Well, Captain," she said, "the voyage progresses. It will not be long before we're on the leads—Macbeth in line with Kinsolving's Sun. And then . . ."

He said, "That will be the hardest part. The leads might have been, by sheer chance, dead accurate when Maudsley brought *Polar Queen* back to the Rim from Outside—but they won't be so accurate now. There's galactic drift, you know."

She said, "I'm a navigator. I know."

"But a few simple calculations," he went on, "combined with a search pattern."

"Yes." She sipped from her bulb. She said suddenly, "I wish that your clever Mr. Brentano had this cabin bugged. I wish that your wife could overhear this conversation."

"Keep her out of it," said Calver sharply.

"Why? She's probably assuming the worst—and here we are, quietly swigging brandy and talking shop."

He said, "That's why I invited you here."

She said, "You're a bloody liar, Derek, and we both of us know it."

Calver said, "So I'm a bloody liar. So what?"

"I like to be frank," she told him.

"But can't you see," insisted Calver, "that it would be quite impossible, here, in this ship? Things are bad enough now; let's not make them worse."

"They couldn't be worse," Sonya said practically. "Everybody knows that the new Mate is the Master's mistress. We might as well be hung for sheep as lambs."

"I'd prefer not be hung," he said, then corrected himself pedantically. "Hanged, I mean."

"Hanged or hung—what's the difference? You still get a sore throat."

"Have some more gargle," suggested Calver.

"Thank you, dear. But isn't this domesticated? Remind me next time to bring my knitting."

"I'll do that," promised Calver.

"Seriously, Derek, what's wrong with us?"

"You know. It just wouldn't be decent to do anything here and now."

"My good man," she said patiently, "we've been over all that before. Furthermore, your everloving wife won't let you sleep with her. She's applying sexual sanctions. If she were here, in this cabin, as she should be, I should not be here. Nature abhors a vacuum—and that applies to human nature as well as to physics."

"But . . ."

"Fellow shareholders or no fellow shareholders, you're still the Master. You're the law and the prophets. For example, if you were to say to me, 'Miss Verrill, take off your shirt,' I should obey the order."

He said, "Sonya, I didn't say anything of the kind."

"You've been thinking it," she told him. "I've been watching you eying the cleavage ever since I parked my fanny in your best armchair."

She unfastened the last button and shrugged

herself free of the garment. She made no attempt to hide her breasts—and, thought Calver, it would have been criminal to have hidden them. She said, "Well?"

"I spent a few weeks on Hygea," he told her carefully. "You know it, no doubt. Nudism, vegetarianism, total abstinence."

"And we aren't vegetarians," she said, "neither are we total abstainers. So any incidental nudism doesn't count. Or does it?"

Calver unstrapped himself from his chair and pushed away from it so that he floated gently towards the door. He snapped the catch on the lock. When he turned he saw that Sonya was divesting herself of her shorts. He felt absurdly—or not so absurdly?—guilty as he started to throw aside his own garments.

But if he was going to be blamed for something he might as well do whatever it was he was being blamed for.

And, in any case, he wanted to do it.

Badly.

"It's been too long," whispered Sonya.

"Too long," he whispered.

"We . . . We needed this . . ."

The intercom phone was buzzing irritably. Reluctantly, Calver let go of the girl, drifted away from her, reluctant to let his attention wander from the pale, lovely body floating there in the semi-darkness. He fumbled along the bulkhead until his hand closed on the instrument. He pulled it from its clip and raised it to his mouth.

"Captain here."

"Acting Third Officer here," said Elise Renault

stiffly. "There is an emergency."

"Well, what is it?" demanded Calver sharply.

"It's your wife. She's locked herself in the Mannschenn Drive Room."

Calver cursed bitterly as he fumbled for his shorts and sandals. He pulled them on and rushed out into the alleyway.

14

CALVER DARED to hurry to the Mannschenn Drive Room; as yet there were no indications that the gyroscopes had been tampered with, that the temporal precession field was fluctuating. He hurried, pulling himself hand over hand along the guide rails, kicking off from bulkheads, swimming through the air, through shafts and alleyways, with the speed possible only to an experienced spaceman. He hurried—and yet there were long pauses, too long, the drifting from bulkhead to bulkhead, during which he was able to think, to worry and to blame himself. He had heard stories of what happened to people when they were in too close a proximity to a misbehaving Mannschenn Drive Unit, and they were not pretty stories. Even when turned inside out, literally, a human being will survive for a while, too long a while.

He realized that Sonya was following him. He paused, half turned his head, snarled, "You'd better keep out of this."

"But, Derek, as Chief Officer."

"As Chief Officer you should be in the control room in an emergency—especially when the Master is required elsewhere."

"All right," she said. "You know where to find me."

Calver continued his nightmare fall through the free falling ship, the ship that, at any moment, might fall through and into a nightmare beyond all imagination. *No,* thought Calver, *not a nightmare, not a bad dream, but an evil reality of hopelessly twisted space and time. . . .*

But outlines were not wavering yet, and colors were not sagging down the spectrum, and there was, as yet, no insane repetition of words and thoughts and actions. There was still time. Almost as clearly as though he were in the Interstellar Drive Room himself he could visualize Jane standing before the gleaming intricacy of spinning and ever precessing gyroscopes, hypnotized by their uncanny motion, mind and will drawn from her, dragged from her and sent whirling down the dark infinites. . . . Or, perhaps, at this moment she was selecting some heavy tool from the rack, some spanner or the like, to send crashing into the heart of the weird, shimmering complexity.

Bendix was there in the alleyway outside the Mannschenn Drive Room, and with him were Renault and Lloyd. Lloyd was stammering, "But, Mr. Bendix, I just slipped out for a couple of minutes to the toilet. . . . How was I to know . . . ?"

"You should have called me," growled his chief.

"But Mrs. Calver had just looked in. . . . She said that she'd stood an occasional M.D. watch in other ships."

"That's true," said Calver. "She knows enough to be able to shut it down in a hurry if things go wrong."

"Oh," grunted Bendix. "You're here at last, Calver. Well, this is your ship, and that's your wife locked in there with my tame gyroscopes—although how long they're going to stay tame I shouldn't like to say. What are you doing about it?"

"Cut off the power supply at the mains," said Calver promptly.

Bendix swore disgustedly, then said, "And do you think I never thought of that? Oh, it'd work all right —as long as there was somebody there able—and willing—to do all the right things. Jane might be able —but is she willing? You know what will happen if the gyroscopes start toppling, don't you?"

Calver knew.

He knew as much as anybody—although that was not much. He had heard the stories of ships lost in time rather than in space, had himself visited planets that must have been colonized by human beings millenia before man sent his first clumsy rockets climbing painfully towards Luna, let alone dispatched his first ships to the stars. He had heard and read the stories, and had seen some of the evidence supporting them.

The intercom speaker on the bulkhead crackled sharply and the men heard Jane's voice, "Is my husband there?"

Silently Renault handed Calver a microphone. Calver said quietly, "Yes, I'm here, Jane. Will you come out of the Mannschenn Drive Room, please, and let Mr. Lloyd resume his watch?"

"No," she said.

He asked coldly, "What do you intend doing in there?"

She replied, "I'm not quite sure yet, my dear." She made the term of affection sound like an epithet. "I'm not quite sure. I'm leafing through the manual at the moment. Who knows what ideas I may get from it? But I can tell you one thing I shall do—if there are any attempts to break down or to burn open this door, then I shall take a heavy spanner to the governor."

"This is mutiny," said Calver coldly.

"So it is, my sweet, so it is," she agreed. "And mutiny's a crime, isn't it? And adultery isn't. Unfortunately."

He snapped, "Jane, don't be so absurdly possessive."

"Possessive, is it?" She laughed. "Do you remember how you carried on, Derek, when I went out for a few drinks at Port Tharn with the captain of *Rim Wyvern*? Or was that, somehow, different?"

"Courtney," said Calver, "is one of the more notorious wolves in the Rim Runners fleet."

"But you," she pointed out, "can carry on with one of the more notorious bitches in the Intelligence Branch of the Survey Service."

Calver was silent.

"The double standard," she went on, after a pause. "Convenient, isn't it, for men like you." She paused again. "Of course, it wasn't the blackmail that I minded so much. I know you well enough to realize that you'll stop at nothing to get what you really want. The blackmail was bad enough, but it was the broken promises afterwards that were just a little too much. You forced me into helping you to attain your crazy ambition—and then, *then,* you work things so that your tow-headed trollop sails in this ship—*our* ship."

"That," said Calver without expression, "was none of my doing."

"Wasn't it?" She laughed without mirth. "Wasn't it? Whom do you think you're fooling, Derek Calver? Not I, for a start."

"It was none of my doing," repeated Calver.

"Oh, you poor, little, innocent woolly lamb, helpless in the jaws of the big, bad, bitch wolf. My heart bleeds for you. Or it would, if I didn't despise you so much."

"I would suggest," said Calver, "that you leave all this name calling until later and tell us just what the hell you are playing at."

"But there may not be a later," she told him. "There won't be if I manage to bring back yesterday —or the day before, or the decade before or whenever. What period do you wish to return to, Derek? That sort of honeymoon of ours on Mellise, just before the hurricane? Although the hurricane itself wasn't bad. It was better than this. Or would you prefer that time on Grollor when you got entangled with the commissioned popsy again and were stashed away aboard *Star Rover?* Play the scene over again—and then you can make a few changes. You can sell out to the Survey Service then instead of waiting until now. It will save quite a deal of trouble and ill feeling."

Bendix was whispering, "Keep her talking, Captain, and I'll get the cutting and burning tools along."

She said lightly, "That's a very sensitive microphone you have there, Derek. Not that it matters. As soon as you tried to break in, I'd know—and then we'd all find out what happens when a really heavy spanner is slung into the works."

Calver turned to the Interstellar Drive Chief. "And what will happen if a spanner is slung into the works, Bendix?"

Bendix said, "I'd sooner not find out, Captain."

"These big, strong men," scoffed Jane. "All of you wanting to push out into the unknown, the unknowable—but when you have the unknown on your very front doorstep you shy away from it. This is it, Derek. You wanted the unknown so very, very badly, my dear. Now you shall have it, served up on a silver tray and trimmed with parsley."

"Jane!" roared Calver. "That's enough of this tomfoolery. Stop whatever you're doing and come out of there. At once."

"Ay, ay, Captain. Ay, ay, my left foot. But what will you promise if I agree to come out? What will you promise this time? And how long will you keep your promise?"

"She's enjoying making you squirm, Calver," said Bendix, not without a certain glum satisfaction. "The trouble is that she's making us all squirm."

"That's all very well," put in Renault, "but it's time that somebody did something about something."

"You could remember to use your depilatory cream each morning," suggested Jane. "Just for a start, that is." She started to giggle, and Calver felt the beginnings of hope. "Oh, there's so much, so very much that could be done to clean this ship up. You're all of you lazy, untidy..." She giggled again. "How would it be if we went back in time to the Stone Age? Don't you think that you'd all be much happier scratching around on a kitchen midden? Or just gnawing your mammoth bones more or less clean and tossing them out of the cave to fall where they might? Men," she went on, "are quite impossible, really. Untidy, undisciplined, lecherous." She added confidentially, "You know, they drink too. Boozing and wenching—the male's idea of paradise. Slurping up anything that tastes like liquor and carrying on with little blonde trollops. It wouldn't be so bad if they weren't married, of course. But when they are, it's rather much." There was quite a long silence, and when she resumed, her voice betrayed the beginnings of hysteria. "But I'm changing all that. Or punishing it. I'm sending this ship full of swine back to some pigsty in the past. . . . If I can . . . If . . . I . . . can . . . Damn thish print! Why musht the barshtardsh make it sho shmall? An' all theshe blashted shwitchesth an' dialsh an' metersh . . . But why worry? There'sh shpanner, ishn't there? Where'sh bloody thing got to? Ah, here. Shpanner, one number, chrome plated, coming up . . . Coming . . ."

. . . *down!* thought Calver with sick desperation.

And nothing happened. The four men, their faces white and tense, stared at each other, but nothing had happened, nothing was happening. The thin, high whine of the Mannschenn Drive, from behind the locked door, did not vary.

Sonya Verrill came along the alleyway. There was a smugness in her expression that Calver did not like. She said briskly, "Mr. Bendix, you can break in now."

"Not so fast," snapped Calver. "Miss Verrill, what have you done?"

"S.O.P. in the Survey Service," she told him airily. "The procedure worked out to deal with situations such as this. It's not unknown for people to go round the bend in the Mannschenn Drive Room—and if we have time we pump anaesthetic gas through the ventilating system. I called out Dr. Malone to supply the anaesthetic, and Mr. Brentano to lend a hand with the isolating valves."

"She's not hurt?" asked Calver anxiously.

"Not physically. She'll not even have a hangover."

"There are more and deeper hurts than the physical," whispered Calver.

"And if she isn't hurt," growled Bendix, "it will be no thanks to either of you."

They waited in silence while Lloyd went to fetch the cutting torch.

15

CALVER KEPT to his own quarters, seeing nobody unless required to do so on ship's business. He was thinking too much and he was drinking too much. He hoped that the drinking would inhibit his thought processes, but it did not. He was thinking too much and he was remembering too much, harking back to the old days before the skein of his life became so hopelessly tangled. He could not blame Jane for this, but neither could he blame Sonya. He tried to blame himself, but even this he found difficult. He had acted as he had acted because he was himself, Derek Calver, his personality the resultant of his years of experience both in deep space and on various planetary surfaces. He had reacted to external stimuli as surely as the dogs—still famous after how many centuries?—which had been the subjects of the experiments made by the ancient Russian Pavlov.

Old Doc Malone came to see him.

"Derek," said the ship's physician, his usually jovial face grave, "we have to land Jane."

"Where?" asked Calver, sipping from his bulb of brandy.

"You're the navigator."

"It will mean delay," said Calver.

The doctor exploded. "For the love of all the odd gods of the galaxy, man, snap out of it! The Outsiders—if there are any Outsiders—have been waiting for centuries, or millenia. There's no urgency. A few weeks, or months, are neither here nor there. If you keep Jane cooped up aboard this ship a minute longer than you have to, I'll not answer for the consequences."

Calver squeezed out the last of the brandy from the bulb and tossed it towards the disposer. It missed and drifted aimlessly in the air of the cabin, a tiny, deflated, crumpled balloon. The doctor looked at it and looked at a half dozen or so of its predecessors. He said, "This was a happy ship. Now she's bound to hell in a handbasket."

"Is she?" asked Calver, without much interest.

"Damn it all, you're the Master. Take charge, can't you?"

"I am in charge. And all my officers are highly efficient."

"Your Catering Officer is not. If it's of any interest at all to you—which I'm beginning to doubt—she's been suspended from her duties, and Tanya Brentano's taken over."

"That explains the Slavic flavor to the cuisine," murmured Calver. "I was rather wondering. But why?"

"Because, Captain, none of us want to wake up in the morning to find ourselves dead of poisoning. You may be surprised to learn that it's neither you nor

your popsy that's being blamed for the present state
of affairs, but your wife. If she'd taken a kitchen knife
to either you or Sonya everybody would have said
that she was quite justified, but she didn't. Instead
she tried to hit at you through the ship, thereby hazarding the lives of all on board. So nobody loves poor
Jane, and poor Jane loves nobody. All of which
makes any sort of cure quite impossible as long as she
remains in this tin coffin."

"Cure for what?" asked Calver. "You assured me
that the anaesthetic gas you used was perfectly safe."

"And so it is safe. It did no harm at all to her,
either physically or mentally. What did the harm
was the period of emotional stress which, under the
circumstances, is continuing, and then staring too
long into those damned, uncanny gyroscopes. I've
always been scared of the bloody things myself."

"Have a drink," offered Calver, extending a long
arm to his locker.

"I'd like one, but I'm not having one with you,
Derek. Not now. I'll not encourage you. Alcohol's a
good staff, but a poor crutch, and you're making too
much of a crutch of it."

"Am I?"

"You are. Now, just leave that bulb in the cabinet
and talk things over sensibly. We have to deviate
from our trajectory, and it's up to you to decide
where we deviate to. We have to land Jane so that she
may receive proper treatment and attention."

"Of course," Calver pointed out, "if we deviate
and make for the nearest port, it might be better to
keep Jane on board and pay off Sonya."

"It would not. The ship holds too many memories,
unhappy ones, for Jane. Furthermore, I haven't the
drugs and the apparatus, even if I knew how to use

them. You know as well as I do that ship's doctors are never able to keep up with the latest advances in any field of medicine. Too, I'll admit that I want to get to the bottom of this Outsider mystery as much as you do and I realize that Sonya, with her Survey Service experience, will be very useful indeed."

"I thought," said Calver, "that everybody hated her guts, everybody but me, that is."

"That might have been the case at first," admitted Malone. "But she's a good Chief Officer, and now that she's keeping out of your hair—or are you keeping out of hers? She's proving herself to be a good shipmate. She's got the women eating out of her hand now, and that helps a lot."

"So she's poisoned their minds against Jane," said Calver.

"She has not, Derek. She's frank and honest, and has made it quite plain that she operates according to her own code of morals and that she's never been in the habit of picking anything up unless its been cast aside by its rightful owner."

"I suppose I was cast aside," interjected Calver.

Malone ignored this. He went on, "One result has been, of course, that all the wives have made it quite plain that each of them consider her husband to be the most marvelous man in the universe. Which hasn't been at all a bad thing for the husbands."

"That's what Jane should have done," said Calver.

"Precisely. That's what Jane should have done, and then we shall all have been spared a lot of trouble. But Jane is Jane."

"Jane is Jane," agreed Calver, "and I wouldn't want her changed."

"Wouldn't you, now?"

"H'm. I suppose I could suggest a few improvements. . . . If she were a little less possessive, for example. I'm inclined to think that her possessiveness has been the real cause of most of the trouble."

"Go on," urged Malone. "Go on."

"It's a pity that we haven't a couch in here," said Calver wryly, "although it's not really required in free fall, is it? But I'll go on. Yes, she's very possessive. And I think she was jealous—is jealous— of the Outsiders as much as of Sonya. Women who get married and become domesticated when they're past their first youth often are that way."

"Go on," said Malone. "Go on. And just study in your spare time and work for a degree or so in medicine and you'll be able to go ashore as a psychiatrist."

Calver grinned. "That's far, very far, from my intentions. But you know as well as I do that anybody who has served for a long time in passenger ships is bound to acquire a rough and ready working knowledge of psychology."

"Then why the hell haven't you used it?" demanded Malone.

"Because," admitted Calver, "I've been too lazy, or too cowardly, or both, to use this knowledge in my dealings either with myself or with my nearest and dearest."

"But there's hope for you yet," encouraged Malone.

"Thank you."

"Now, Derek, listen to me. I know you're the Captain and I'm only the ancient, barely competent quack. I admit that I couldn't take a ship from Point

A to Point B—come to that, neither could you without the help of your assorted technicians—but I've knocked around the galaxy for rather more years than you have. And there's one firm conclusion I've come to; slinging blame around never serves any useful purpose. No, not even when you blame yourself. But . . . but you should know yourself, and, as far as it is possible, know others. And the more you know, the less you'll be inclined to blame."

"I have been thinking along those lines," admitted Calver.

"Good. Then you've made a start. And I hope that you'll be able, now, to land Jane to a hospital without feeling too much of a heel about it. And if you want to sleep with your blonde popsy, do so, as long as the ship doesn't suffer. Just be yourself. You're not a bad sort of a bastard, when all's said and done."

"But it's all so . . . so callous," objected Calver.

"I suppose it is. But remember this—in all the millenia of man's recorded history it's been the sentimentalists, the nobly self-sacrificing types, who've done the most damage. Sonya's selfish and honest about it, but she's done far less damage to this ship and this enterprise than you have done."

"I'll do some more thinking on those lines," promised Calver.

"Do just that, but don't brood. And now, if you don't mind, I'll be taking that drink. I've earned it."

"I'll have one with you," said Calver, "and then I must get up to Control to see about this deviation."

16

SLOWLY, SLOWLY, *The Outsider* dropped down to her berth at Port Forlorn. It was unfortunate, thought Calver, sitting glumly in the captain's chair in the control room while Sonya Verrill handled the ship, that Lorn had been the most suitable planet to which to deviate, in terms of both distance and medical facilities. It was unfortunate, he thought, and then reproved himself for his egocentricity. He knew how he was feeling, but how was Jane feeling? It must be worse for her.

For Lorn held so many memories, too many memories. Lorn was the world upon which it had all started: his entering the Rim Runners' service, his signing on the Articles of *Forlorn Lady*, his first meeting with Jane. And now the ship was gone, lost off Eblis during her attempt to salvage the Trans-Galactic Clipper *Thermopylae*—and Maclean, who had been her Mate, was gone—killed in a drunken brawl on Tharn. And Captain Engels was gone, his tired old heart having ceased to beat during the hurricane on Mellise.

And now Jane was going.

Sonya was saying something.

"Yes?" asked Calver, snapping out of his morbid reverie.

"Do you wish to take over now, Captain?"

"No thank you, Miss Verrill. You've done a good job so far."

And hasn't she just? he thought. Then—*No, that's unfair. She's been no more than the catalyst, happening along at the right moment—or the wrong one. If I hadn't been so willing to be led astray. . . . And if Jane had tried to hold me in a more intelligent manner.*

He stared out through the viewports to the uninviting scene below, to the vista of barren hills and mountains scarred by mine workings, to the great slag heaps that were almost mountains themselves, to the ugly little towns, each one of which was dominated by the tall, smoke-belching chimneys of factories and refineries, to the rivers that, even from this altitude, looked like sluggish streams of sewage.

He heard Sonya swear, heard her mutter, "A cross wind, blast it."

He said, "It's always windy on Lorn, and the wind is always cold and dusty and stinking with the fumes of burning sulphur."

Brentano said, "What a pity we have to leave Jane on a world like this."

"Doc assured me," Calver told him stiffly, "that the facilities here for dealing with any form of space neurosis are as fine as those anywhere in the galaxy."

Port Forlorn was close now, too close for further conversation, the dirty, scarred concrete apron rushing up to meet them. *The Outsider* dropped through a swirling cloud of coruscating particles, the dust raised by her back-blast and fired to brief incandescence. She touched, sagged tiredly, her structure creaking like old bones. The sudden silence, as the rockets died, seemed unnatural.

Sonya Verrill broke it. "Secure all, Captain?"

"Secure all," he said.

"That looks like the ambulance," stated Brentano.

"Will you go down to the airlock, Mr. Brentano, to see to the arrangements?" said Calver.

The others left the control room. He was alone with Sonya.

She said, a little bitterly, "I suppose you're blaming me."

He said slowly, "No. I'm not sure that I blame myself, even." He shrugged. "Life's a mess, really. You can want too much, and when you get it it's no use to you. No use at all."

She told him, "If you like, Derek, I'll drop off here."

"That will solve nothing, Sonya." He grinned wryly. "After all, we still have to find the Outsiders. And as you pointed out, some time ago, you have Survey Service experience." More to himself than to her he added, "Might as well save something out of the wreck."

"There are times," she whispered, "when I hate you. And this is one of them. You know that I want to find whatever's out there as much as you do, for my own reasons. But . . ." She flared suddenly, "Damn it all, there are decencies."

The intercom phone buzzed. Calver picked up the instrument. "Yes," he said after a pause. "Yes. I'll be right down." His face, when he turned back to Sonya, was old and strained.

Sonya said, "Derek, if it will help at all, tell her that I'm leaving here."

He demanded, "What will that solve? The Mannschenn Drive is as much responsible for her state as any emotional strain. She has to have proper attention, ashore. It is quite out of the question for her to remain on board."

"But for her to know that the ship has blasted off from Port Forlorn, with myself still a member of the crew."

"We need you," said Calver. "And we need your experience. This isn't an ordinary commercial voyage, as you have already pointed out."

The telephone buzzed again.

"Are you afraid to say goodbye to her?" asked the girl.

"No," he snapped. He spoke sharply into the instrument. "Yes, Mr. Brentano. I'm on my way."

He left the control room and took the elevator down to the after airlock. Brentano was there, and Doc Malone, engaged in conversation with the Port Doctor. And there were two white-coated orderlies standing by the stretcher upon which was the blanket-shrouded form of Jane. Calver knew that she was drugged and wondered if she were conscious. He found himself hoping that she was not, and hated himself for his cowardice.

Her eyes opened and her white face turned to him.

"Derek," she said in a dull voice.

"Jane," he said.

She said, "I'm . . . sorry . . ." She formed her words with an effort, her voice seeming to come from

very far away. "But you can . . . find the Outsiders
. . . It means so much . . . to you . . . more than . . .
me . . . more than . . . Sonya . . ."

"No more than you," he lied.

"But . . . it does . . . otherwise . . ." She managed
a brief flicker of a smile. "Well, my dear . . . good
luck . . ."

He said, "Sonya is willing to leave off here."

"No . . ." she murmured. Then, in a stronger
voice, "No. You must have . . . a good . . . Mate . . .
We've all put so much into this . . . expedition . . . It
must have . . . a chance of . . . success . . ."

"Derek," Malone broke in, "this is doing my patient no good at all. See her again in hospital, before
we blast off. But I insist that she be taken ashore
without further delay."

Calver took Jane's hand in his. She did not return
the pressure. He said, "We'd better do as Doc says.
But I shall be seeing you before we shove off."

"If . . . you want to . . ." she whispered.

"Jane," he said inadequately.

And then he had to relinquish her hand, and the
white-coated attendants were wheeling the stretcher
down the ramp to the waiting ambulance.

17

As soon as the formalities consequent upon the ship's unscheduled arrival had been dealt with, Calver hurried ashore, taking a cab from the spaceport to the hospital. He had not wasted time by changing out of uniform, which made things easier for him as a visitor arriving after official visiting hours. But his visit did little to allay his fears, the anxiety that was increasing as the hour set for departure approached. He was allowed to see Jane, but she could not see him. He could look at her through the thick glass of an observation window, could stare through into the cold chamber in which her motionless body was stretched on the white bed, and that was all.

"Narcotherapy, Captain," the overly cheerful ward Sister told him. "The best cure for any form of space neurosis, even Recession Cafard. When your wife wakes up she'll be as healthy and happy as ever."

"And when," he asked, "will that be, Sister?"

"That's entirely up to Dr. Wilcox. He's taken full charge of the case. He wants to see you before you leave."

"I want to see him," said Calver.

He gazed through the icy glass at Jane. Her face was as white as the sheet that covered her. He could detect no respiratory motion. And he wanted desperately, absurdly, to bring her to life with a kiss, to warm her body with his own. But until matters were resolved, one way or another, there would be little point in restoring her to consciousness.

He looked long and longingly at Jane and then, suddenly, realized that he was envying her. But . . .

He asked abruptly, "Do they dream?"

"Do who dream?" said the Sister.

"The patients. The people who're undergoing this narcotherapy . . ."

"I . . . I don't know." She looked archly up into the face of the tall spaceman. "It could be rather . . . pleasant."

"Perhaps," said Calver. He quoted:

> *To sleep, perchance to dream,*
> *Ay, there's the rub . . .*

"What was that, Captain?"

"Just something that a Prince of Denmark was supposed to have said once."

"Denmark? Where's that? As far as I know, the only human royalty in the galaxy is in the Empire of Waverley."

"It doesn't matter," said Calver. Then, "Thank you, Sister. And do you think that Dr. Wilcox will see me now?"

"I'll take you right up," replied the girl.

The doctor was too professional, too . . . inhuman. He was, decided Calver, a biological engineer rather than a physician, far too prone to regard a sick man or woman merely as a malfunctioning machine. *It's just as well*, thought Calver, *that in space we get only the relative failures of the medical profession. This man would be as efficient as all hell, but he'd be a lousy shipmate.*

The stiffly white-clad man looked coldly at Calver across the gleaming expanse of his desk top and said, "Please be seated, Captain." He pulled upon a drawer, brought out a folder, and glanced at its contents. "Yes. Your medical officer told me something of the background of the case. Mrs. Calver looked too long at your Interstellar Drive Unit while it was in operation, and as a result her mental balance is upset."

"And how long will the cure take?" asked Calver. "How long will she be sleeping? As you may have heard, this is not a commercial voyage that we are making, and I can hold the ship."

"I'm sorry, Captain. I cannot give you a definite answer. The data has yet to be processed and evaluated."

Calver said, "Surely you can give me some idea."

The doctor regarded the spaceman over his steepled fingers. "Captain," he said, "I take it that you contemplate being by the patient's bedside when she is awakened."

"Too right," Calver told him.

"Has it never occurred to you, Captain, that there are times, even in marriages in which both partners have led strictly moral lives, when loathing ousts love? And in your case. . . ." He picked up the folder, looked at it with a certain distaste. "Your Medical Officer, I fear, is too loyal to his captain ever to make a good doctor. However, I was able to obtain all the background details from Mrs. Calver before she was put into the deep sleep—although she, too, evinced what, in my opinion, was an unearned loyalty."

"You used drugs, of course," said Calver.

"Of course. And, frankly, I was shocked by what I learned. However," he went on, "morals are no concern of mine." He did not add the word "unfortunately," but Calver, watching the cold, narrow face, knew that he was thinking it.

"So?" asked Calver.

"So in my opinion, Captain, it would do little to improve my patient's chances of complete recovery if she awoke to see you."

"You don't approve of my conduct, I take it?"

"No."

"Are you married, Doctor?" asked Calver.

"Your impertinent query has no bearing upon the case, Captain."

"But it has on your attitude." Calver got to his feet. "I take it, then, that you can give me no definite date."

"That is so."

"I suppose I can take a second opinion?"

"And a third if you wish, Captain. And a fourth. And a good day to you."

Malone was waiting for Calver in the entrance lobby of the hospital. He said, "I knew you'd be seeing Wilcox, so I hung on until you were through."

"I've been seeing Wilcox," said Calver grimly.

"A good man," Malone told him. "One of the best in his field. Brilliant. But . . ."

"But what?" demanded Calver. "Look, Doc, I've no intention of leaving Jane in his hands if there's any doubt—"

"There's always doubt," said Malone. "But there's less of it with Wilcox than with anybody else. He's so damn' competent that everybody wonders what he's doing here, on this one horse planet away to hell and gone on the edge of the ultimate night. But he likes the Rim worlds. And he hates people— as people. Patients, as far as he's concerned, are no longer people." He laid his hand on Calver's sleeve. "But this is no place to talk. Too drafty altogether. And the sun's well over the yardarm."

"I should be getting back to the ship," said Calver.

"What for?" demanded the old doctor. "You've a bunch of good officers; they can see that she's all buttoned up for deep space without your hovering over them and getting in their hair."

Calver allowed himself to be steered across the road to the nearest bar. He relaxed a little in the form-fitting chair by the low table and allowed Malone to dial the order. With the glass of whisky in his hand he relaxed a little more.

He said, "I'm still thinking of holding the ship here until Jane's recovery. If the other shareholders are willing, that is."

Malone said, "What do you take me for, Derek? That was the first point that I raised with Wilcox, and he, as you know, advises strongly against it. And he has something there. When we return, loaded with honor and glory, things might be different. Better."

"Honor and glory." Calver laughed mirthlessly. "You know, Doc, now that we're on the last lap I wonder if it's been worth it."

Malone dialed again. He said, "Somebody, sometime, had to find out what was behind all the Outsider legends. And it might as well be us."

Calver looked at his watch. "After this drink we'd better be on our way back to the ship."

"But what's the hurry, Derek? This may be our last chance for a drink ashore for one helluva long time, and we may as well make the most of it. I always maintain that no liquor tastes as it should out of a drinking bulb in free fall. And grown men were never meant to take their alcoholic nourishment out of feeding bottles."

Calver ignored this. "Doc," he said abruptly, "now that you've seen Wilcox and know what the treatment is, what do you think of Jane's chances?"

"Very good. I'll even go so far as to say excellent."

"You mean that?"

"Have you ever known me to lie to you, Derek? Even white lies?"

"No."

"Then let's have another drink to Jane's recovery."

Calver looked at his watch again. "And then we must go."

"But what's the hurry, man? It's quite pleasant here, and you and I haven't had a real chance to talk things over, away from the ship, for quite some time. And by things I'm not meaning your own somewhat involved personal muck-up. Let's talk shop."

"Yours or mine, Doc?"

"Yours, of course. After all, I'm the layman who's

being shanghaied away on this wild goose chase. I'd still like to know just how you intend to find Maudsley's Outsiders."

"All we can do, Doc, is follow his sailing directions. Put the two leading stars in line, exactly astern, and then run for fifty light years out."

"And there the Outsiders will be, waiting for you."

"There they will not be. As a spaceman you should know, by this time, that everything is in motion relative to everything else—and out here, on the Rim, the mathematicians still haven't been able to plot the relative motions. And the Outsiders themselves are an unknown factor."

"So if they aren't waiting for us at the end of our fifty light year extension of radius, what then?"

"A search pattern, of course. A three dimensional search pattern."

"Radar should help."

"Of course. But the trouble is that radar is useless while the Drive's in operation. I'll try to put it into words of one syllable for you. The principle of radar is no more—and no less—than the accurate measurement of time, the interval between the emission of a radio pulse and its reception after it's been bounced back by the target. But the Mannschenn Drive does funny things to time, as we all know. It's principle is Tempora Precession. So, putting it crudely, the two don't mix."

"H'm . . . I think I can see that. But surely there's some sort of gadget, some sort of detection device that can be used while the Drive's running."

"There is, the Mass Proximity Indicator. It was developed by the Survey Service. Its use isn't restricted to the Federation naval forces, but the Federation high brass has made sure that it's very, very expensive."

"What about *Faraway Quest?*" asked Malone.

"Yes. She's got one. I don't know what strings Grimes pulled to get it. As a matter of fact, the last time we were here, I tried to persuade him to hire me the thing—it's in Rim Runners' store now, gathering dust—but he conveyed the impression that he'd be willing to let me have his right arm, but not the M.P.I. Oh, well, if the late Mr. Maudsley managed without one, we can."

"It would be a handy thing to have, all the same," said Malone.

"Too right it would." Calver made as though to stop Malone as he dialed for another round, then changed his mind. "I'll not say that it would wash out the necessity for a search pattern entirely, but it would help a lot. The most annoying part of it all is that Grimes flatly refuses to admit that there's any substratum of truth in the Outsider legends. If he thought that we should find something, he'd play."

"He can be very pigheaded," said Malone.

"You're telling me." Calver looked at his watch again. "And after this drink we'll pay our bill and go."

When, at last, they boarded a cab for the return to the ship, Calver was beginning to feel suspicious. The effects of the alcohol were wearing off, and it seemed to him that Malone was fighting a strong delaying action. The doctor had thought of all sorts of last minute shopping and was insisting on making his purchases in out-of-the-way establishments. But eventually, Calver's patience having worn dangerously thin, they were driving through the spaceport gates.

And—"What the hell's been going on?" exploded Calver as the vehicle rounded the corner of a tall warehouse and the ship came into view.

There was the giant traveling crane in position, the end of its jib feet clear of *The Outsider*'s stem. High on the hull, at control room level, there was the flaring blue incandescence of welding torches. Clustered around the vaned landing gear was a small fleet of Rim Runner maintenance and repair trucks.

"What the hell's been going on?" he demanded again.

"You'll find out," said Malone smugly.

The cab pulled up at the airlock ramp. A young man marched sharply down the incline and saluted with a flourish. He was wearing a Chief Officer's uniform, but the badge on his cap bore the winged wheel of Rim Runners.

"Vickery, sir," he snapped. "Miss Verrill's relief. Everything's in hand, and we shall be ready for space as soon as the welding's been completed and tested."

"Mr. Vickery," said Calver coldly, "report to me in my cabin please."

"Derek," broke in Malone, "I suggest that you let Mr. Vickery carry on with his job, for the time being. I'll do the explaining."

18

"WELL, DOCTOR?" asked Calver stiffly, officially.

"This will come as rather a shock to you, Captain," said Malone.

"Rather a shock? Really, Doctor, you excel at the art of masterly understatement. I return on board expecting to find my ship buttoned up for space, and I'm met at the airlock by a brand new Chief Officer whom I wouldn't know from a bar of soap, and I find that all sorts of unauthorized repairs have been put in hand during my absence."

"No repairs," Malone told him. "Just an addition. A farewell gift from Sonya."

"Yes. Sonya. Miss Verrill. Why did she leave, and by whose authority?"

"The Purser made up her wages and, quite legally, the Second Mate signed her discharge."

"All right. I'll be having a word with Mrs. Bendix and Mr. Brentano later. But why did she leave?"

"Because she's a woman. Because she's a member of the oldest trade union, the oldest lodge of all.

When it came to a real showdown she was on Jane's side—more than any of us men were. She talked matters over with me, and we agreed that if Jane learns, when she breaks surface, that Sonya did not accompany you, it will do much for Jane's state of mind. It could easily make all the difference." He paused. "And even now that the Rim worlds are independent of the Federation, the Survey Service still draws a lot of water out here. She was able to talk Commodore Grimes into releasing young Vickery for the expedition."

"An inexperienced Chief Officer."

"He's not. And he's had far more experience on this class of vessel than Sonya ever had."

"Even so, Sonya's got Survey Service experience. Exploration . . ."

"And so has young Vickery," went on Malone patiently. "Not actually in the Survey Service, the Federation Survey Service—but he was Second Mate on *Faraway Quest* the last time that Grimes took her out on his own survey work. He's experienced all right. Make no mistake about that. And he'll be able to look after Sonya's farewell gift to you."

"What the hell do you mean?" demanded Calver.

The old doctor gestured towards the Captain's desk. "There's a letter waiting for you. From Sonya. You'd better read it before you start ramping through the ship blowing your top. I'll leave you to it." He got to his feet. "And I think that it will put you in a somewhat better frame of mind."

When Malone was gone Calver picked up the envelope. It was addressed to him in Sonya's bold, almost masculine hand. He tore it open and ex-

tracted the folded sheets of paper. He hesitated
before reading the letter. What had Sonya to say to
him, and what was the mysterious farewell gift about
which Malone had been blathering? And there was
the faintest suggestion of the perfume that the girl
had always worn hovering around the paper. . . .
Calver shrugged. And so what? Everything, it
seemed, was over now, and he was glad, and he was
sorry. But Jane's recovery was all that there was of
any importance now, and he would always be grateful to Sonya for doing what she could to ensure it.

He opened the letter. He read:

Dear Derek,
I'm sorry that I wasn't around to see your expression when you returned to the ship, to find me
gone and all sorts of mysterious works in progress
around the sharp end. Frankly, I'm sorry that I
wasn't around. Period. But you can see, you must see
that it had to be this way. I want happiness, and that
knowledge would have poisoned everything for us.
With all her faults Jane is far too fine a person to be
handed the dirty end of this particular stick. As a
woman, I can imagine all too well what it would have
been like for her to be revived from that deep freeze
to the knowledge that you and I were out beyond the
stars together, with all that that implies. As things
are, I shall make sure that she is told that I left the
ship here, in Port Forlorn. Just one last thing I ask of
you—that you write to me and tell me what it is that
you find. You know why it's important to me.

But I have made one last contribution to the venture. I went to beard Commodore Grimes in his den.
He's not a bad old bastard—a bit gruff, but suscep-
tible to feminine charm. And I turned on the charm,

believe me. Olga Popovsky the Beautiful Spy, in person, singing and dancing. And I got what I wanted.

For you.

As you know, this *Faraway Quest* of his is his real sweetheart. The best isn't too good for the bitch. She's got gear that's not all that common in the Survey Service. She's got a Mass Proximity Indicator. Or, to be more precise, she had one. If all has gone according to plan, by the time you're able to read this the instrument will already have been installed in your control room—and an officer who's conversant with the workings of the brute will have taken my place. The way I was able to swing things, the Indicator was never purchased outright by Rim Runners, was only on hire from the Survey Service. And as the Service's senior (and one and only) representative in Port Forlorn I was able to bring just a little pressure to bear.

But I was just kidding as far as that's concerned. It was sales talk more than pressure. I told him that the Survey Service is interested in the Outsider legends, and after I'd proved to him that poor Bill Maudsley was one of our officers he was willing to admit that there might be something in the stories after all. And then I really went to town. 'The Outsiders,' I said, 'are, after all, on the back doorstep of the Rim worlds. And yet you're letting private interests investigate something that might be of vital importance to you.'

By this time he was toying with the idea of commissioning *Faraway Quest*, but she's in the throes of quadrennial survey and refit. I mentioned the *Quest*'s Mass Proximity Indicator, and he said that even if he were willing to let you have it, it was far too expensive and delicate a piece of equipment to be handled and maintained by untrained personnel. I told him that the solution was obvious—to lend you an officer as well as the instrument. That way, I pointed out, the Rim worlds would have a representative along on the expedition. And so, after a lot more talk on this and that, it was decided. My last official act as Chief Officer was to sign, in the absence of the Master, the contract. It's not a bad one. You hire the Indicator for a nominal fee of $1.00 (Rim currency) per mensem (Galactic standard) and Mr. Vickery is directly responsible, to Commodore Grimes, for its operation and maintenance. On the other hand, you are to allow Mr. Vickery to make full observations of anything worth observing and to make his report to the Commodore. But don't forget that the Federation Survey Service, as represented by myself, has now pulled out, so you're no worse off than you were before. Anyhow, Julia has the contract with all the other ship's papers, so you'll be able to check it all for yourself when you get around to it.

And so much for business.

You needn't worry, Derek. I'm not going all slushy on you. Perhaps in one of the alternative universes we're shipmates forever and all the rest of it, but not in this one. This, as far as we're concerned, is the end of the penny section. Please don't think that I'm not sorry. I am—more so, perhaps than you will ever know. But, things being as they are, this is the only way. You see that, don't you? This is the only way.

So, darling, look after yourself. And all the best of luck, always.

Your
Sonya.

* * *

So, thought Calver, *this is it. She's right, of course. She's right. But . . .*

He sat there, staring at the letter. He started to crumple it up, intending to throw it into the disposal chute. Then he changed his mind and carefully smoothed the sheets out again, stowing them in the top drawer of his desk. As he was doing so Malone, after briefly rapping on the door, entered the room.

"So you know now," he said.

"Yes. I know."

"She was a good Chief Officer," said Malone.

"Yes," agreed Calver. "She's good." *In many ways,* he thought.

"I shall rather miss her," said Malone.

"And I," said Calver.

"But Vickery's a good lad," went on the doctor. "He's taken charge quite well, and at short notice."

Somebody was tapping at the door. "Come in," called Calver.

It was the new Mate. He stood there at attention, his cap under his arm. He reported, "New installation completed, sir. Hull airtight. Vessel ready for deep space in all respects."

"I hope you're right, Mr. Vickery," said Calver tiredly.

In his somehow deflated mood he did not feel like making any personal inspections.

19

AND SO *The Outsider* lifted from Port Forlorn, climbed on her thundering jets through the smog-filled sky to the cleanliness of outer space. In her control room the Captain and his officers made their calculations, independently feeding data into the computer, checking and rechecking, then put the ship on to the trajectory that would bring them to within half a light year of Kinsolving's Sun. They ran under Interstellar Drive, with the warped, convoluted lens of the galaxy on their port hand and the Outside emptiness to starboard. They wondered, inevitably, what that aching nothingness held and they talked, often, of the drunken, frightened Maudsley and of the stories and legends that were part of the culture of the Rim worlds. Vickery, at first, had been skeptical but Calver could tell that after only a few days he was as eager to participate in the solution of the mystery as the rest of the crew.

At the appointed time the ship re-entered normal space and time and the navigators congratulated themselves on the accuracy of their work. Clear and distinct against the hazily glowing lens were the lead stars, almost in line. A carefully calculated hop of only minutes' duration, demanding—and getting— the utmost skill on the part of the Mannschenn Drive engineers, put *The Outsider* into position.

Directional gyroscopes whined and slowly the ship swung about her short axis. The lens was directly astern of her now. Calver and Vickery and Brentano checked and double checked, even went out through the airlock in spacesuits to make visual observations. Renault and Bendix stood by in their respective enginerooms, and Levine concentrated his mental powers on the task of punching a message across the light years to his telepathic colleagues in the Rim world spaceports.

The great rockets rumbled and flared, building up acceleration and velocity, roared and flared and suddenly died. And the singing, spinning, gleaming wheels of the Drive blurred and faded, blurred and faded as they resumed their time-twisting precession. Astern of the ship the Galactic Lens took on the appearance of an oddly crumpled Mobius Strip.

Ahead of her the Outside looked as it had always looked—a great, wide expanse of sweet damn all.

For fifty light years they ran, but not, as Maudsley had put it, with all hands choking on the stink of frying lubricating oil from the Interstellar Drive Unit; Bendix was too good an engineer for that. For fifty light years they ran, and then, with the Drive shut down, fell outwards through the emptiness. Neither radar nor the Mass Proximity Indicator gave warning of anything at all in their vicinity. Levine, shut up in his cabin with his organic amplifier, reported hearing only faint, routine signals from Rim world shipping and shore installations. Elise Renault, who was at least as good an electronic technician and communications officer as Brentano, was picking up nothing of greater interest than signals that were, at latest, half a century old.

Ten light years west they ran, ten light years in, twenty light years east and another twenty out. North they ran and south. There were still no results, and Calver ordered the volume of the search pattern increased. In the tank of the plotting chart the glowing, skeletal cube expanded slowly—hour by hour, day by day, week by week—and still there was nothing.

And, for the first time, Calver was beginning to doubt, although he would not admit it. And with the doubt was a growing bitterness. He had paid so heavily, and others had paid, for the privilege of being able to lead this expedition. Because of his ambition Jane had suffered, was suffering. And Sonya had suffered. And himself. It would be the supreme irony if nothing was found.

But, he told himself unconvincingly, there must be *something*. The legends could not be laughed off. Neither could the weird, ancient artifacts found, from time to time, on the Rim worlds. And there was Maudsley, and the manner of his dying. . .

But . . .

The stars are fading, he thought.

The stars are fading, and the caravan

Starts for the dawn of nothing. . .

And Calver, sitting alone in his cabin, grinned wryly at that oddly retentive memory of his, the memory that could and would always dredge up tags of verse apposite to any and every occasion.

And then—it was during the running of their fourth search pattern—they found it. *It* was a pulsing light and a flickering needle on the panel of the Indicator. *It* was a sense of vague unease in Levine's mind that worsened as the range decreased. *It,* at last, was a growing blip on the radar screen, but that was not until the Mannschenn Drive had been shut down and the ship proceeding cautiously under rocket power.

They saw *it* at last, stared at *it* through the high powered telescope in the control room. It was faintly self-luminous, and it was big, and seemingly metallic, and of far too irregular of shape to be a ship —or to be a ship built by any race with a passion for symmetry.

Cautiously, with carefully timed and calculated rocket blasts, Calver nosed *The Outsider* in towards the . . . the wreck? . . . the derelict? He obtained readings of the mass of the thing and gasped his disbelief. But his instruments were not lying, and he was able to throw his ship into a tight orbit about it. Then, with the others, he stared out through the ports at the fantastic structure—the domes and turrets, the battlements and crenelations. It was like a huge castle. It was like a castle where no castle had any right to be.

"Levine," he called into the telephone. "Levine, can you pick anything up? Is anyone there? Is anything there?"

"There's something there . . ." The Psionic Communications Officer's voice sounded uneasy, frightened. "There's something there. Something. But it's not human."

"We didn't expect it to be," said Calver.

"But . . . It's not alive, even . . ."

"Do you believe in ghosts?" asked Brentano suddenly.

"Look at the instruments," ordered Calver sharply. "That thing's too solid and has too much mass to be a Rim ghost."

Vickery's voice was awed, subdued. "Sir," he asked, "a boarding party?"

"Yes, Mr. Vickery."

"Then I'll call for volunteers, and get suited up myself."

Calver said, "I'm sorry, but you'll not be going. You're the second in command. You will stay here, standing by to render aid—or to get the hell out if you have to." He added, more to himself than to the others, "I want to see what it is that I've paid for."

Brentano said, "I'd better come with you. You'll need somebody who knows something about electronics."

"And I," said Tanya Brentano. "There may be work for a biologist."

"You'd better stay here," her husband told her, "until we know whether or not the thing is safe."

"Like hell I will," she said.

Calver let them fight it out. He felt very lonely. He should have been having a similar argument with Jane.

Or with Sonya.

20

THE BOARDING PARTY did not leave, however, until
after a great deal of discussion, some of it
acrimonious. Calver argued that its composition was
the concern of the Master, not that of a meeting of
shareholders. He managed at last to convince the
others of the legality of his stand, and made the point
that it would be criminal folly to leave the ship
without a large enough crew to take her back to the
Rim. He was taking Brentano, he said, because of
that officer's known versatility. He was taking Tanya
because she was not indispensable. If anything
should happen to her, Julia was quite capable of adding the Catering Officer's duties to her own, and old
Doc Malone had, more than once in the past, done
duty as Biochemist. Even so, he did not like having a
woman along, but knew that Tanya would prefer to
face any risk side by side with her husband.

Suited up, laden with equipment, the three of
them left the airlock together. Together they stood on
The Outsider's pitted shell plating, waiting for the

circular door to close. The curve of the hull hid the control room ports from them, but they knew that the little compartment would be crowded, that all their shipmates would be waiting there to watch them jet across the emptiness to the faintly glowing enigma hanging in the black sky.

"Captain to Chief Officer," said Calver into his helmet microphone. "We are outside."

"Chief Officer to Captain. I hear you, sir. Are there any further orders?"

"No, Mr. Vickery. You have my instructions. Captain to boarding party. Are you ready?"

"All ready, they replied.

"Then follow me."

He kicked the magnetic soles of his boots clear of the plating and activated his suit reaction units. He allowed himself briefly to wonder what it would be like to be lost out there, alone in a suit and with the darkness, unbroken by the friendly stars, all around him. He told himself as it would be no different from being lost anywhere else in interstellar space; the chances of survival would be just the same—infinitesimal.

The bulk of the . . . the *thing* loomed ahead of him. It had seemed huge from the ship, but there had been no yardstick for comparison. He had his yardsticks now—the spacesuited figures of Brentano and Tanya. If this giant construction were indeed a ship, then an *Alpha* Class liner would serve as one of its smaller lifeboats.

Skillfully using their personal rockets, Calver and his two companions made a feet first landing on a flat area of hull that was not cluttered with turrets and sponsons and enigmatic antennae. Calver expected the soles of his boots to take hold by their built-in magnetism, but they did not. There was none of that odd stickiness experienced when a magnetic field is employed as surrogate for gravity. And yet he did not bounce back into space after the impact of the landing, but was maintained in place by a field that could only be gravitational. It was even stronger than those wildly improbable readings taken in the ship's control room.

"Captain to *The Outsider*," he called urgently. "This thing has some sort of artificial gravity that's just been switched on. Adjust orbit accordingly."

"What do you think I'm doing?" came Vickery's aggrieved reply. Calver saw the flare of rocket drive at the stern of his distant ship. He waited for the Chief Officer to get things under control. Then, "Sorry, sir," said Vickery in a more even voice. "That sudden gravitational surge took me by surprise."

"And me," said Calver.

"Something," remarked Tanya Brentano quietly, "is looking at us."

Calver turned, saw that two of the antennae, like slender, flexible masts, had bent so that they were pointing at the boarding party, and were following their movements.

"Mr. Vickery," said Calver, "put Mr. Levine on the phone." There was a brief delay. As soon as Calver heard Levine's voice he said, "There's something here, something intelligent. Are you sure that you can't pick up anything definite?"

"Yes . . ." said Levine slowly. "Yes . . . It's less vague now. . . . The uneasiness is still there. But there's more now. There's curiosity, but it's unemotional . . . And there's a sort of a hope."

"Is there any animosity?"

"No."

"Can you get through to . . . *it?*"

"I'm trying, Captain. I'm . . . trying." Levine chuckled suddenly. "It's . . . like . . . Have you ever tried to make love to a robot?"

"Have you, Derek?" asked Tanya Brentano.

He laughed, and heard the laughter of the others. Levine's outrageous simile had broken the tension. Then he said briskly, "It knows we're here. If it were hostile it could have dealt with us by now. We're assuming that it's not, anyhow, and we're trying to find a way in."

"Service," said Tanya. "With a smile?"

With no betraying vibration a circular doorway had opened. The three from the ship approached it cautiously. They looked down into what was obviously an airlock. A short ladder ran from its rim to a level deck below.

" 'Will you come into my parlor, said the spider to the fly?' " quoted Brentano in a dubious voice.

"To judge from what happened to Maudsley," said Calver, "the worst that can happen to us is to be driven to drink. And it's happened to us before." He saw through the transparency of the girl's helmet her expression of protest. "Sorry, Tanya," he amended. "It's never happened to you." Mentally he added, *yet.*

"I'll take the risk," she said.

One by one, Calver in the lead, they dropped into the chamber. Suddenly, smoothly, the door slid shut above their heads. There were no visible controls for reopening it, but Calver was not unduly worried. He and the others carried equipment that could burn or cut through any known metal or alloy. What did worry him, however, was that with the shutting of the door they had been cut off from radio communication with the ship.

"The chamber's being filled with some sort of atmosphere," said Brentano.

"And I've a hunch," Calver told him, "that it's our sort of atmosphere. But we'll not risk taking off our helmets . . . But there's another door opening. Shall we . . . ?"

"Of course," said Tanya Brentano. "What did we come here for?"

"The lighting," whispered her husband. "It's . . . odd. Not a globe or tube along the great long alleyway, and yet it's like broad daylight. How do they do it?"

"That," said Tanya, "is for you to find out. You're the electronics expert. Remember?"

Calver was only half listening to their amicable bickering. He began to stride along the seemingly interminable alleyway. Although the deck was of burnished metal—as were the sides and the deckhead—his booted feet made no sound. And even had he been walking in a vacuum there should have been vibration, but there was none. He looked down and saw his reflection, as clear as in a mirror. He looked to the side and saw his reflection, with those of the others, in the walls, stretching to infinity, and endless series of diminishing images. It was like one of those mirror mazes found in amusement halls—but it was not amusing.

He walked, and the others walked with him. Accustomed as they were to free fall they found the exercise tiring. Twice they stopped, sitting down to rest and sipping water from their suit tanks. On the second occasion they made a careful check of their air supply gauges, found that it would be all of six hours before it would be necessary to connect up the spare bottles that they had brought with them. Calver was tempted, even so, to sample the air in the alleyway, but decided against it.

They walked, and they came at last to a door. Like everything else it was of highly polished metal. For lack of any visual evidence to the contrary it could have been no more than a bulkhead, but Calver *knew* that it was not. He knew that the alleyway had to lead to somewhere, and that to have it leading to a blank wall would make no sense whatsoever.

"But why should it make sense?" he whispered, puzzled. "Why should it make sense? Why should we assume that our logic is the only logic, that our way of doing things is the only way of doing things?"

But he was not surprised when the door opened.

Stiffly, like a robot, he walked into the huge chamber beyond the door, the compartment that was more like a great cave than any space aboard a ship, and . . .

21

I hate her, thought Derek Calver. *I hate her*. His mother was out of the room, busy in the kitchen. The boy glared at his baby sister gurgling happily in her cot, at the little, drooling monster that had robbed him of the love and affection that were his right. *I hate her*, he thought again. He got up from his chair, walked over to the cot, and struck the infant across the chubby face with the magazine that he had been reading. He was back in his seat before the first outraged wail broke the silence.

"Derek," demanded his mother, picking up the bawling child, "what happened?"

"I don't know," he said. "I was reading."

"What are those marks on her face?"

"Where? Oh, I suppose she must have jumped around and hit her face on the side of the cot." He went on in what he now knew to be an insufferable manner, "In any case, Mother, most parents send their babies to the robot nursery."

* * *

"Bumble bee! Bumble bee! Fly back to your stinking hive, bumble bee!" yelled the children.

The Shaara drone, who had wandered away from his ship, away from the spaceport environs, and who had imbibed sufficient whisky in several taverns seriously to affect his powers of locomotion, tried to ignore them. But he could not ignore the ill-favored mongrel dog, belonging to one of the boys that, egged on by its master, faced the unhappy extra-Terrestrial, its ugly face creased in a vicious snarl. The drone swiped the dog with one clawed foreleg and then clumsily took to the air, flying only a few yards before tumbling to the ground. He tried to walk, but the movements of his six legs were ridiculously uncoordinated. The dog nipped a piece out of one trailing wing. He turned to defend himself, and this time inflicted a wound so painful that the mongrel fled, yelping.

"He's hurt my dog!" screamed Derek Calver.

He picked up a stone and threw it. The others followed his example. But the police arrived before any serious damage was done.

"Cadet Calver," asked the Captain Commandant of the Academy gently, "do you swear on your honor, as a probationary officer and as a gentleman, that you played no part in last night's race brawl?"

"I so swear," said Calver solemnly, thinking, *After all, I was on the outskirts of the crowd and I never even got a chance to kick the black bastard...*

"You'll come back, Derek," pleaded the girl.

"Of course, darling," lied Fourth Officer Derek

Calver, secure in the knowledge that he was to be promoted and transferred at the end of the voyage and that with any luck at all he'd never be on the Polaris Sector run again.

"Mr. Calver," ranted the notoriously irascible Captain Jenkins, "never in all my days in space have I tried to push such a sloppily loaded ship up through an atmosphere. You were in direct charge of the distribution of mass. What have you to say?"

"There must be something wrong with the Ralston, sir," said Second Officer Derek Calver.

And there soon will be, he thought, *if I can get my hands on it before the old bastard makes his personal check.*

"So you're quite determined," whispered Dorothy Calver. "Does this home I've made for you mean nothing to you? Do I mean nothing to you? Don't you care what happens to the children?"

"No," replied Calver.

"I should have realized," said his second wife bitterly, "that you can't make a silk purse out of a sow's ear."

Calver tried to keep his temper under control. He said, "I was Chief Officer of one of the Commission's big ships. I was happily married with a family. I threw all that away so that I could marry you. But I'm not, repeat not, going to be made over to please you. I'm a spaceman, not one of those planet-bound puppies that you're always running around with."

"Happily married?" she laughed. "That wasn't what you told me. And you told me, too, that you were sick and tired of deep space and that you'd be happy to stay on the one planet the rest of your life, as long as you had me there with you. . .

"Your trouble, Derek, is that you're selfish. I've changed, in lots of ways, just to try to make you happy. You must grasp the fact that adjustments by both partners are essential to a happy marriage. But you won't adjust. You'll never adjust."

"I try to," he said.

"You say that you try to. You say this, and you say that, you promise this and you promise that, but that's as far as it ever goes. You're so conceited that you're quite convinced that Derek Calver is the end product of evolution, with no room for improvement. . . And let me tell you, my dear, that my father is getting just a little restive and wondering why he should be paying an executive's salary to a glorified office boy."

"My nose bleeds for your father," said Calver nastily. Then, "Where are you going?"

"It's no business of yours. If you must know, I've been asked to the Sandersons'. And if you must know something more, Sylvia pleaded with me not to bring —I quote—'that drunken oaf of a spaceman'."

"What courteous friends you have," said Calver. "As courteous as you are, darling."

"Get out!" she flared. "Get out!"

Both Calver and his wife ignored the tawdry, frightened, little blonde who was struggling hastily into her clothing. Calver, getting slowly out of the rumpled bed, said, "This is my home."

"This," said his wife, "was your home. But it's my apartment. And unless you're out of here within half an hour, I'll call the police to have you evicted."

"If I had known," he said, "that you'd be home so early."

"Get out, you no-good swine!" she said with cold viciousness.

Captain Derek Calver, with Jane Arlen at his side, stood in the Master's cabin aboard the Trans-Galactic Clipper *Thermopylae*.

"Captain Calver," said Captain Hendriks, "my thanks are inadequate."

"I did what I could, Captain," said Calver.

"At least," said Hendriks, "I shall do what I can, too. Sometimes, in wrangles over salvage awards, the owners of the ships involved are remembered and their crews, who have done all the work, are forgotten. But I am not without influence."

"That aspect of the matter had never occurred to me," said Calver.

"You must hate it out here," said Hendriks. "But you'll be able to return now, to the warmth and light of the Centre."

"So we shall," said Calver with a mild amazement. "So we shall."

And I shall be a rich man, he thought. *I shall be rich, and no longer dependent on the charity of Jane's father and perhaps, if she has not remarried, or even if she has.*

He turned his head slightly to look at the other Jane, at Jane Arlen, his lover and loyal shipmate.

She'll manage, he thought. *She'll have her share of the salvage money. But perhaps money's not everything. . . .*

His hand found Jane Arlen's and closed upon it, and felt the answering warmth and pressure. "But I belong on the Rim," he said. "We belong on the Rim."

And he despised himself for the smug nobility with which he had made the gesture.

* * *

And as it went on he despised himself the more. On the stage of his memory there were scenes played with Jane, and scenes played with Sonya, and scenes played with both. And yet he was able to stand outside and watch, and to pity as well as to despise, and, towards the end, to understand. He was the creature of heredity and of environment. He was cruel at times, and clumsy most of the time, but he had tried to act with a certain bumbling honesty, had not been all bad all the time. . .

To despise was wrong, and to pity was wrong. . . . Somehow he knew that.

Understanding was the goal, the only goal. He would endeavor to understand his own behaviour, and Jane's behaviour, and perhaps he would be able to bring her out here, and perhaps, when she had learned to face herself, a fresh start could be made.

To understand, to face and to understand . . .

To face, without fear, without contempt and without pity . . .

They were standing in the huge chamber, with its oddly flowing lines and fantastic perspective—Calver and Brentano and Tanya. Calver could see the faces of the others through the transparencies of their helmets, pale and with lines of strain that had not been there before, with the lines of strain still evident, and yet at peace. Their eyes were the eyes of those who had looked at too much in too short a time. Yet they both essayed a tremulous smile, and Calver smiled in answer. He saw how they were holding each other tightly and he was briefly envious.

"I assume," he said, "that we all went through the same experience."

"I always had rather a high opinion of myself," whispered Brentano. "Until now."

"But what did it all mean?" murmured his wife.

"I think I know," said Calver. "I think I know—or I can guess. Or I can remember. I can remember a story I read once—it was when I was passing through a phase of reading every twentieth century author I could lay my hands on. This was by a man called Wells, and its title was *A Vision of Judgment*. Wells imagined a judgment day, with all living and all who had ever lived on Earth called by the last trump to face their maker, to be tried and punished for their sins or, perhaps, to be rewarded for their good deeds. Everyone had his session of hell as his naked soul stood in full view of the multitude and the Recording Angel recited the long, long catalogue of petty acts of meanness and spite. All the trivial (but not so trivial) shabby things, all the things in which even the most perverted nature could take no pride, no matter how much pride he took in some quite spectacular wrong-doing."

"So you think that we have been judged?" said Tanya slowly. "By whom, Derek? And why?"

"And how?" demanded Brentano.

"There are other doors opening," said Tanya. "There is machinery beyond them . . . Apparatus . . ."

"Dare we?" asked Brentano.

You dare, said the voice in their minds. *You dare. The secrets are yours for the asking, to use as you will. Soon, now, you will cross the gulf, and you will be welcome.*

22

THEY, THE members of the boarding party, were back aboard *The Outsider,* and were discussing their experiences with their shipmates.

"From Bernhardt's Nebula it must have come," said Calver. "How long ago? I don't know, but we shall be finding out. It's an intergalactic spaceship and, at the same time, an electronic brain that makes anything built by ourselves no more than a glorified abacus.

"And it's a quarantine station."

"A quarantine station?" echoed Vickery.

"Yes. And it's far more logical than any of ours. Ours are used after travelers arrive at their destination, this one is used before they set out. That's the idea I got, anyhow, and Tanya and Brentano gained the same impression. And truly alien entities need not fear biochemical infections; the destructive idea is the only one really communicable disease of intelligent life. So this quarantine station screens for that. Perhaps when Levine goes across with the next boarding party he may be able to establish better rapport with the mind of the thing than we did, and learn more than we have done. There's an utterly alien way of thought behind their machines, for example, and what we take to be the Intergalactic Drive Unit is altogether outside—*outside,* not beyond —our technology.

"But the quarantine station . . .

"The way I see it is this. There's intelligent life, highly intelligent life, on the worlds of Bernhardt's Nebula. It could well be that their manned ships have already visited this galaxy from time to time; after all, there is evidence. It could be, it seems to me, that the people of the Nebula want to make contact with us; for trade, perhaps, or cultural exchange, or just neighborliness.

"But . . .

"It could be that our neighbors in this next galaxy are, to all external appearances, horrible monsters, some utterly alien life form, something so different as to be frightening, or sickening, yet something that still has, under the repulsive surface, a very real and warm humanity. After all, we've come across nothing yet in our own galaxy on those lines. Every race with which we've come into contact has run very much to one or another of the standard patterns—mammalian, saurian, arthropodal."

"But the quarantine station?" demanded the Mate again.

"I was coming to that, Mr. Vickery. Please give me time. It was left here, out beyond the Rim—there may be others—in the hope that with the development of interstellar flight it would be discovered. It was left here to test the fitness of its discoverers to use the treasures of scientific knowledge and technical know-how that it contains, to build the ships capable of making the big crossing. We, the three of us, passed the test without cracking. Had we cracked, there is little doubt that we should have been bundled outside as unceremoniously as Maudsley must have been—bundled outside with the memories of the fear and the horror and some sort of post-hyp-notic inhibition to stop us from ever talking about it. It's possible that some of Maudsley's crew did pass the test—but they died with *Polar Queen*.

"It is possible," he said, "that some of you will not pass." He added, with a new humility, "But if I did, there is little likelihood that any of you will fail.

"It's an ingenious test, and amazingly simple. It's ... It's a mirror that's held up to you, in which you see ... everything. Yes, *everything*. Things that you've forgotten and things that you've wished for years that you could forget. After all, a man can meet any alien monster without fear, without hate, after he has met and faced the most horrible monster of all. . . .

"Himself."

POUL ANDERSON

Ursula K. Le Guin

10705	**City of Illusion**	$2.25
47806	**Left Hand of Darkness**	$2.25
66956	**Planet of Exile**	$1.95
73294	**Rocannon's World**	$1.95

Available wherever paperbacks are sold or use this coupon